A Law Unto Herself

A Law Unto Herself

REBECCA HARDING DAVIS

Edited and with an introduction
by Alicia Mischa Renfroe

University of Nebraska Press
Lincoln and London

LIBRARY OF CONGRESS
Cataloging-in-Publication Data

Davis, Rebecca Harding, 1831–1910, author.
A law unto herself / Rebecca Harding
Davis; edited and with an introduction
by Alicia Mischa Renfroe.

pages   cm.—(Legacies of
nineteenth-century American
women writers)

Includes bibliographical references.
ISBN 978-0-8032-3814-5 (paperback)
ISBN 978-0-8032-5670-5 (pdf)
ISBN 978-0-8032-5671-2 (epub)
ISBN 978-0-8032-5672-9 (mobi).
1. Women—Legal status, laws, etc.—
United States—Fiction. 2. Women—
United States—History—19th
century—Fiction. 3. Law reform—
United States—Fiction. 4. Gender
identity—Fiction. I. Renfroe, Alicia
Mischa, editor. II. Title.
PS1517.L3 2015   813'.4—dc23
2014015253

Set in Adobe Carlson Pro
by Renni Johnson.
Designed by A. Shahan.

Contents

Acknowledgments

I would not have been able to complete this edition without the support of others. I am especially grateful to Sharon M. Harris for her advice, encouragement, and enthusiasm throughout this project. My work on Davis has benefited greatly from conversations with Sherry and Robin Cadwallader; they graciously welcomed me into the Society for the Study of Rebecca Harding Davis and Her World and have generously shared their work on Davis. I continue to be motivated by the example of Mary Papke, who first introduced me to nineteenth-century women writers in an undergraduate class at the University of Tennessee; her work in the recovery of Kate Chopin and Edith Wharton surely planted the seeds of this project long before I had ever heard of Rebecca Harding Davis.

This project also benefited from the support of my institution, Middle Tennessee State University, and the National Endowment for the Humanities. I received two MTSU Faculty Research and Creative Activity grants in 2010 and 2011 that provided summer support and a one-course release for preliminary research and writing. Mark Brynes, the dean of the College of Liberal Arts, approved travel funds for a trip to the University of Virginia to use the Richard Harding Davis Collection. I am especially grateful to my department chair, Tom Strawman, for his support and encouragement. I would also like to thank the National Endowment for the Humanities for funding my participation in two fantastic summer institutes: "The Rule of Law: Legal Studies and the Liberal Arts" directed by Matthew Anderson and Cathrine O' Frank in 2009 and "Transcendentalism and Social Action in the Age of Emerson, Thoreau, and Fuller" directed by Sterling "Ric" Delano, David Berry, and Diane Whitley Bogard. These experiences continue to shape my research in unexpected and fruitful ways.

My research is closely related to my teaching. I was fortunate to share my preliminary work with students in my graduate seminar on Louisa May Alcott and Rebecca Harding Davis. I thank Joy Smith, Cori Mathis, Shelley Maddox, Sarah Gray-Panesi, Brittany Hall, Jacquelyn Hayek, Jessica Hanson, Kazunori Oda, Sarah King Rivas, Sally Vandenberg, and Shellie Michael for their insights and encouragement. The introduction and footnotes were greatly improved by their questions and comments. I would also like to thank my research assistant, Mo Li, for her work on the project. She found elusive sources and proofread several drafts with a smile and a willingness to help with whatever I asked. My colleague Martha Hixon generously offered her advice regarding Davis's references to fairy tales.

I am particularly thankful for my friends and family. Kelly Kilgore Bratcher, Angela Byers, Lisa Durham Mendenhall, and Pat Bradley willingly listened to all things Davis. My wonderful canine assistant, Baby, made sure I took time away from my desk for a quick walk. Jim and Jan Hart offered their encouragement and support throughout the project. I am especially grateful to my parents, Ronald and Helen Renfroe, for fostering my intellectual curiosity in ways that continue to shape my academic career; I would not be editing a book today if I had not read so many good books as a child.

Last, I would not have been able to complete this project without John Hart. My partner in all things, he willingly and patiently wore the hats of literary critic, writing center tutor, and head chef as needed. He continues to enrich my life in ways I never imagined.

Editor's Introduction

In *A Law Unto Herself*, Rebecca Harding Davis transforms a typical Gothic plot device of a lost inheritance into a vehicle for a realistic critique of the legal status of women. Originally serialized in *Lippincott's Magazine* in 1877 and published in book form in 1878, *A Law Unto Herself* appeared during a time of cultural change and contradiction. Women's legal rights and cultural roles shifted dramatically throughout the nineteenth century. With the passage of married women's property laws throughout the century, the common law doctrine of *coverture*—which held that a married woman was legally "under the cover" or protection of her husband and thus not a legally recognizable "person"—was gradually replaced through statutory reform. Enacted in several waves beginning in the 1830s and culminating in the 1890s, these statutes theoretically transformed a married woman into a legal subject, capable of making her own contracts, inheriting and owning property in her own name, and keeping her own wages. Women also entered male-dominated professions, such as law and medicine, in increasing numbers. However, despite these gains, in *Bradwell v. Illinois* (1873), the United States Supreme Court held that Myra Bradwell did not have a constitutional right to be admitted to the state bar to practice law because the right to practice a profession was not protected by the Fourteenth Amendment. Drawing on contemporary domestic ideology and the legal doctrine of coverture in his concurring opinion, Justice Bradley observed that as a married woman, Bradwell could not enter the contracts necessary to the profession without her husband's permission. He noted:

> The civil law, as well as nature herself, has always recognized a wide difference in the respective spheres and destinies of man and woman. Man is, or should be, woman's protector and defender. The

natural and proper timidity and delicacy which belongs to the female sex evidently unfits it for many of the occupations of civil life. The constitution of the family organization, which is founded in the divine ordinance, as well as in the nature of things, indicates the domestic sphere as that which properly belongs to the domain and functions of womanhood.

Thus, for much of the nineteenth century, the legal system and its basic principles remained bound in patriarchal assumptions about gender.

Though changes to property law offered married women new forms of agency, the impact of these changes on the everyday lives of women remained ambiguous at best. By the end of Reconstruction in 1877, African American men had voting rights on paper but not in practice, while universal women's suffrage would have to wait until the passage of the Nineteenth Amendment in 1919, even though women in Wyoming had the right to vote as early as 1869 and many other states had granted partial suffrage throughout the late nineteenth century. As Brook Thomas suggests in *American Literary Realism and the Failed Promise of Contract*, these issues may also be situated as part of a larger cultural shift from an emphasis on status-based relationships, characterized by hierarchical arrangements such as slavery and marriage, to contract-based relationships, presumably freely chosen and negotiated in the marketplace (2). As William Graham Sumner explains, "a society based on contract . . . gives the utmost room and chance for individual development, and for all the self-reliance and dignity of a free man" (qtd. in Thomas 2–3). Yet, as Thomas cautions, a contractually organized society does not guarantee equality, especially when status-based relationships persist, often disguised in new forms.

Read in light of the Philadelphia Centennial Exposition in 1876, the novel raises questions about the application of universal norms—such as freedom and equality—to women, African Americans, and other marginalized groups; *A Law Unto Herself* provides a sustained inquiry into the legal rights of women and thus lends support, though indirectly, to the women's rights movement. Organized to celebrate the signing of the Declaration of Independence, the exposition surely reminded Rebecca Harding Davis and her contemporaries of the nation's founding on the promise of "inalienable rights" for its citizens.[1] Yet, the passage of the Fifteenth Amendment in 1870 granted the right to vote to African American men but failed to mention women, a point that Susan B. Anthony and others foregrounded through a public reading of "A Declaration of Rights" on July 4, 1776. The group could not get permission to be part of the exposition's official program and instead staged a demonstration outside the lecture hall (Cordato 130–31). Emphasizing an Enlightenment conception of "the natural rights of each individual," the "Declaration of Rights" describes a host of wrongs against women, even noting that "*The Writ of Habeas Corpus*, the only protection against *lettres de cachet*, and all forms of unjust imprisonment . . . is held inoperative in every State in the Union, in case of a married woman against her husband,—the marital rights of the husband being in all cases primary, and the rights of the wife secondary." In *Rebecca Harding Davis and American Realism*, Harris observes that Davis's "literary stance on women's rights" can best be characterized as "interest, but from a distance" (193). Though Davis never officially joined the women's movement, her fiction speaks to contemporary debates about women's work, marriage, and property ownership.

Describing the women writers of the era, Elaine Showalter suggests that "the heroine of women's writing in the 1870s was 'the coming woman,' the emancipated woman of the future" and that "women's fiction . . . was a series of female Declarations of Independence" (164, 166). Neither the true woman nor the new woman, the 1870s woman lived in a time of transition. Her ancestor was the true woman, immortalized in the pages of domestic fiction and characterized by her commitment to the virtues of purity, piety, submissiveness, and domesticity.[2] In contrast, characterized by their search for "feminine self-realization," the New Women of the 1890s were social nonconformists who "rejected conventional female roles, redefined female sexuality, and asserted their rights to higher education and the professions" (Showalter 210). The "bohemian New Women" of the city might be "art students, editors, actresses, and journalists" who saw themselves "as daring modern heroines" (210). With three fascinating female characters that can be read as reflections of the title, *A Law Unto Herself* registers many of these contradictions, provides one of Davis's most complex treatments of the "woman question," and offers a powerful critique of what it means to be a woman within, and subject to, the law.

Brief Biography of Rebecca Harding Davis

Best known for her critique of industrialism, "Life in the Iron-Mills" (1861), Rebecca Harding Davis was a prolific writer whose career spanned over fifty years. She serialized sixteen novels, published ten novels in book form, and published several hundred short stories and essays in a host of periodicals.[3] The daughter of Rachel Leet Wilson (1808–1884) and Richard W. Harding (1796–1864), Rebecca Blaine Harding was born on June 24, 1831, at the home of her aunt and uncle (Rebecca Wilson Blaine and James Blaine) in Washington, Pennsylvania.[4] The young Rebecca lived with her parents in Alabama until 1836 when the family moved again to Wheeling, Virginia (now West Virginia).

Rebecca Harding began her education at home with her mother and private tutors. In 1845 Harding moved to Washington, Pennsylvania, where she lived with her aunt and uncle while attending the Washington Female Seminary for three years before graduating as valedictorian of her class. The curriculum included "geometry, literature, music, and drawing" as well as "courses in Evidences of Christianity, Mental Philosophy, and Butler's Analogy" (Harris and Cadwallader xii). After graduation, she returned to Wheeling and informally continued her education by studying with her brother, who attended Washington College.

Other details about Harding's life during this period are scarce. From about 1849 to 1861, she apparently contributed to the *Wheeling Intelligencer*, edited by Archibald Campbell (Harris, *RHD and Realism* 25–26). Other than her newspaper experience, little is known about her early writing until she sent "Life in the Iron-Mills" to James T. Fields at *The Atlantic Monthly*, where the publication of the story in the April 1861 issue caused an immediate sensation for its indictment of industrial capitalism. Shortly thereafter, Harding met her future husband, Lemuel Clarke Davis, a Philadelphia law clerk and editor. After a brief correspondence, they married on March 5, 1863, and had three children,

Richard Harding Davis (born April 18, 1864), Charles Belmont Davis (born January 24, 1866), and Nora Davis (born October 16, 1872).

Despite the demands of a growing family, Davis was her most prolific during the 1860s and 1870s when she used her pen to examine a variety of social issues. Drawing on her experience in the border state of West Virginia, she wrote several frank treatments of the Civil War for *The Atlantic Monthly*, including "John Lamar" (1862), "Blind Tom" (1862), and "David Gaunt" (1862) and examined the complexities of Reconstruction in her ambitious novel, *Waiting for the Verdict* (1868). Throughout her career, she penned Gothic thrillers and mysteries for *Peterson's Ladies Magazine*, eventually producing over ninety stories and fourteen serialized novels for that venue. Though neglected by scholars, these stories record her lifelong commitment to social justice. Noting in passing Davis's "obsession with inheritance" (45), Ruth Stoner observes that her *Peterson's* tales include "some of the most subversive literature written in the nineteenth century—radical declarations of women's status as chattel and portraits of women's sexual repression, embedded within very conventional imagery and formulaic sentimental plots" (44).

As this edition of *A Law Unto Herself* seeks to demonstrate, Davis clearly understood that law is a form of power. Her interest in law may have been fueled by her husband, who had legal training and edited *The Legal Intelligencer* for about ten years. Even a small sampling of her work reveals her consistent engagement with the treatment of women, children, workers, the insane, and otherwise disabled within the legal system. For instance, "In the Market" (1868) describes the limited options for female self-development, including marriages in which women "endure in legal prostitution" (207). "Polly" (1871) examines "distinctions in the law" (50), including consent, legal guardianship, inheritance, and marriage that affect women's everyday lives. "Josey's Dower" (1876) describes a gift in which two sisters "give up" the "right of choice" of their inheritance to another sister who does not deserve the reward (329). Women who attempt to subvert typical roles also face legal obstacles. "A Day with Dr. Sarah" (1878) focuses on a female physician who "had fought her way into her profession, and out of the Christian Church, and . . . had clinched with Law, Religion, and Society in a hand-to-hand fight because of their treatment of women" (611). Published just one year after Twain and Warner's *The Gilded Age: A Story of Today* (1873), the novel *John Andross* (1874) is a fictionalized account of William Tweed's Whiskey Ring that examines issues of political corruption and capitalistic greed. Ahead of her time, Davis recognizes the dangers of a monolithic, powerful corporation. Explaining his role in the Tweed Ring, the protagonist John Andross observes, "For years I have been in the hold—not of a man, nor a devil, but of a corporation. . . . It buys and sells at will the government and interests of the city where it belongs: it controls the press, the pulpit, the courts" (52). More specifically, "it buys the law" (53). A contributing editor to the *New York Tribune* from 1867 to 1889 and the *New York Independent* from 1868 to 1908, Davis came to understand this issue firsthand when she wrote an exposé about corporate greed for the *Tribune* and then resigned when she learned that her work had been censored because the corporation was a major advertiser (Harris, RHD *and Realism* 233).

After 1880, Davis focused primarily on her short fiction and journalism, producing essays about race relations, labor reform, and other issues of the day. She published three more novels: *Kent Hampden* (1892), *Doctor Warwick's Daughters* (1896), and *Frances Waldeaux* (1897). She also continued to write thrillers for *Peterson's* and juvenile fiction for the *Youth's Companion* and *St. Nicholas*. Her final published story, "Two Brave Boys," appeared in *St. Nicholas* in July 1910 just two months before her death on September 29, 1910, at Richard Harding Davis's home in Mount Kisco, New York.

Critical History

Like many of her contemporaries, Davis blends characteristics from multiple literary genres such as sentimentalism, the Gothic, and romanticism. Her work also prefigures realism and naturalism—both most often associated with late nineteenth-century male writers. She draws on wide-ranging classical, literary, and biblical allusions as well as contemporary events. As Lisa Long suggests, Davis's work "has much to teach us: about the limits of generic classifications and the perils of literary history; [and] about the continuing need for critical work that elucidates the many American women writers who remain if not 'lost,' at least hidden" (262). Writing of several such midcentury writers (Alcott, Stoddard, Woolson, and Phelps), Anne Boyd claims that "our understanding of American women's literary history as advancing from sentimentalism to domestic literature to local color to modernism obscures the value of many women writers who do not fit neatly into any of these categories" (249). Like many of her contemporary women writers, Davis resists easy categorization, and as a result, much of her canon continues to be neglected.

For early reviewers such as Henry James, Davis's use of sentimental conventions may have obscured her contributions to the emerging literary forms of realism and naturalism. Like her sentimental predecessors, Davis often focuses on the plight of women in conventional, domestic settings. Popularized by antebellum women writers like E.D.E.N. Southworth, Susan Warner, Maria Cummins, and Harriet Beecher Stowe, sentimental literature gained a major share of the antebellum literary market and sparked negative reactions such as Hawthorne's infamous remark about "that damn-d mob of scribbling women" (qtd. in Person 24). Usually featuring an abused or disempowered protagonist (such as Charles Dickens's Oliver Twist or Harriet Beecher Stowe's Uncle Tom), sentimental literature often foregrounds the victim's suffering in order to elicit an emotional response and thus work as a call to action on its audience.[5] With its fraught literary history, as Nina Baym observes, "the term 'sentimental' is often a term of judgment rather than a description" (*Woman's Fiction* 24).

In a scathing review of *Waiting for the Verdict* published in *The Nation*, a young Henry James misreads Davis as a sentimental writer, noting that though some of her short stories are "distinguished by a certain severe and uncultured strength," they are also "disfigured by an injudicious straining after realistic effects" (221). He also takes issue with her choice to write about lower-class characters; though they may be appropriate subject matter,

> they are worth reading about only so long as they are studied with a keen eye versed in the romance of human life. . . . Mrs. Davis's

manner is in direct oppugnancy to this truth. She drenches the whole field beforehand with a flood of lachrymose sentimentalism, and riots in the murky vapors which rise in consequence of the act. (221)

Her characters ultimately emerge as "frowning, grinning automatons," and "the reader . . . cries aloud for the good, graceful old nullities of the 'fashionable novel'" (222). His review of *Dallas Galbraith* one year later echoes many of these concerns. Though he admits that "Mrs. Davis, in her way, is an artist," he concludes that she "takes life desperately hard and looks upon the world with a sentimental—we may even say, a tearful—eye" (224, 225). In *Reading for Realism*, Nancy Glazener aptly points out that "James probably attacked Davis so vehemently and elaborately because she might have been taken for a realist even though she did not, in James's view, observe realist-professional emotional proprieties" (127).

Though realism and naturalism had not been "officially" defined by spokespersons like William Dean Howells and Frank Norris, several reviews of *A Law Unto Herself* prefigure the concerns of both and situate Davis as an early contributor to these emerging forms. Often interpreted as a reaction against the "unreality" of romantic, sentimental, and Gothic literature, realism focuses on everyday life and commonplace experiences, emphasizes character development over plot, and resists the use of stock character types to represent good and evil. Realism also strives for veracity, for being true to everyday life; as William Dean Howells succinctly defined it, "realism is nothing more and nothing than the truthful treatment of material" (966). An unsigned review in *The Nation* compares Davis to Howells, noting that "she succeeds in giving a truer impression of American conditions than any writer we know except Mr. Howells, while there is a vast difference between his delicately illuminated preparations of our social absurdities and Mrs. Davis's grim and powerful etchings" ("Recent Novels" 264). The reviewer clearly has some reservations with Davis's brand of realism: she "writes stories which can hardly be called pleasant, and which frequently, as in 'A Law unto Herself,' deal with most unpleasant persons, but there is an undercurrent of recognized rectitude and a capacity for calling a spade a spade which sets her writings in a category far removed from French morality" ("Recent Novels" 264). In a similar vein, a short unsigned piece in *Godey's Lady's Book* acknowledges that the novel is "powerfully written, full of interest, but written also in a style somewhat broad and coarse, especially from the pen of a woman" ("Literary Notices" 435). Foreshadowing objections to the subject matter of realists and naturalists, the review also takes issue with the occasional use of profanity: "It does not, in our opinion, add to the strength of a really powerful book, to add profanity to its expressions, and put oaths in the mouths of women as well as men" ("Literary Notices" 435). Continuing this trend, the *New York Times* notes that in chapters 3 to 5 (a section that includes a powerful scene in which Jane takes the law into her own hands), Davis provides "good enough stuff in the story to make the reader wonder uncomfortably when he is to be shocked by some coarseness or lack of good art such as this writer seldom fails to supply" ("Lippincott's Magazine" 3). The reviewer also describes the protagonist, Jane Swendon, as "a young woman unlike the conventional Miss in almost every regard except beauty" ("Lippincott's Magazine" 3). As these reviews suggest, many of her contemporaries recognized Davis's affinities with realism; like her male counterparts, she describes the individual's relation to his or her environment and the commonplace details of everyday life.

Many of her contemporaries also recognized the complexities of her career and of the options available for women writers. In *Women Authors of Our Day in Their Homes*, Julia Tutwiler praises Davis for her "willingness to leave questions open, to acknowledge that every verdict must be an individual verdict" (272). Though Davis is "the house-mother . . . innocent of ambition" (272), her "intellectual outlook is not confined to her home and literature. She is abreast with the thought and movement of the day, entering into the life around her with the enthusiasm which is one of her most helpful and inspiring qualities and which is tempered and individualized by the habit of reflection" (276). In another assessment of Davis in her own time, Elizabeth Stuart Phelps remarks in "Stories that Stay,"

Rebecca Harding may have been too terribly in earnest. Her intensity was essentially feminine, but her grip was like that of a masculine hand. She may have had her faults in style, but those were minor matters. Her men and women breathed and suffered, loved and missed of love, won life or wasted it with an ardor that was human, and a power that was art. (120)

Other early analyses emphasize her kinship with Russian realism or French naturalism. A lengthy obituary in the *New York Times* praises her "stern but artistic realism" that "suggested a man of power not unlike Zola's" ("Rebecca H. Davis" 13). In *American Authors*, published in 1938, Stanley Kunitz and Howard Haycraft write, "Mrs. Davis's earlier novels . . . were grimly realistic, belonging to the 'naturalistic' school of Zola. She was consciously pioneering this field in America, thirty years before Stephen Crane, forty years before Theodore Dreiser" (208). Similarly, in the *Dictionary of American Biography*, Fred Pattee describes her works as "Russian-like in their grim and sordid realism" (143), and "Today's Women," published in the *Washington Post* in 1929, credits Davis for "introduc[ing] the labor question in American fiction" (Minderman 9). However, despite this recognition of her work, Davis was virtually erased from American literary history with the canonization of mostly male writers in the mid-twentieth century.[6]

In 1972 Davis was reintroduced to a new generation of readers with Tillie Olsen's pioneering Feminist Press edition of *Life in the Iron Mills and Other Stories*. By far Davis's most frequently anthologized and taught text, "Life in the Iron-Mills" has since generated over a hundred articles and book chapters, and the importance of Olsen's role in sparking interest in Davis cannot be overstated. Unfortunately, Olsen erroneously identified Davis as the author of a conservative argument against women's rights, *Pro Aris et Focis (For our Altars and our Hearths)* (137), a mistake that may have impacted Davis's reception by early feminist critics involved in the recovery of many women writers in the early 1970s.[7] Olsen also initiates the "poor Rebecca" depiction of Davis as a thwarted and somehow diminished artist. Noting that "a scanty best of her work is close to the first rank" and "even that best is botched," Olsen concedes that "botched art or not—a significant portion of her work remains important and vitally alive for our time" (155). Elaine Showalter concurs, concluding in *A Jury of Her Peers* that "Davis could not sustain the prophetic power of her early work" (137), and Judith Fetterley goes even further, claiming that, like Hugh Wolfe, "Davis, too, chose a form of suicide; artistic compromise turned her pen against herself" (313). These early assessments rely on Olsen's limited collection of Davis's work and thus overlook the complexity of her long career.

The pioneering scholarship of Sharon M. Harris, Jean Pfaelzer, Jane A. Rose, Robin Cadwallader, and others has done much to complicate these readings and to recognize her contribution to nineteenth-century literary history. Noting the lack of sustained critical attention to Davis's canon, Rose points out that her "work fits no neat critical category" (RHD xi), while Harris notes her ability to blend literary styles, "most often using the techniques of both romanticism and sentimentalism . . . to draw readers into stories wherein the realities of quotidian life were of primary significance" (RHD *and Realism* 7). Situating Davis as "a founder of American realism," Jean Pfaelzer argues that "from within these critiques of sentimentalism and transcendentalism, Davis founded a prototypical realist discourse" (*Parlor Radical* 21). Pfaelzer also suggests that Davis often "managed to use contemporary popular genres against themselves, in a sense deconstructing them as she went along" ("Legacy Profile" 41).

This edition of *A Law Unto Herself*, which has been out of print since its original book publication in 1878, continues the project of recovering Rebecca Harding Davis for a new generation of readers. Through the novel's protagonist, Jane Swendon, Davis draws on familiar literary conventions (the female bildungsroman, romanticism, domestic fiction, and Gothic fiction) to suggest that the audience is unable to "read" Jane "right," either through familiar genre-specific narratives about the female heroine, or, more significantly, through the lens of the law and its conceptions of women and legal identity. Framed in light of debates about citizenship, suffrage, and other rights, the novel speaks to the myriad complexities of its cultural moment and invites consideration of changing gender roles; opportunities for women as artists; the treatment of the poor; the impact of immigration, urbanization, and industrialization; and the reform movements designed to address these issues.

A Law Unto Herself: Cultural Context

From the first chapter of *A Law Unto Herself*, Davis employs self-reflexive references to genre that invite critique of genre conventions. The novel opens with a reminder about the dangers of reading for genre by invoking familiar Gothic tropes. The action begins in a typically Gothic setting—"a raw, cloudy afternoon" as a carriage travels "down a lonely road" to "an apparently vacant house . . . set back from the road . . . [and] long abandoned to decay" (3). The house appears to Captain Swendon (Jane's father) and Cornelia Fleming (a family friend) "as if it were an open grave" (4). Against this haunting backdrop, readers learn the details of the "ghastly errand: to drag out the secrets of the grave" by using a spiritualist medium to communicate with the spirit of Jane's dead mother about her inheritance (3). Readers are thus prepared for a Gothic heroine, surrounded by danger and mystery.

Like many Gothic heroines, Jane is disinherited and lacks the male guidance and support to claim her legal rights. Here, Davis perceptively uses a conventional plot device to expose real-world legal doctrines that shaped the lives of nineteenth-century American women. In the opening chapter, readers learn that Jane's grandfather (Old Morôt) disinherited Jane's mother (Virginie Morôt Swendon) when she married Jane's father. He left his estate to his nephew, Phillip Laidley. Though Morôt regretted his decision, he died before formally changing his will and instead "charged" Laidley to "do justice to his daughter" (11). In the first will, Laidley apparently honored this request, leaving his property to Jane after her mother died. However, before the action of the novel begins, Laidley has had a change of heart. His new will leaves everything to Pliny Van Ness's charity, and he plans to "do justice" to Jane by arranging her marriage to Van Ness. The novel opens with the séance to contact Jane's mother for her approval. This typical Gothic plot raises a host of issues regarding Jane's property rights as a single or married woman and the legal power of a husband to control not only his wife's property but her destiny as well; by disinheriting Jane, Laidley erases her legal identity as an heir and attempts to ensure her complicity through an arranged marriage. As Teresa Goddu suggests, Gothic literature is not necessarily an escapist form designed to entertain through evoking fear; indeed, "the Gothic registers its culture's contradictions" (3). Davis uses this plot to reveal the links between property ownership, citizenship, and legal rights for women.

Though the title *A Law Unto Herself* refers most obviously to Jane, it can easily be applied to her foils, Charlotte and Cornelia, because both women subvert nineteenth-century gender roles and provide alternative models of female agency. As a medium and confidence woman (a con artist), Charlotte asserts the female power often associated with the Gothic, while the Bohemian writer Cornelia embraces the independence and freedom of the new woman. Both offer models of female identity that depart from the domestic ideals of true womanhood and invite comparison to Davis's other explorations of the woman question, particularly in *Earthen Pitchers* (1874) and *Kitty's Choice or A Story of Berrytown* (1873).

A character who could have been taken from a Gothic novel, Charlotte (disguised as the renowned clairvoyant Mrs. Miriam Combe) claims to be a spiritualist medium, able to materialize the spirits of the dead. In *Radical Spirits*, Ann Braude notes that "spirit mediums formed the first large group of American women to speak in public or to exercise religious leadership" (xix). Further, spiritualists differed from other women religious leaders in their "commitment to women's rights" (xx). Thus, for many women, spiritualism provided a source of cultural power and an active public identity. Though she is quickly revealed to be a fake, Charlotte also seems to have "the evil eye" associated with a mesmerist's powers.[8] In a reversal of Nathaniel Hawthorne's Westervelt and Priscilla in *The Blithedale Romance* (1852), Charlotte "materializes" a veiled woman pretending to be Virginie Morôt, called back to advise Laidley about his will. Read as a female mesmerist, Charlotte transgresses boundaries. As Theresa Gaul observes, "the culture that celebrated sentimentalism . . . feared the power possessed by the mesmerist, viewing it as threatening to gender roles and standards of sexual propriety" (835).

Like Alcott in "Behind a Mask" (1866), Davis codes Charlotte's sexuality through her mesmeric power—she is "charged with electricity" and her gaze produces strong reactions in most of the men (14).

Though described as "a regular confidence woman" (125), Charlotte is not a one-dimensional villain. Davis makes clear that Charlotte's profession actually pays better than honest work, a point she revisits in "Low Wages for Women" (1888) where she argues that women must have access to meaningful work and be able to do it well in order to achieve economic security. When Jane later encounters Charlotte disguised as a Russian princess, she keeps Charlotte's secret because "she remembered she had once taken the bread from the wretched woman's mouth" and "would not do it again" (107). Drawing on domestic ideology, Davis also humanizes Charlotte through her regard for her son. Thinking of his future, Charlotte briefly considers Jane's offer of "honest work" as a seamstress but then she "remember[s] the time when some fussy, good women had put her in charge of a fashionable Kindergarten" (114, 115).[9] Despite a good salary and teachers to help with the work, Charlotte broke "the finical apparatus to pieces, left a heap of bonbons for the children, scrawled a verse of good-bye with the chalk on the blackboard, and [took] to the road again without a penny" (115). A law unto herself, Charlotte provides a genre-defying model of female agency that resists domestic gender codes.

Like Charlotte, Cornelia Fleming is also a potential model of female agency. Reminiscent of Hawthorne's Zenobia in *The Blithedale Romance*, Cornelia is a prototypical bluestocking artist and a forerunner of the independent new woman of the 1890s. Described by Carroll Smith-Rosenberg as "single, highly educated, economically autonomous" (qtd. in Showalter 210), the new woman forges her own path. The only character explicitly described as an artist, Cornelia is "an Arab among her own sex" who "stepped freely up . . . to level ground with men, and struck hands and made friendships with them precisely as if she were one of themselves" (12, 6). However, Cornelia is not the typical suffragist or artist. Literally a law unto herself, she avoids both "the emancipated lonely sisterhood, who set social laws at defiance" and "the whole tribe of literary and artistic adventurers" (27). She describes herself as "independent as any—female doctor" (130), invoking a profession often denied to women in the nineteenth century.[10] Like Louisa May Alcott's Jo March, Cornelia is often figured in masculine terms: a "clever, candid boy" and "an innocent, manly boy" (6, 161). She admits to an "antipathy . . . to everything in the world that was not masculine" (98), and like the men in the novel, she frequently misreads Jane. Though she notes that Jane "can turn a penny to the best advantage," Cornelia sees her as a "child" who "irritated her, just as a machine did, or an animal or any other creature whose motive-power she could not comprehend" (27). Cornelia's masculine identity stands in sharp contrast to the feminine exemplar of sentimental, domestic fiction.

Like her contemporaries Louisa May Alcott in *Work* (1873) and Elizabeth Stuart Phelps in *The Story of Avis* (1877), Davis draws on the tradition of the female bildungsroman. Jane's plight suggests elements of the typical domestic plot in which a young woman "has lost the emotional and financial support of her legal guardians . . . but . . . goes on to win her own way in the world" (Baym, *Woman's Fiction* ix). The protagonist is eventually rewarded with "domestic comfort, a social network, and a companionable husband" after learning the value of the "overcoming of obstacles through a hard-won, much tested 'self-dependence'" (ix). Left to her own devices by her ineffectual father, Jane forges an independent identity of sorts, yet she lacks a fully realized, mature sense of self. For instance, at the beginning of the novel, during Charlotte's performance, Jane seems independent and decisive because she is the only one to see through the charade. Readers later learn that she manages the family finances and helps her father make his patent models though she still has child-like traits: "she made the models, she draughted them, she worked with carpenter's tools, needles, pencils, clay, by turns, and was both swift and skillful" (28). However, though Jane has some artistic ability, she is frequently described as a "child" (28), and her suitor Bruce Neckart initially believes that "the girl is like her dog" (45). Further, unlike the typical domestic heroine, Jane seldom justifies her actions through appeals to traditional Christianity. For instance, when Judge Rhodes's daughters offer their "domestic feminine influence," they learn that Jane "did not know a word of any catechism" and offer "religious novels to convert her" (101). Jane takes the books "but never cut[s] the leaves" (101). Thus, Jane does not have access to the traditional sphere of influence afforded by true womanhood ideology.

Despite Jane's practical traits and ability to see through deception, her suitors consistently misread her in sentimental and romantic terms, a misreading that may also suggest Davis's awareness of her own position (the sentimental authoress in James's reviews, for instance) in a rapidly changing literary marketplace.[11] Throughout the novel, Bruce Neckart attempts to "read" Jane "page by page" but does so according to the wrong genre (62). Like the protagonist of a domestic novel, Jane appears to Neckart as part of "quiet, pretty picture" (31), and to her other suitor, Pliny Van Ness, as "the most noticeable point in the picture" (121). Framed in this way by her male "readers" as an artistic representation, Jane is open to interpretation, and misinterpretation, throughout the novel.

A reflection of the late-nineteenth-century market economy, Neckart is a public man. As an editor and businessman, he is involved with the political issues of the day and is always aware of the market; for instance, when he negotiates a contract with a local man, he refuses to follow the local practice to "talk rates when the day's over" (36). Instead, he insists on making the bargain as strangers, requiring a price up front and claiming that "I pay to a penny, and I exact to a penny" (36). He even recognizes that the marriage market is akin to a slave auction but fails to recognize his own complicity in the system: "Item, so much amiability; item, so many pounds of healthy flesh; item annual income so much. . . . [I]f she prove satisfactory, he will marry her" (71).

His romanticized view of Jane reflects the contemporary ideology of separate spheres. When he sees Jane, he "vaguely remembered the jargon of sentimental novels, the heroines of which always keep their heads on Nature's breast. He did not mean to chaff any woman, but he would gladly have proved this one sentimental and weak to explain his strong antipathy to her" (43). With Jane, who seems "a part of the shore, as much as sea or sand" (44), Neckart begins "to feel the physical effect of coming from close streets and striving work into this vast open space" and realizes that "the influence that had quieted him so unaccountably had been in the girl" (44, 45). Reading Jane through the lens of domesticity, Neckart believes that her presence creates a private space and offers a haven from the hectic public sphere. Characterized by his "dwarfed bulk and massive head set in its black mane," Neckart calls to mind Charlotte Brontë's Rochester in *Jane Eyre (1847)*, a point that is reinforced not only by Jane's name but also by the description of her as "his little friend" and his desire to "claim . . . a guardianship over her" (62). Yet, it is precisely this type of male guardianship, and its legal implications, that the novel encourages readers to question.

"But his blood is good": Reform, Race, and Ethnicity

A Law Unto Herself also engages contemporary conversations about race, ethnicity, and biological inheritance. In contrast to her stark treatment of race in her fiction of the 1860s (*Waiting for the Verdict* [1868] features a mulatto doctor and examines contemporary concerns about miscegenation, for instance), Davis does not directly examine the plight of African Americans in *A Law Unto Herself*, an interesting choice since the novel was published near the end of Reconstruction. Only a few African American characters appear at the margins of the novel, and all of them are stereotypes who speak in dialect and play the role of slave turned domestic servant. These flat depictions may subtly suggest the failures of Reconstruction; though free citizens, many African American men must continue to behave like slaves in order to survive in white society.

Perhaps a reflection of the emerging cultural interest in proto-eugenics and social Darwinism, Davis shifts to broader questions about "blood" as a marker of race, ethnicity, and destiny. For instance, Jane is desirable for her status as a pure white woman; an example of "the great women of her race," she is consistently marked by her whiteness and her Swedish blood (62). Though Jane lacks the "true American vim" (32), Neckart is attracted to "her clear Scandinavian face" (45). Interestingly, this "Swedish blood" is desirable in a woman but not necessarily a man; Captain Swendon's "Swedish blood had infused a gentle laziness into his temper," and he forgives Laidley "as no American with English grandfathers would have done" (25). Further, consistent with eugenic ideas about desirable marriages, insanity is an "obstacle" that "make[s] it simply criminal" to marry and risk passing the disease to offspring (40).

These ideas also inform contemporary discussions about the poor. Through conversations about charitable reform, Davis examines contemporary theories about benevolence. She suggests that some organized reform efforts are suspect because they do not adequately address the underlying capitalist system that produces poor working conditions, inadequate wages, and poverty.[12] In *The Dangerous Classes of New York* (1872), Charles Loring Brace, a near-contemporary of Davis and the inspiration for many of the reforms addressed in the novel, focuses primarily on the plight of homeless urban children and argues that they should be sent to the rural West via orphan trains to build new lives with foster families with Christian values. Davis encourages readers to question this approach by linking Brace's reforms to a variety of schemes in the novel, including a "State Home for destitute children" and "Orphans' Homes in the Gulf States," often supported by letters of authentication from clergy (112, 109).[13] These schemes depend on upper-class guilt to raise money to help "friendless children" and raise the "dangerous classes" (90) and replicate "the vast system of organized charities through which the kindly wealthy class touch [sic] the poor beneath them" (111). Another con game involves selling lots in "Temperance City" to "colonists who are tee-totallers and members of some church" (111). As an investor observes, "Shares go off this summer like hotcakes. There's nothing like religion . . . to back up business enterprise" (111). Through this section, Davis calls attention to the dark side of industrialization and contemporary strategies for reform that often linked capitalism and Christianity.

A reflection of emerging Social Darwinist theories, Judge Rhodes believes that the poor cannot be helped: "What with ignorance and whiskey and conceit, the dangerous classes even here are too heavily handicapped to make any running. They will need two or three lives after this . . . to bring them up to a fair starting point" (75). In contrast, Captain Swendon suggests "to give to 'em all, and so be on the safe side" even though he admits that "the organized charities tell us they are all impostors; and then every day some organized charity turns out to be a swindle" (75). Jane tries to find middle ground in her solution. She purchases Hemlock Farm, "a great untrimmed tract of farm and woodland on the Hudson" and creates a kind of utopian community for urban refugees, "a colony of Philadelphia paupers," as Cornelia puts it (63, 96). Building on her earlier treatments of industrialism and urbanization in "Life in the Iron-Mills," *Margret Howth* (1861), and "The Promise of the Dawn" (1863), Davis describes poverty and disease. Twiss, the shoemaker "who used to live—or starve—in the back ally of their garden," is the "head-gardener"; Nichols, the "consumptive sempstress," is "growing quite fat" while she handles the dairy; and the new stable boy has escaped "the printing office, where he was going to the devil" (77). As Twiss's situation indicates, poverty is not simply a matter of unemployment or disability—some people are poor because they do not earn a living wage. Jane's solution suggests that authentic, individual action, rather than organized reform, can lead to positive change.

However, though Jane's actions are perfectly consistent with the moral influence attributed to women by domestic ideology, her approach elicits criticism; because she simply helps people who have been kind to her, Jane does not distinguish between the deserving and the undeserving poor, an important point of distinction for many nineteenth-century reformers. Reinforcing other descriptions of Jane as a child, Cornelia claims that "very young girls are apt to be impetuous in their charities and damage more than they help" (96). Thus, some forms of aid can actually harm the recipient. Similarly, echoing Emerson's position in "Self-Reliance" that a dollar given to the poor is "a wicked dollar" (322), Judge Rhodes argues that "every bit of bread given to a beggar degrades human nature and rots society to the core" (97). He also suggests that such efforts are "hopeless," noting that "the more efforts you make to reform the dangerous classes the more hardened you will grow" (98). When the captain notes that "the Good Samaritan wasn't afraid of pauperizing that poor devil on the road," Judge Rhodes counters, "Let him starve. He will have self-respect. The Good Samaritan knew nothing of political economy" (97). Underlying many of these ideas about the poor is the assumption that "blood" is an indicator of who or what a person can become.

Law, Gender, and Identity

With its emphasis on the legal status of women, *A Law Unto Herself* may also be productively read in light of recent interdisciplinary scholarship interested in the convergence of law and literature. The work of Robert Ferguson, Brook Thomas, Wai-Chee Dimock, and others suggests the ways in which reading literature with regard to its legal context can help us better understand the cultural significance of both. In *Cross-Examinations of Law and Literature*, Thomas suggests that "if law, like literature, is related to the narratives a culture tells about itself, so literature, like law, responds to its historical situation by seeking ways to resolve social contradictions" (6). Focusing on literature as a means to expose and critique the limitations of law, Wai-Chee Dimock cites "Life in the Iron-Mills" as a powerful example of her claim that through literature "the problem of justice is given a face and a voice" (10). Recent work on women writers and law suggests several promising directions for Davis scholarship. Melissa Homestead's recent analysis of "the implications of the copyright debates for nineteenth century scenes of reading and writing" invites inquiry into the influence of other legal doctrines on both the literary texts and everyday lives of nineteenth-century women writers (4); further, her work on the intersection of married women's property laws and copyright protections might be extended to postbellum writers, including Davis.

Most relevant for my analysis here, in *Criminal Conversations*, Laura Korobkin persuasively argues that sentimentalism may be productively understood as a cultural discourse that shapes not only literature but its rational "other"—the law. For Korobkin, the rhetoric of sentimentality "permeates the legal process" and "provides the controlling mode for jury arguments that strive to convince jurors that their own deepest beliefs and emotions are at stake" (15). Thus, in the courtroom, sentiment coexists with reason as lawyers rely on emotional appeals to reinforce a particular narrative about the "facts" of the case.[14]

In his legal analysis of Jane's situation, Judge Rhodes exemplifies this point. Described by Cornelia Fleming as "one of those shrewd, common-sense men who, when lifted out of their place into the region of sentiment or romance, swagger and generally misconduct themselves" (8–9), Judge Rhodes represents the rational order of the legal system, but his views often stem from sentimentalism, especially his assumption that a society built on status-based relationships will provide justice when the letter of the law fails. When Cornelia points out that the estate "legally" belongs to Van Ness as Laidley's new heir, the judge agrees but with a caveat: "Of course this sort of crime is unappreciable in the courts. But society, Virginia society, knows how to deal with it" (11). He agrees to "do justice" by encouraging an arranged marriage for Jane rather than investigating her legal options, such as a will contest or a caveat proceeding, that might help her claim the estate. Viewing Jane as a "poor creature" (21), he never imagines that Jane might take the law into her own hands. Through his legal analysis of her situation, Judge Rhodes reflects prevailing legal ideology that the private sphere of family relationships should be outside the law's reach. Also, as a Southerner, Judge Rhodes exemplifies the unreconstructed South and its inability to adjust to rapid cultural changes.

Through her depictions of male characters, Davis exposes the limitations of the patriarchal assumption that the father / husband should be the de-facto legal representative of the family. In her critique of law as a form of gendered oppression, Davis emphasizes several issues: a woman's legal identity, her property rights, and her mental capacity as determined by the law. Jane's plight highlights the gray area between a legally defined (and thus legally actionable) crime and a moral wrong that may not be defined as a crime by the law. Jane's lack of legally viable options to secure her inheritance highlights her status as a woman, and it is not surprising that she chooses to break the law to claim her property. In her treatment of these issues, Davis clearly recognizes the interdependence of sentimental and legal discourse suggested by Korobkin's analysis.

As a young, unmarried woman, Jane has limited legal options, and in the nineteenth century, her father would be expected to contest Laidley's second will through a caveat proceeding, an action that seems unlikely given his inability to act as a true head of the household.[15] Described as a "good for nothing" and a "well-born tramp," Captain

Swendon serves as a failed exemplar of romantic individualism (12). Though he enlists in the army for practical, not ideological, reasons—"to keep the wolf out of the house at home" (7)—he devotes himself to his inventions and seems just as divorced from reality as Davis recalled Emerson and Bronson Alcott.[16] Though Jane has managed the family finances for several years, her father persistently reads her a sentimental heroine, as weak and in need of male guardianship. A literal example of the "dead hand of the law," he finally forces Jane to consent to a marriage that she would not choose for herself.

Through the complicated inheritance plot, Davis also reveals the limitations of guardianship and trust arrangements, legal relationships through which a male relative or family friend controlled property on behalf of a woman or child. Though Phillip Laidley is not Jane's legal guardian or a trustee, Old Morôt's deathbed request for "justice" suggests a fiduciary relationship because Laidley has control over an estate that was originally intended for Jane's use. His decision to leave the estate to charity reveals the problems with assuming that a male guardian or trustee will automatically make sound legal decisions on behalf of his female ward.

When Jane confronts Laidley about his will, his reaction emphasizes his position as a kind of guardian and foregrounds the reasons why she lacks legal status—the related issues of her age, her mental capacity, and her natural state as a woman according to God's law. First, he asks, "Do I understand what you say? . . . That you, a child, come here to a dying man to assert your claim to his property! It is incredible that you came of your own free will. Who sent you?" (51). His response mirrors several important legal questions—though readers do not know her precise age, his reference to Jane as a "child" is an accurate reflection of her legal status. Because Jane is an unmarried woman, her legal rights, to the extent they exist at all, reside in her father until she comes of age. Similarly, Laidley questions Jane's "free will," an important concept in nineteenth-century American law, and assumes that, even if she is legally of age to do so, she lacks the capacity to act on her own. Even when he acknowledges that she has a "crude, illegal claim" on his "property" (51), he justifies his decision with an appeal to higher law:

How can you understand the relations of a dying man to his Maker? It has been shown to me how with this money I could make peace with—with Him. . . . Why, the rich man was commanded to "sell all that he had and give to the poor, and he should have treasure in heaven." The place is marked in the Bible there. . . . Why should I take from the poor to give to your father? (51, 52)

According to Laidley, the laws of God and of man concur on this issue. Jane's answer is a simple assertion of ownership that goes to the question of female agency at the heart of the novel; she replies, "Because it is not yours to take or give" (52). With Jane's defiant action in the moment that follows, Davis encourages her readers to reconsider their conceptions of free will, consent, and justice. Her response implicitly asserts her identity as a legal subject and citizen capable of owning and controlling property.

The issue of consent plays an important role throughout the novel. In *From Bondage to Contract*, Amy Dru Stanley describes contract as both a "worldview" that "idealized ownership of self and voluntary exchange between individuals who were formally equal and free" and a "social relation assumed in American culture to rest of principles of self ownership, consent and exchange" (x). Borrowing these principles, early women's rights activists often linked slavery and marriage to expose the legal status of married women. However, as Stanley points out, "legal and political thinkers . . . held that marriage was peculiar among free contracts, that it alone—unlike either contracts of sale or contemporary wage contracts—created a related of status" (180). Judge Rhodes illustrates precisely this type of thinking.

Through Jane, Davis highlights the paradox of consent as it applies to women. As Stanley explains, "Like all other contracts, marriage hinged on the principles of mutual consent and exchange. But, unlike any other contract, the marriage contract ordained male proprietorship and absolute female dispossession, establishing self ownership as the fundamental right of men alone" (11). Put another way, when a woman consents to the marriage contract, she may give up her ability to consent to any other contract. Davis makes this point apparent in the way that she handles Jane's marriage ceremony. Like Esther Lashley in *The Second Life* (1863), Jane "consents" only at her father's deathbed request (a point that clearly suggests coercion), and though she ultimately avoids Esther's fate, Jane risks being declared mad and committed to an institution, a Gothic plot twist that foregrounds Jane's new legal status as wife. Her marriage amounts to a patriarchal bequest rather than a freely chosen agreement; as Captain Swendon explains, "I can give her to you. I can die in peace" (143). This important scene underscores the significance of consent. When Jane flees, her husband quickly requests an official marriage certificate, explaining that "if my wife is living and wandering insane through the country, it will be necessary to prove my right to claim her" (152). This language reflects Jane's status as property. Paradoxically, given Jane's alleged insanity, the minister seeks clarification: "Are you quite sure she consented freely to the marriage? There was no moral compulsion used?" (152).

Married women's property laws were enacted gradually over the nineteenth century to counteract the legal doctrine of coverture. In his *Commentaries on the Laws of England*, Sir William Blackstone provides a succinct definition of the doctrine of marital unity: "The very being or legal existence of a woman is suspended during the marriage, or at least is incorporated and consolidated into that of the husband; under whose wing, protection, and cover, she performs everything" (bk. 1; ch. 15). Thus, a wife had little or no legal identity apart from her husband. Passed in the 1830s and '40s, the first married women's property laws "dealt primarily with freeing married women's estates from the debts of their husbands" and "left untouched the traditional marital estate and coverture rules" (Chused 1398). The second group, enacted over a twenty-year period from the early 1840s until well after the Civil War ended, "established separate estates for married women" through which they might have limited control of their own property (Chused 1398). The final statutes were passed in the late nineteenth century and provided that married women could keep their wages (Chused 1398).[17] In the absence of these statutory guarantees, most states allowed married women to hold property in a trust through a separate estate. In most cases, a male relative, usually a father or brother, set up a trust in order to shield the wife's inheritance from a husband who lacked business skills or, even more likely, was estranged from his wife's family. However, as legal scholars demonstrate, "the virtual universality of married women's property acts did not mean . . . that uniformity reigned in America" (Shammas 83). Jane's rights in New York might not be consistent with her rights if she lived in Virginia or New Jersey. Further, the mere existence of married women's property laws did not guarantee that women could automatically gain meaningful control of their property. In her study *In the Eyes of the Law*, Norma Basch argues that "married women's acts cannot be construed as a revolution" because they often "failed to obliterate the historic barriers the common law had thrown around married women" (200).

If we assume that Jane's marriage is valid, then her husband would control her property to the extent allowed by the married women's property law in her home state, New York. As New York was among the most liberal jurisdictions in the United States at the time, its married women's property law suggests that Jane might maintain at least some control of the property she owned prior to her marriage; the 1848 statute reads in part, "the real and personal property of any female who may hereafter marry, and which she shall own at the time of marriage . . . shall continue her sole and separate property, as if she were a single female."[18]

The turn to insanity, which Davis treats in depth in her novella *Put Out of the Way* (1870), points to another important issue—the capacity to consent and the legal mechanism for evaluating that capacity. By declaring Jane insane, her husband might be able to control her property despite the protections afforded by married women's property laws. In *Put Out of the Way* (1870), Davis examines unethical civil commitment procedures that allow sane individuals to be institutionalized without a physician's authorization or due process review.[19] The protagonist, Philip Wortley (based on his real-world counterpart Morgan Hinchman) was committed to an asylum by unscrupulous relatives who wanted control of his property. By purchasing a physician's certificate and paying for Wortley's board, they literally put him "out of the way" until he was able to contact a judge by secretly sending a letter. Though Pennsylvania passed new legislation (L. Clarke Davis was appointed to the investigating committee) in 1874 to provide due process guarantees and greater oversight of physicians and institutions, Davis continued to call attention to the issue in stories such as "The Case of Jane Boyer" (1877). In a study of nineteenth-century civil commitment reform, Applebaum and Kemp report that "rather than an abrupt switch from relaxed procedures to stringent safeguards, Pennsylvania law underwent a slow accretion of procedural protections, with the essential role of families, friends, and physicians left undisturbed" (352).

Jane's plight becomes a metaphor for the plight of all women in a patriarchal legal system, a system in which resistance can be an indicator of madness. With the understanding that "the law would ensure him immediate possession of his wife" (167), Jane is forced to recognize that "it was the Law" (168). She realizes that though "the law within her gave a savage answer," "she must answer according to the judgment of the outside world" (168). Even a sympathetic friend advises her, "Suppose you don't like him so much at first? You'll grow into it. Hundreds of women marry without love. You must give up to the law" (170).

The emphasis on law throughout the novel also invites consideration of the title. What does it mean for Jane to be "a law unto herself" in the context of a legal system that systematically excludes her participation? A familiar idiom, the title phrase might have resonated in several ways with Davis's audience. It appears in Nathaniel Hawthorne's *The Scarlet Letter* (1850) as a description of Pearl: "It was as if she had been made afresh, out of new elements, and must perforce be permitted to live her own life, and be a law unto herself, without her eccentricities being reckoned to her for a crime" (112). In this scene, Chillingsworth proclaims that "there is no law, nor reverence for authority, no regard for human ordinances or opinions, right or wrong, mixed up with that child's composition" (112). In contrast, for Dimmesdale, Pearl has "the freedom of a broken law" (112). In this context, the phrase suggests that Pearl has the potential to create herself without reference to law or social custom. This allusion to *The Scarlet Letter* is particularly haunting if we consider Jane as Pearl's figurative descendent. Jane cannot create herself in a world that figures her as a child rather than an autonomous adult.

Sophocles's *Antigone* is another likely source that reinforces the novel's central themes. The most popular Greek heroine in nineteenth-century America, Antigone would certainly have been a familiar figure for Davis and her audience. The last installment of Sophocles's *Oedipus* trilogy, *Antigone* centers on the clash between positive law (Creon's edict forbidding the burial of traitors) and natural law (the law of the gods that demands the burial of a family member). In violation of Creon's law, Antigone symbolically buries her brother and defends her action on the grounds that she is following the law of the gods. The line that may have inspired Davis's title comes late in the play, after Antigone has been sentenced to death, and most translations emphasize the Chorus's recognition of Antigone's autonomy. Commenting on her situation, the Chorus describes her as "answering only / To the law of yourself, you / Are the only mortal who / Will go down alive into Hades" (881–884). In an 1842 edition (available at the Philadelphia Public Library where Davis often worked), Thomas Francklin translates the same phrase as "above thy sex, and to thyself a law" (59). More recently, Diane Raynor comments on the connotations of the original Greek: "The Chorus disapprovingly calls her 'autonomos' (following her 'own law' or being a law unto herself)" (84).[20] In this context, the phrase refers to Antigone as an autonomous subject.

In *The Mirror of Antiquity*, Caroline Winterer examines the use of classicism by American women for a range of political and personal goals and argues that the many permutations of Antigone across the nineteenth century reflect the tension between public and private roles for women. According to Winterer, "Antigone became the crux of one of the major questions of the post–Civil War period: Could women become political actors and on what grounds?" (190). Winterer describes Antigone's resonance with American women: "Antigone was popular . . . because she dramatized clearly how Americans might accept female political participation in an age that still insisted on the essentially apolitical nature of women" (191). However, this interest was not without complications; Winterer observes that many nineteenth-century commentators "took an overtly political story and made it a study in feminine self-perfection. . . . During these decades, *Antigone* spoke less for a universal *human* dilemma of choosing between self and state . . . than for a peculiarly *female* moral story of religious obligation, family duty, and martyrdom to true womanhood" (205, italics in original). Thus, the Antigone of Davis's cultural moment resonates powerfully both with Jane's defiant action and the novel's complex ending.

Like Antigone, Jane becomes a "law unto herself," and her justification also appropriates natural law but with a twist: "She was absolutely certain of her own honesty, and she hoped that God believed in it. What did it matter if by the laws of men and society she was a thief?" (139). This description resists both natural law and positive law, implying instead that a woman must be her own moral compass, a move that suggests the title and foreshadows the complicated ending. Indeed, the novel persistently asks readers to examine the relationship between positive law (man-made law) and natural law (God's law or some higher notion of justice). Davis's contemporary, Harriet Beecher Stowe, creates a powerful example of this clash in *Uncle Tom's Cabin* (1852) when Mrs. Bird asserts God's law to counter the man-made Fugitive Slave Law, a law her senator-husband helps to enact and then must break. Mrs. Bird's justification provides a typical nineteenth-century invocation of natural law grounded in Christian religious principles, and she is also a typical example of the nineteenth-century true woman of sentimental fiction, acting from her position as the moral center of the domestic space. In contrast, Jane's justification for her decision elides the typical definition of natural law in religious terms. Rather than an appeal to "God's law," Jane justifies her actions by asserting honesty and an implied sense of personhood that she hopes God will understand.

Pointing to the heart of Davis's legal critique, the phrase "a law unto herself" appears twice in the novel, both times in relation to marriage. Near the novel's midpoint, Jane reluctantly discusses the expectation that she marry. She admits, "I don't know what I was made for" (103), and her father urges her to "be like other people" (103). Here, it is important to recognize that Jane has not been "made" to be anything other than a dependent, child-like woman. Though she acts independently to manage her father's affairs, others consistently misread her as a child.

Concerned that Jane has "loved but one or two people in the world," he continues, "You cannot be a law to yourself, child. . . . [Y]ou are out of the groove which other girls are in" (103). Recognizing her father's distress, Jane promises, "I will give myself up, body and soul, to Society or Philanthropy—anything you choose—rather than see you so shaken" (105). Jane's lighthearted declaration, spoken simply to soothe her father, proves prophetic when he forces her into a marriage she would not choose.

The phrase appears again in the final scene when Jane admits, "I know that I made many mistakes when I was a law to myself. You are my law now." (175). Yet, the narrator's last comment further undercuts Jane's apparent concession to her husband's law: "There are times when she seems, even to him, a woman whose acquaintance he has scarcely made, and whom he can never hope to know better" (175). In the context of the concluding line, Jane may well remain a "law unto herself" and unknowable to others, a reading that complicates the conventional ending of the female bildungsroman. Through the ending, Davis posits an identity for Jane that is not a completely relational self—she keeps a part of herself as private property—but not quite an autonomous self as she submits to her husband's law according to the cultural ideology of the day.

In her final act of defiance, she continues to emphasize her legal right to her inheritance, asserting her identity as a property owner by making a "free gift" of it to a charity (175). This gift, however, is a paradox; as Hildegard Hoeller explains, in nineteenth-century America, "the gift collides with and reflects on the market" (13), and by the end of the century, "the gift appears to be a more and more difficult, yet always utterly necessary, concept to uphold" (14). On the one hand, by asserting her right to the property through making a legal gift, Jane resists the idea of marital unity inherent in the doctrine of coverture; she acts through her own legal identity. However, her gift raises the specter of coercion because her husband may have unduly influenced her decision. Through this assertion of a legal identity and a private self, Jane claims a kind of property interest in herself but one that exists in isolation, suggesting the alienated and fragmented self of modernity.

Notes

1. In "A Rainy Day" (1882), Davis describes the exhibition from the perspective of a young visitor, Amy Pollok, who does not visit the women's exhibit.
2. See Barbara Welter's classic article, "The Cult of True Womanhood."
3. For a bibliography of Davis's work, see Jane A. Rose, "A Bibliography of Fiction and Non-Fiction by Rebecca Harding Davis." For subsequent additions, see "Newly Discovered Works by RHD."
4. For biographical details, I am indebted to Langford, *The Richard Harding Davis Years*; Harris, *Rebecca Harding Davis and American Realism*; Harris and Cadwallader, "Introduction" in *Rebecca Harding Davis's Stories of the Civil War*; Jean Pfaelzer, *Parlor Radical*; and Jane A. Rose, *Rebecca Harding Davis*.
5. Critical assessments of sentimentalism vary greatly. See Ann Douglas, *The Feminization of American Culture*; Jane Thompkins, *Sensational Designs*; and Shirley Samuels, *The Culture of Sentiment*.
6. See Nina Baym, "Melodramas of Beset Manhood."
7. See Eppard, "Rebecca Harding Davis: A Misattribution," and Harris "Rebecca Harding Davis: A Continuing Misattribution."
8. See Davis's "Mesmerism vs. Common Sense" (1881).
9. Just two years earlier in "Two Women" (1875), Davis described two types of women that "represent two phases of city life" and "are born antagonists" (5). Jane McCall is a practical woman who is "a huckster in the Farmer's Market" and is "honest, but sharp as a steel trap" (5), and like Cornelia, Madame Constantia de Gonzalon "is clever with her pen," and like Charlotte, she once had charge of a kindergarten but left her charges "tearing through the house like sheep without a shepherd" when she took to "vagabondage" (5).
10. For more on the woman physician in Davis's work, see Harris, "Rebecca Harding Davis's Kitty's Choice and the Disabled Woman Physician."
11. My approach here is informed by Laura Korobkin's claim that "sentimental texts . . . interpret the lives of their readers" (78). If Jane functions on one level as a text (the description of her as a book to be read page by page certainly invites such an interpretation), then what does she reveal about her readers?
12. For an overview of benevolence literature by American women writers, see Bernadi and Bergman, *Our Sisters' Keepers: Nineteenth Century Benevolence Literature by American Women*.
13. As Karen Halttunen argues in *Confidence Men and Painted Women*, both types of con artists exemplify cultural anxieties about identity by revealing "that they themselves and those around them were 'passing' for something they were not" (xv).

14. To illustrate her general argument, Korobkin focuses on "criminal conversation," the civil tort for adultery cases (16). She suggests that "appeals court judges appropriated stories about domesticity and marriage from literary fictions and used them to instantiate the legal parameters of spousal rights and obligations" (18).

15. Also, successful will contests were rare due to a high burden of proof. The estate typically pays for the proceeding and is thus diminished in the process of litigation (Dickens's famous *Jarndyce v. Jarndyce* litigation in *Bleak House* [1853] comes to mind here).

16. See "Boston in the Sixties" in *Bits of Gossip* (1904).

17. For a general history of married women's property law, see Peggy Rabkin's *Fathers to Daughters: The Legal Foundation of Female Emancipation* and Norma Basch's *In the Eyes of the Law: Women, Marriage, and Property in Nineteenth-Century New York.*

18. The 1848 New York statute known as the Married Women's Property Act reads as follows:

    Section 1: The real and personal property of any female who may hereafter marry, and which she shall own at the time of marriage, and the rents, issues and profits thereof shall not be subject to the disposal of her husband, nor be liable for his debts, and shall continue her sole and separate property, as if she were a single female.

    Section 2: The real and personal property, and the rents issues and profits thereof of any female now married shall not be subject to the disposal of her husband; but shall be her sole and separate property as if she were a single female except so far as the same may be liable for the debts of her husband heretofore contracted.

    Section 3: It shall be lawful for any married female to receive by gift, grant, devise or bequest, from any person other than her husband and hold to her sole and separate use, as if she were a single female, real and personal property, and the rents, issues and profits thereof, and the same shall not be subject to the disposal of her husband, nor be liable for his debts.

    Section 4: All contracts made between persons in contemplation of marriage shall remain in full force after such marriage takes place. See Laws of New York, 1848, Chapter 20.

19. For an examination of Davis's collaboration with her husband, L. Clarke Davis, on this issue, see David Dowling, "Davis, Inc.: The Business of Asylum Reform in the Periodical Press."

20. In Plumptre's Harvard Classics edition, his translation emphasizes Antigone's free will: "But of thine own free will, in fullest life, to Hades tak'st thy way" (946–47).

Works Cited

Alcott, Louisa May. "Behind a Mask, or A Woman's Power." 1866. *Behind a Mask: The Unknown Thrillers of Louisa May Alcott*. Ed. Madeline Stern. New York: Harper, 2004. 1–104. Print.

———. *Little Women*. 1868. Eds. Anne K. Phillips and Gregory Eiselein. New York: Norton, 2003. Print.

———. *Work: A Story of Experience*. 1873. Ed. Sarah Elbert. New York: Schocken, 1977. Print.

"A law unto oneself." *The Facts on File Dictionary of Allusions*. Eds. Martin S. Manser and David H. Pickering. New York: Facts on File, 2009. *Scribd*. Web. 12 Dec. 2012.

Appelbaum, P. S., and K. N. Kemp. "The Evolution of Commitment Law in the Nineteenth Century." *Law and Human Behavior* 6.3–4 (1982): 343–54. Print.

Basch, Norma. *In the Eyes of the Law: Women, Marriage, and Property in Nineteenth-Century New York*. Ithaca NY: Cornell University Press, 1982. Print.

Baym, Nina. "Melodramas of Beset Manhood: How Theories of American Literature Exclude Women Writers." *American Quarterly* 33 (1981): 123–39. Print.

———. *Woman's Fiction: A Guide to Novels by and about Women in America, 1820–70*. 2nd ed. Urbana: University of Illinois Press, 1993. Print.

Bergman, Jill Annette, and Debra Bernardi, eds. *Our Sisters' Keepers: Nineteenth Century Benevolence Literature by American Women*. Tuscaloosa: University of Alabama Press, 2005. Print.

Blackstone, Sir William. *Commentaries on the Laws of England*. 4 vols. Oxford: Clarendon, 1765–69. *The Avalon Project: Documents in Law, History, and Diplomacy*. Yale Law School. Web. 1 June 2012.

Boyd, Anne. *Writing for Immortality: Women and the Emergence of High Literary Culture in America*. Baltimore: Johns Hopkins University Press, 2004. Print.

Brace, Charles Loring. *The Dangerous Classes of New York and Twenty Years' Work Among Them*. New York: Wynkoop, 1872. Google Book Search. 1 June 2012.

Bradwell v. Illinois. 83 U.S. 130. Supreme Court of the US. 1873.

Branton, Harriet K. "Sarah Foster Hanna and the Washington Female Seminary." *The Western Pennsylvania Historical Magazine* 61.3 (1978): 221–31. Print.

Braude, Ann. *Radical Spirits: Spiritualism and Women's Rights in Nineteenth-Century America*. 2nd ed. Bloomington: Indiana University Press, 2001. Print.

Carroll, Bret E. *Spiritualism in Antebellum America.* Bloomington: Indiana University Press, 1997. Print.

Chused, Richard. "Married Women's Property Law: 1800–1850." *Georgetown Law Journal* 71 (1983): 1359–425. Print.

Cordato, Mary Frances. "Toward a New Century: Women and the Philadelphia Exposition, 1876." *The Pennsylvania Magazine of History and Biography* 107.1 (1983): 113–35. *JSTOR.* Web. 7 June 2012.

Davis, Rebecca Harding. *Bits of Gossip.* 1904. Rpt. in *Rebecca Harding Davis: Writing Cultural Autobiography.* Eds. Janice Milner Lasseter and Sharon M. Harris. Nashville: Vanderbilt University Press, 2001. Print.

———. "Blind Tom." *Atlantic Monthly* Nov. 1862: 580–85. Rpt. in *Rebecca Harding Davis's Stories of the Civil War Era: Selected Writings from the Borderlands.* Eds. Sharon M. Harris and Robin L. Cadwallader. Athens: University of Georgia Press, 2010. Print.

———. "The Case of Jane Boyer." *Peterson's Magazine* Jul. 1877: 33–37. *American Periodicals.* Web. 2 Mar. 2011.

———. "David Gaunt." *Atlantic Monthly* Sept.–Oct. 1862: 257–71, 403–21. Rpt. in Harris and Cadwallader. 24–84. Print.

———. "A Day with Dr. Sarah." *Harper's New Monthly* Sept. 1878: 611–17. *American Periodicals.* Web. 2 Mar. 2011.

———. *Earthen Pitchers. Scribner's Monthly* Nov. 1873: 73–81; Dec. 1873: 199–207; Jan. 1874: 274–81; Feb. 1874: 490–94; Mar. 1874: 595–600; Apr. 1874: 714–21. *American Periodicals.* Web. 2 Mar. 2011.

———. "In the Market." *Peterson's Magazine* 1868: 49–57. *American Periodicals.* Web. 2 Mar. 2011.

———. *John Andross.* New York: Orange Judd Company, 1874. *Google Book Search.* Web. 18 May 2011.

———. "John Lamar." *Atlantic Monthly* Apr. 1862: 411–23. Rpt. in Harris and Cadwallader. 1–23. Print.

———. "Josey's Dower." *Peterson's Magazine* Nov. 1876: 324–28. *American Periodicals.* Web. 2 Mar. 2011.

———. *Kitty's Choice or Berrytown and Other Stories.* Philadelphia: Lippincott, 1873. Print.

———. *A Law Unto Herself.* Philadelphia: Lippincott, 1878. *Google Book Search.* Web. 10 Jan. 2009.

———. "Life in the Iron-Mills." *Atlantic Monthly* Apr. 1861: 430–51. Rpt. in Olsen. 9–66. Print.

———. "Low Wages for Women." *The Independent* 8 Nov. 1888: 1. *American Periodicals.* Web.

————. "Mesmerism vs. Common Sense." *Peterson's Magazine* Jul. 1881: 52–57. *American Periodicals*. Web. 10 Jan. 2009.

————. "Polly." *Peterson's Magazine* Jan. 1871: 46–54. *American Periodicals*. Web. 2 Mar. 2011.

————. "The Promise of the Dawn: A Christmas Story." *The Atlantic Monthly* Jan. 1863: 10–25. Rpt. in Harris and Cadwallader. 95–121.

————. *Put out of the Way. Peterson's Magazine* May 1870: 355–67; June 1870: 431–43; Jul. 1870: 30–41; Aug. 1870: 109–18. *American Periodicals*. Web. 10 Jan. 2009.

————. "A Rainy Day." *Peterson's Magazine* Jan. 1882: 49–53. *American Periodicals*. Web. 10 Jan. 2009.

————. *The Second Life. Peterson's Magazine* Jan. 1863: 33–39; Feb. 1863: 121–30; Mar. 1863: 204–11; Apr. 1863: 293–300; May 1863: 348–53; Jun. 1863: 420–30. *American Periodicals*. Web. 10 Jan. 2009.

————. "Two Women." *The Independent* 14 Oct. 1875: 5–6. *American Periodicals*. Web. 12 June 2012.

————. *Waiting for the Verdict*. 1868. Upper Saddle River NJ: Gregg Press, 1968. Print.

"A Declaration of Rights of the Women of the United States by the National Suffrage Association, July 4 1876." *Selected Papers of Elizabeth Cady Stanton and Susan B. Anthony*. Vol. 3. Ed. Ann D. Gordon. New Brunswick NJ: Rutgers University Press, 2003. The Elizabeth Cady Stanton and Susan B. Anthony Papers Project. Web. 12 June 2012.

Dimock, Wai-Chee. *Residues of Justice: Law, Literature, Philosophy*. Berkeley: University of California Press, 1996. Print.

Douglas, Ann. *The Feminization of American Culture*. New York: Knopf, 1977. Print.

Dowling, David. "Davis, Inc.: The Business of Asylum Reform in the Periodical Press." *American Periodicals* 20.1 (2010): 23–45. Print.

Emerson, Ralph Waldo. "Self Reliance." 1841. *Transcendentalism: A Reader*. Ed. Joel Myerson. New York: Oxford University Press, 2000. 318–40. Print.

Eppard, Philip B. "Rebecca Harding Davis: A Misattribution." *The Papers of the Bibliographical Society of America* 69 (1965): 265–67. Print.

Fetterley, Judith, ed. "Rebecca Harding Davis." *Provisions: A Reader From Nineteenth Century America Women*. Bloomington: Indiana University Press, 1985. 306–42. Print.

Francklin, Thomas. *The Antigone of Sophocles*. New York: Harper, 1842. Print.

Gaul, Theresa Strouth. "Trance-Formations: Mesmerism and 'A Woman's Power' in Louisa May Alcott's *Behind a Mask*." *Women's Studies: An Interdisciplinary Journal* 32.7 (2003): 835–51. Print.

Glazener, Nancy. *Reading for Realism: The History of a U.S. Literary Institution, 1850–1910*. Durham: Duke University Press, 1997. Print.

Goddu, Teresa A. *Gothic America: Narrative, History, and Nation*. New York: Columbia University Press, 1997. Print.

Halttunen, Karen. *Confidence Men and Painted Women: A Study of Middle-Class Culture in America, 1830–1870*. New Haven CT: Yale University Press, 1982. Print.

Harris, Sharon M. *Rebecca Harding Davis and American Realism*. Philadelphia: University of Pennsylvania Press, 1991. Print.

———. "Rebecca Harding Davis: A Continuing Misattribution." *Legacy* 5.1 (1988): 33–34. Print.

———, and Robin L. Cadwallader. Introduction. *Rebecca Harding Davis's Stories of the Civil War Era: Selected Writings from the Borderlands*. Eds. Sharon E. Harris and Robin Cadwallader. Athens: University of Georgia Press, 2010. Print.

———. "Rebecca Harding Davis's *Kitty's Choice* and the Disabled Woman Physician." *American Literary Realism* 44.1 (2011): 23–45. Print.

Hawthorne, Nathaniel. *The Blithedale Romance*. 1852. Ed. William Cain. New York: Bedford, 1996. Print.

———. *The Scarlet Letter*. 1850. Ed. Ross C. Murfin. New York: Bedford, 2005. Print.

Hoeller, Hildegard. *From Gift to Commodity: Capitalism and Sacrifice in Nineteenth-Century American Fiction*. Durham: University of New Hampshire Press, 2013. Print.

Homestead, Melissa. *American Women Authors and Literary Property, 1822–1969*. Cambridge: Cambridge University Press, 2005. Print.

Howells, William Dean. "Editor's Study." *Harper's New Monthly Magazine* Nov. 1889: 966. *Making of America*. Web. 30 Nov. 2012.

James, Henry. Rev. of *Dallas Galbraith* by Rebecca Harding Davis. *Nation* 22 Oct. 1868. Rpt. in Literary Criticism. Eds. Leon Edel and Mark Wilson. Vol. 1. New York: Library of America, 1984. 222–29. Print.

———. Rev. of *Waiting for the Verdict* by Rebecca Harding Davis. *Nation* 21 Nov. 1867. Rpt. in Edel and Wilson. 218–22. Print.

Korobkin, Laura. *Criminal Conversations: Sentimentality and Nineteenth-Century Legal Stories of Adultery*. New York: New York University Press, 1998. Print.

Kunitz, Stanley J., and Howard Haycraft. *American Authors, 1600–1900: A Biographical Dictionary of American Literature*. New York: H. W. Wilson, 1938. Print.

Rev. of *A Law Unto Herself*. *The Independent* 28 Feb. 1878: 9. *American Periodicals*. Web. 30 Nov. 2012.

Langford, Gerald. *The Richard Harding Davis Years: A Biography of Mother and Son.* New York: Holt, Rinehart and Winston, 1961. Print.

"Lippincott's Magazine." Rev. of *A Law Unto Herself* by Rebecca Harding Davis. *New York Times* 20 Jul. 1877: 3. *Proquest Historical Newspapers.* Web. 30 Nov. 2012.

"Literary Notices." *Godey's Lady's Book and Magazine* May 1878: 435. *American Periodicals.* Web. 30 Nov. 2012.

Long, Lisa. "The Postbellum Reform Writings of Rebecca Harding Davis and Elizabeth Stuart Phelps." *The Cambridge Companion to Nineteenth-Century American Women's Writing.* Eds. Dale M. Bauer and Phillip Gould. Cambridge: Cambridge University Press, 2001. 262–83. Print.

Minderman, Earl. "Today's Women." *Washington Post* 24 June 1929: 9. *Proquest Historical Newspapers.* Web. 2 May 2013.

"Newly Discovered Works by RHD." *The Rebecca Harding Davis Society Newsletter* 1.1 (2009). Web.

Olsen, Tillie, ed. Afterword. *Life in the Iron Mills and Other Stories.* By Rebecca Harding Davis. Old Westbury NY: The Feminist Press, 1985. Print.

Pattee, Fred. "Rebecca Harding Davis." *Dictionary of American Biography.* Vol. 5. Eds. Allan Johnson and Dumas Malone. New York: Scribner's, 1930. Print.

Person, Leland. *The Cambridge Introduction to Nathaniel Hawthorne.* Cambridge: Cambridge University Press, 2007. Print.

Pfaelzer, Jean. "Legacy Profile: Rebecca Harding Davis." *Legacy* 7.2 (1990): 39–45. Print.

———. *Parlor Radical: Rebecca Harding Davis and the Origins of American Social Realism.* Pittsburgh: University of Pittsburgh Press, 1996. Print.

Phelps, Elizabeth Stuart. "Stories that Stay." *Century* Nov. 1910: 118–23. *American Periodicals.* Web. 6 June 2011.

———. *The Story of Avis.* Ed. Carol Farley Kessler. New Brunswick NJ: Rutgers University Press, 1985. Print.

Rabkin, Peggy. *Fathers to Daughters: The Legal Foundation of Female Emancipation.* Westport CT: Greenwood, 1980. Print.

Raynor, Diane J. *Sophocles' Antigone: A New Translation.* Cambridge: Cambridge University Press, 2011. Print.

"Rebecca H. Davis, Novelist, Dead." *New York Times* 30 Sept. 1910, spec. ed.: 13. *Proquest.* Web. 7 Aug. 2012.

"Recent Novels." *The Nation* 18 Apr. 1878: 263–65. *The Nation Archive.* Web. 30 Nov. 2012.

Rose, Jane A. "A Bibliography of the Fiction and Non Fiction of Rebecca Harding Davis." *American Literary Realism* 22.3 (1990): 67–86. Print.

———. *Rebecca Harding Davis*. New York: Twayne, 1993. Print.

Samuels, Shirley. Ed. *The Culture of Sentiment: Race, Gender, and Sentimentality in 19th Century America*. New York: Oxford University Press, 1992. Print.

Shammas, Carole, Marylynn Salmon, and Michel Dalin. *Inheritance in America: Colonial Times to the Present*. New Brunswick NJ: Rutgers University Press, 1987. Print.

Showalter, Elaine. *A Jury of Her Peers*. New York: Knopf, 2009. Print.

Sophocles. *Antigone. Trans.* E. H. Plumptre. *The Harvard Classics*. Vol. 8. New York: Collier, 1909–14. Web. 12 Dec. 2009.

———. *Antigone. The Complete Sophocles: Volume 1: The Theban Plays*. Eds. Peter Burian and Alan Shapiro. Oxford: Oxford University Press, 2010. Print.

Stanley, Amy Dru. *From Bondage to Contract: Wage Labor, Marriage, and the Market in the Age of Slave Emancipation*. Cambridge: Cambridge University Press, 1998. Print.

Stoner, Ruth. "Rebecca Harding Davis's 'Second Life'; or 'Her Hands Could Be Trained as Well as His.'" *Legacy* 19.1 (2002): 44–52. Print.

Stowe, Harriet Beecher. *Uncle Tom's Cabin*. Ed. Elizabeth Timmons. New York: Norton, 2000. Print.

Thomas, Brook. *American Literary Realism and the Failed Promise of Contract*. Berkley: University of California Press, 1997. Print.

———. *Cross-Examinations of Law and Literature: Cooper, Hawthorne, Stowe, and Melville*. Cambridge: Cambridge University Press, 1987. Print.

Thompkins, Jane. *Sensational Designs: The Cultural Work of American Fiction, 1790–1860*. New York: Oxford University Press, 1985. Print.

Tutwiler, Julia. "Rebecca Harding Davis in Philadelphia." *Women Authors of Our Day in Their Homes: Personal Descriptions and Interviews*. Ed. Francis Whiting Halsey. New York: James Pott, 1903. Print.

Welter, Barbara. "The Cult of True Womanhood: 1820–1860." *American Quarterly* 18.2 (1966): 151–74. Print.

Whorton, James C. *Nature's Cures: The History of Alternative Medicine in America*. Oxford: Oxford University Press, 2002. Print.

Winterer, Caroline. *The Mirror of Antiquity: American Women and the Classical Tradition, 1750–1900*. Ithaca NY: Cornell University Press, 2007. Print.

Yellin, Jean Fagan. Afterword. *Margret Howth: a Story of To-Day*. By Rebecca Harding Davis. 1861. New York: The Feminist Press, 1990. Print.

A Note on the Text

This edition of Rebecca Harding Davis's *A Law Unto Herself* is based on the only book edition, published by J. B. Lippincott & Co. of Philadelphia, Pennsylvania, in 1878. The book version is divided into six parts that indicate the breaks for serialization. Otherwise, the text of the book edition is identical to the original serialization; see *Lippincott's Magazine* 2 (Jul.–Dec. 1877): 39–49, 167–82, 292–308, 464–78, 614–28, 719–31.

This edition retains Davis's nineteenth-century spellings, usage, punctuation, and hyphenation. She frequently uses dashes to indicate shifts, as in a line of dialogue that includes phrases directed at different characters.

A Law Unto Herself

PART I

Chapter 1

On a raw, cloudy afternoon in early spring a few years ago a family carriage was driven slowly down a lonely road in one of the outlying suburbs of Philadelphia, stopping at last in front of an apparently vacant house. This house was built of gray stone, and stood back from the road, surrounded by a few sombre pines and much rank shrubbery: shrubbery and trees, and the house itself, had long been abandoned to decay.

"Heah am de place, sah," said the footman, opening the carriage-door.[1]

An old gentleman in shabby clothes, embellished dramatically by a red necktie, an empty sleeve pinned to his breast, sprang out briskly; a lady followed, and stood beside him: then a younger man, his head muffled in a close fur cap, a yellow shawl wrapped about his neck, looked feebly out of the window. His face, which a pair of pale, unkindled eyes had never lighted since he was born, had been incomplete of meaning in his best days, and long illness had only emphasized its weakness. He half rose, sat down again, stared uncertainly at the house, yawned nervously, quite indifferent to the fact that the lady stood waiting his pleasure. His money and his bodily sufferings—for he was weighted heavily with both—were quite enough, in his view, to give him the right to engross the common air and the service of other men and women. Indeed, a certain indomitable conceit thrust itself into view in his snub nose and retreating chin, which made it highly probable that if he had been a stout day-laborer in the road yonder, he would have been just as complacent as now, and have patronized his fellows in the ditch.

"Will you take my arm, William?" said the old man waiting in the road. "This is the house."

"No. I have half a mind to drop the whole matter. Why should I drag out the secrets of the grave? God knows, I shall find them out soon enough!"

"Just so. Precisely. It's a miserable business for this April day. Now, I don't want to advise, but shall we drive out on the Wissahickon and fish a bit? You'll catch a perch, and Jane shall broil it over the coals, eh?"

"Oh, of course I'm going through with it," scowling and blinking through his eye-glasses. "But we are ten minutes before the time. I can't sit in a draughty room waiting. Tell David to drive slowly down the road until four, Captain Swendon."

"Certainly, certainly," with the nervous conciliatory haste of a man long used to being snubbed.—"You hear Mr. Laidley, David?—We'll arrange it in this way, then. Miss Fleming and I will stroll down the road, William, until the time is up.—No, Jane," as his daughter was going to leave the carriage. "Stay with your cousin." The captain was his peremptory self again.

Like every man conscious of his own inability, he asserted himself by incessant managing and meddling for his neighbors.

The carriage jolted down the rutted road. The little man inside tossed on the well-padded cushions, and moaned and puffed spasmodically at his cigar.

Buff and David, stiff in green and gold on the box, nodded significantly at each other. "He's nigh unto de end," said Buff. "De gates of glory am creakin' foh him."

"Creakin', shore nuff. But 'bout de glory I'm not so shore. Yoh see, I knows," rubbing his gray whiskers with the end of the whip. "I have him in charge. Mass' Swendon gib orders: 'Yoh stick by him, Dave.' 'S got no friends: 's got no backbone. Why, wid a twinge ob toothache he squirms like an eel in de fire—swears to make de debbil turn pale. It'll be an awful sight when Death gits a holt on him. But I'll stick."

Captain Swendon and Miss Fleming, left alone under the pines, both turned and looked at the house as if it were an open grave.

"So it is here the dead are to come back?" said the captain with a feebly jocular giggle. "We'll go down the road a bit. 'Pon my soul, the atmosphere here is ghastly."

They struck into the meadows, sauntered through a strip of woodland where the sparrows were chirping in the thin green boughs overhead, and, crossing some newly-ploughed fields, came suddenly upon

4

a row of contract-houses, bold, upright in the mud, aggressively new and genteel. They were tricked out with thin marble facings and steps. A drug-shop glittered already at one end of the block, and a milliner's furbelowed window closed the other with a red-lettered sign, which might have served as a motto for the whole: "Here you buy your dollar's worth of fashion for your dime of cash."

"Ah!" cried the captain, "no ghostly work here!—the last place where one would look for any miraculous stoppage of the laws of Nature."

"Stoppage, you should say, of the social laws of 'gents' and their ladies, which are much more inexorable," said his companion. "Oh I know them!" glancing in at the windows, as she tramped through the yellow mud, with keen, amused eyes. "I know just what life must be in one of these houses—the starving music-teacher on one side of you, and the soapboiler on the other: the wretched small servant going the rounds of the block to whiten the steps every evening, while the mistresses sit within in cotton lace and sleazy silks, tinkling on the piano, or counting up the greasy passbook from the grocer's. Imagine such a life broken in upon by a soul from the other world!"

"Yet souls go out from it into the other world. And I've known good women who wore cheap finery and aped gentility. Of course," with a sudden gusty energy, "*I* don't endorse that sort of thing; and I don't believe the dead will come back to-day. Don't mistake me," shaking his head. The captain was always gusty and emphatic. His high-beaked, quick-glancing face and owlish eyes were ready to punctuate other men's thoughts with an incessant exclamation point to bring out their true meaning. Since he was a boy he had known that he was born a drill-sergeant and the rest of mankind raw recruits. "Now, there's something terribly pathetic to me," he said, "in this whole expedition of ours. The idea of poor Will in his last days trying to catch a glimpse of the country to which he is going!"

Cornelia Fleming nodded, and let the subject drop. She never wasted her time by peering into death or religion. She belonged to this world, and she knew it. A wise racer keeps to the course for which he has been trained, and never ventures into the quagmires beyond. She stopped beside a tiny yard where a magnolia tree spread its bare stalks and dull

5

white flowers over the fence, and stood on tiptoe to break a bud. The owner of the house, an old man with a box of carpenter's tools in his hand, opened the door at the moment. She nodded brightly to him. "I am robbing you, sir. For a sick friend yonder," she said.

He came down quickly and loaded her with flowers, thinking he had never heard a voice as peculiar and pleasant. The captain, a little behind, eyed her critically from head to foot, his mouth drawn up for a meditative whistle, as she stood on tiptoe, her arm stretched up among the creamy buds. The loose sleeve fell back: the arm was round and white.

"Very good! ve-ry good!" the whistle meant; "and I know the points of a fine woman as well as any of these young fellows."

Two young fellows, coming up, lingered to glance at the jimp waist and finely-turned ankle, with a shrug to each other when, passing by, they saw her homely face.

The captain gallantly relieved her of her flowers, and paraded down the road, head up, elbows well out, as he used, thirty years ago, to escort pretty Virginie Morôt in the French quartier of New Orleans. It was long since he had relished conversation as he did with this frank, generous creature. No coquetry about her! It was like talking to a clever, candid boy. Every man felt, in fact, with Cornelia, that she was only a younger brother. He liked the hearty grasp of her big white hand; he liked her honest, downright way of stating things, and her perfect indifference to her own undeniable ugliness. Now, any other woman of her age—thirty, eh? (with a quick critical glance)—would dye her hair: she never cared to hide the streaks of gray through the yellow. She had evidently long ago made up her mind that love and marriage were impossible for women as unprepossessing as she: she stepped freely up, therefore, to level ground with men, and struck hands and made friendships with them precisely as if she were one of themselves.

The captain quite glowed with the fervor of this friendship as he marched along talking energetically. A certain subtle instinct of kinship between them seemed to him to trench upon the supernatural: it covered every thought and taste. She had a keen wit, she grasped his finest ideas: not even Jane laughed at his jokes more heartily. She appreciated his inventive ability: he was not sure that Jane did. There were topics, too, on which he could touch with this mature companion that were caviare to Jane. It was no such mighty matter if he blurted out an oath before her, as he used to do in the army. Something, indeed, in the very presence of the light, full figure keeping step with his own, in the heavy odor of the magnolias and the steady regard of the yellowish-brown eyes, revived within him an old self which belonged to those days in the army—a self which was not the man whom his daughter knew, by any means.

They were talking at the time, as it happened, of his military experience: "I served under Scott in Mexico.[2] Jane thinks me a hero, of course. But I confess to you that I enlisted, in the first place, to keep the wolf out of the house at home. I had spent our last dollar in manufacturing my patent scissors, and they—well, they wouldn't cut anything, unless—I used to suspect Atropos had borrowed them and meant to snip the thread for me, it was stretched so tightly just then."[3]

She looked gravely at his empty sleeve.

The captain caught the glance, and coughed uncomfortably: "Oh, I did not lose that in the service, you understand. No such luck! Five days after I was discharged, after I had come out of every battle with a whole skin, I was on a railway-train going home. Collision: arm taken off at the elbow. If it had happened just one week earlier, I should have had a pension, and Jane—Well, Jane has had a rough time of it, Miss Fleming. But it was my luck!"

They had returned through the woods, and were in sight again of the house standing darkly among the pines. Two gentlemen, pacing up and down the solitary road, came down the hill to meet them.

"Tut! tut! It is that Virginia lawyer who has come up to get into practice here—Judge Rhodes. You know him, Miss Fleming. There's an end to our quiet talk. That fellow besieges a woman with his click-clack: never leaves a crack for a sensible man to edge in a word."

Miss Fleming turned her honest eyes full on his for a moment, but did not speak. The captain's startled, foolish old heart throbbed with a feeling which he had not known since that day in the boat on the bayou when Virginie Morôt first put her warm little hand in his. Virginie as a wife had been a trifle of a shrew. Love in the remembrance often has a bitter twang. But this was friendship! How sweet were the friendship and confidence of a woman! Pretty women of late years approached the captain in his fatherly capacity, much to his disrelish. A man need not have his gray hairs and rheumatism thrown in his teeth at every turn. Miss Fleming, now, saw beneath them: she saw what a gallant young fellow he was at heart. He looked down at her eagerly, but she was carelessly inspecting the judge and his companion.

"Who is the fair-haired, natty little man?"

"Oh! Phil Waring, a young fellow about town. Society man. Too fond of cards. Nice lad, but no experience: no companion for you, Miss Fleming."

A vague, subtle change passed over her. It was no definable alteration in mind or body, yet a keener observer than the captain might have suspected a readjustment of both to suit some possible new relation.

Mr. Waring and the judge joined them, and they all walked together toward the house, engrossed with their errand. Miss Fleming never expected from men the finical gallantry usually paid to young ladies, and even the gallant Virginian did not give it to her. The captain indeed, perceiving that she was occupied with Judge Rhodes, gave her up to his escort. "It is almost four. I will go down the road and find the carriage and William," he said, and left them.

Judge Rhodes, as they drew near the house, regarded it darkly: "Decay! death and decay!" waving his pudgy red hands theatrically. "A gloomy gate indeed, through which the dead might well choose to return."

"I should call it a badly-set stage for a poor melodrama," said Miss Fleming coolly.

"But your character is so practical! You are fortunate in that." The judge, who was a stout, bald man, gazed at the house with vague abstraction and dilating nostrils. "Now, I am peculiarly susceptible to spiritual influences. I have been since a boy as sensitive to pain, to, ah— sympathies, to those, ah—electric cords, as Byron says, wherewith we're darkly bound, as—as a wind-harp. I really dread the effect upon myself of the revelations of to-day."[4]

Miss Fleming was silent. The judge, as she knew, was one of those shrewd common-sense men who, when lifted out of their place into the region of sentiment or romance, swagger and generally misconduct themselves, like a workman conscious of his ill-fitting Sunday finery.

One or two carriages drove up to the gate and stopped.

"Who are those people, Mr. Waring?" said the judge, dropping into his ordinary tone.

Mr. Waring put on his eye-glasses. He knew everybody, and had as keen an eye and strong an antipathy for eccentric characters in conventional Philadelphia as a proof-reader for false type. "There is Dehr, the German homoeopath and Spiritualist," he said in a little mild voice, which oddly reminded Miss Fleming of the gurgling flow of new milk. "That woman marching before him is his wife."[5]

"I know," muttered the judge—"strong-minded. Most extraordinary women turn up every day here. This one lectures on hygiene. Mad, undoubtedly."

"Oh no," said Waring—"very dull, good people, both of the Dehrs. Not two ideas to share between them. But there are a dozen tow-headed youngsters at home: they drive the old people into such out-of-the-way courses to scratch for a living. That man in white is the great Socialist, Schaus. The others are scientific fellows from New York and Boston."

"I wish Van Ness was here," said the judge, nodding ponderously. "Van Ness is better known in Richmond than any other Philadelphian, sir. Most remarkable man. Science is well enough as far as it goes, but for clear intelligence, give me Pliny Van Ness."

"No doubt," said Mr. Waring gravely. "Great reformer, I hear. Don't meet him in society. Of a new family."

"Mr. Laidley objected to his coming," said Cornelia.

"He did, eh? I'm astonished at that," said the judge. "I consider Van Ness—But Laidley had the right to object, of course. The meeting is one of the captain's famous schemes—to amuse Laidley. But they tell me that he knows he is dying, and has determined to bring a certain spirit out of the other world to ask an important question."

"I should think," said Miss Fleming dryly, "Mr. Laidley would always require supernatural aid to make up his mind for him. After I talk to him I have the feeling that I have been handling froth. Not clean froth either." When Miss Fleming made the men and women about her the subjects of her skill in dissection, her voice took a neat incisive edge, suggestive of the touch of a scalpel. Little Mr. Waring, pulling his moustache thoughtfully, studied her for a moment without reply.

"Hoh!" laughed the judge. "You have a keen eye! There can be no doubt," suddenly sobering, "that Laidley has been uncommonly fast. But his blood is good—none better in Maryland. High-toned family, the Laidleys. Mr. Waring here could give you his life chapter by chapter if he would. But he would skip over the dirty bits as carefully as he is doing in the road."

"Laidley's life is so very nearly over," suggested Mr. Waring quietly.

There was an awkward silence of a moment.

"Now, I can't understand," blustered the judge, "how Captain Swendon can nurse that fellow as tenderly as he is doing. I've got my share of humanity and forgiveness, and all that. But if any man had thrust my wife and child out of their property, as he has done, he had better have kept out of my sight, sir. I know all about them, you see, for two generations. Captain's wife was a New Orleans girl—Virginie Morôt. It wasn't a matter of property: it was starvation. Poor little Virginie—pretty creature she was too!—would have been alive to-day, there's no doubt of it, if she could have had proper food and medicines. And there's his daughter! What kind of a life has she had for a girl with such blood in her veins? Why, if I should tell you the sum on which that child has supported herself and her father in Baltimore and here since her mother died, you wouldn't believe me. And Laidley did nothing for them. Not a penny! Under the circumstances it was a crime for him to be alive."

"What were the circumstances?" asked Miss Fleming.

"The property, you understand, was old Morôt's—Morôt of New Orleans. Virginie was his only child: she married Swendon, and her father came to live with them in Baltimore. The two men were at odds from the first day. Old Morôt was a keen, pig-headed businessman: he knew nothing outside of the tobacco-trade; worked in the counting-house all day; his one idea of pleasure was to swill port and terrapin half the night. Swendon—Well, you know, the captain. He was a brilliant young fellow in those days, full of ideas that never came to anything—an invention every month which was to make his fortune. They quarreled, of course the wife sided with her husband, and Morôt, in a fit of rage, left the whole property to his nephew, Will Laidley. When he was on his deathbed, however, the old man relented and sent for Laidley. It was too late to alter the will, but he charged him to do justice to his daughter. Laidley has told me that much himself. But it never occurred to him that justice meant anything more than to keep the estate, and allow it at his death to revert to Jane and her father."

"Well, well!" cried Mr. Waring hastily, "that cannot be far off now. Laidley is so nearly a thing of the past, judge, that we might afford to bury his faults with him, decently out of sight."

"I can't put out of sight the years of want for Virginie and her child while he was throwing their money to the dogs in every gambling-hell in Baltimore and New York. Why, the story was so well known that when he came down to Richmond he was not recognized, sir! Not recognized. He felt it. Left the county like a whipped cur."

"Yet, legally, the money was his own," remarked Cornelia.

"Oh, legally, I grant you! But morally, now—" The judge had counted on Miss Fleming's sympathy in his story. Only the day before he had seen the tears come to her eyes over his hurt hound. He was disappointed that she took little Jane's misfortunes so coolly. "Of course this sort of crime is unappreciable in the courts. But society, Virginia society, knows how to deal with it."

"I happen to know," said Waring, "that Laidley's will was made a year ago, leaving the whole property to Miss Swendon."

"And he knows that in the mean time she is barely able to keep herself and her father alive. Pah-h!"

"Really, Jane has quite a dramatic history, and you are precisely the person to tell it with effect, judge," said Miss Fleming, smiling good-humoredly, with that peculiar affable intonation which always numbs the hearer into a conviction that his too excessive emotion is being humored as the antics of an ill-disciplined child.

The judge grew red.

"Yes," continued Miss Fleming, her eyes upon him, "Jane *is* pretty. Your zeal is excusable." The road was muddy at this point, and she passed on in front of them, picking her steps.

"Damn it!" said the judge, "they're all alike! No woman can be just to a pretty face. I thought this girl had sense enough to lift her above such petty jealousy."

"She is not jealous," said Waring, looking critically at her back as he arranged his thin tow-colored moustache. "She is an Arab among her own sex. It's a common type in this part of the country. She fraternizes with men, horses and Nature, and sneers at other women as she would at artificial flowers and perfumery. I don't know Miss Fleming, but I know her class very well."

The Virginian, whose blood revolted at this censure of a lady, rushed to the rescue: "She's honest at any rate. No mean feminine tricks about her. She's offensively truthful. And, after all, she's right: Swendon is a good-for-nothing, a well-born tramp; and Jane is hardly a subject for pity. She's a remarkably healthy girl; a little dull, but with more staying power in her than belongs to a dozen of those morbid, strong-minded women of yours in the North. I suppose I do let my sympathy run away with me."

They joined Cornelia and entered the broken gate. The door of the house swung open at a touch. Within were bare halls and rooms covered with dust, the floors of which creaked drearily under their tread. Following the sound of stifled voices, they went up to a large upper chamber. The walls of this room were stained almost black; the solid wooden shutters were barred and heavily curtained. They made their way to the farther end of the room, a little apart from a group of dark figures who talked together in whispers. Miss Fleming noticed a nervous trepidation in the manner of both men, and instantly became grave, as though she too were more deeply moved than she cared to show.

The whispers ceased, and the silence was growing oppressive when steps were heard upon the stairs.

"Hoh!" puffed the judge. "Here is Laidley at last."

Chapter 2

It was not Laidley who entered, but Mrs. Combe, then the most famous clairvoyant in the United States.[1] According to statements of
men both shrewd and honest she had lately succeeded in bringing
the dead back to them in actual bodily presence. The voice was heard,
then the spirit slowly grew into matter beside them. They could feel
and see its warm flesh, its hair and clothing, and even while they held
it, it melted again into the impalpable air, and was gone. The account
was attested by persons of such integrity and prominence as to command attention from scientific men. They knew, of course, that it was a
trick, but the trick must be so well managed as to be worth the trouble
of exposure. Hence, Mrs. Combe upon her entrance was received with
silent, keen attention.

She was a tall pillar-like woman, with some heavy drapery of black
velvet or cloth about her: there were massive coils of coarse black hair,
dead narrow eyes of the same color, a closely-shut jaw: no point of light
in the figure, but a rope of unburnished gold about her neck. She stood
with her hands dropped at her sides, immovable, while her husband, a
greasy little manikin with a Jewish face, turned on the light and waved
the attention of the audience to her: "This is Miriam Combe, the first
person since the Witch of Endor who has succeeded in materializ-
ing the shpirits of the dead.[2] Our meeting here to-day is under peculiar shircumstances. A zhentleman unknown to me and Mrs. Combe,
but who, I am told, is near death, desires to recall the shpirit of a dead
friend. Zhentlemans will reconize the fact that the thing we propose
to do depends upon the states of minds and matters about us. If these
elements are disturbed by unbelief or by too much light or noise when
the soul shtruggling to return wants silence and darkness, why—it cannot make for itself a body—dat's all."

"You compel belief, in a word, before you prove to us that we ought to believe," said a professor from a Baptist college in New Jersey, smiling blandly down upon him. "Scientifics—"

"I knows noting of scientifics. I knows dat my wife hash de power to ashist de souls to clode demselves wid matter. I don't pretend to explain where she got dat power, I don't know what ish dat power: I only know she hash it. If zhentlemans will submit to the conditions, they shall zhoodge for demselves."

"Now, the ignorance of this man impresses me favorably," said the professor to his friends. "He is evidently incapable of inventing a successful trick even of conjuring. If any great unknown force of Nature has chosen him or his wife as tools, we should not despise the manifestation because the tools are very gross matter. They are the steel wire charged with the lightning, perhaps."

Dr. Dehr came forward and touched the motionless woman, shaking his head solemnly: "She is highly charged with electricity now, sir. The air is vital, as I might say, with spiritual presences. I have no doubt, gentlemen, before we part, that we shall see one of the most remarkable phenomena of the nineteenth century."[3]

"How well she poses!" whispered Miss Fleming to the judge. "But the stage-properties are bad: the velvet is cotton, and the gold brass-gilt."

"Now, to me," said the judge emphatically, "there is a dreadful reality, a dead look, in her face. What Poe would have made of this scene! There was a man who could grapple with these supreme mysteries! No! That woman undoubtedly has learned the secret of life and of death. She can afford to be passive." The judge's very whisper was judicial, though pulpy.

It was not possible that the woman should have heard them, yet a moment after she lifted her eyes and motioned slowly toward them.

"God bless my soul, ma'am! You don't want me!" cried the judge.

Waring half rose, laughing, but with cold chills down his backbone, and then dropped into his seat, relieved: "You are the chosen victim. Miss Fleming."

Cornelia went up to the medium. She was confident the whole affair was a vulgar trick, but there was a stricture at her heart as if an iron hand had been laid upon it. The energy went out of her step, the blood from her face.

The woman laid her hand on her arm. "I need you," she said in a deep voice. "You have great magnetic force: you can aid this soul to return to life if you will. Sit there." She placed both her hands lightly on Cornelia's forehead. Miss Fleming dropped into the seat: she could not have done otherwise.

"Before we opens the séance," proceeded Combe, "zhentlemans can examine de cabinet and convince demselves dere is no trick."

The cabinet was a light triangular structure of black walnut, about seven feet in height, placed in one corner of the room, though with an open space between it and the wall. It moved on casters: the door was on the side facing the audience. Miss Fleming observed with amusement that the seat given her removed her to the farthest distance from this door.

"You will notish dat dere is absolutely noting in de cabinet but a chair—zhoost de walls and de floor and de chair. Miriam will sit there, and de door will be closed. When it opens you will see de embodied spirit beside her."

"Hillo!" cried the judge, "what's this behind the cabinet?"

"It is a window overlooking de garden: I had it boarded up to prevent you sushpecting me of trickery. But you sushpect mine boards, mein Gott! Exshamine dem, exshamine dem! Go outside."

The judge did so. "They are screwed on honestly enough," he said to the spectators. "A ghost had need of a battering-ram to come through that window. It opens on an area thirty feet deep."

The woman went into the cabinet and the door was closed. Steps were heard upon the stairs.

"It ish de zhentleman who calls for de shpirit to appear," said Combe in a whisper.

The door opened, and Laidley, supported by Captain Swendon, entered, giving a quick appealing look about him as he halted for a moment on the threshold. The dignity of approaching death was in his weak, ghastly face, and the judge rose involuntarily, just as he would have stood uncovered if a corpse had gone by. Laidley took the seat which the captain with his usual bluster placed for him opposite the door of the cabinet. Combe turned out the lights: the room was in absolute darkness. The judge moved uneasily near to Waring: "Don't laugh at me, Mr. Waring. But I really feel that there is a Presence in this room which is not human. I wish I had listened to my wife. She does not approve of this sort of thing at all: she thinks no good churchman should meddle with it. But there is *something* in the room."

"Yes, I am conscious of what you mean. But it is a physical force, not spiritual. Not electricity, either. It is something which has never affected my senses before. Whatever it is, it is the stock in trade of these people."

They were ordered by Combe to join hands, and everybody obeyed excepting the captain's daughter, who stood unnoticed by one of the curtained windows.

A profound silence followed, broken by a stifled sob from some overnervous woman. The low roll of an organ filled the void and died. After that there was no complete sound, but at intervals the silence took breath, spoke in a half-articulate wail, and was dumb again.

Pale nebulous light shone in the cabinet and faded: then a single ray fell direct on Laidley's face. It stood out from the night around like a bas-relief—livid, commonplace, a presentment of every-day death. Each man present suddenly saw his own grave open, and the world beyond brought within reach through this insignificant man.

"The spirits of many of the dead are present," said the sepulchral voice within the cabinet. "What do you ask of them?"

Laidley's lips moved: he grasped the arms of his chair, half rose: then he fumbled mechanically in his pocket for his cigar-case, and not finding it sank back helplessly.

"What do you ask of them? Their time is brief."

"I'm a very ill man," he piped feebly: "the doctors give me no hope at all. I want advice about a certain matter before—before it's too late. It is a great wrong I have done that I want to set right."

"Can any of the dead counsel you? Or do you summon one soul to appear?"

"There is but one who knows."

"Call for her, then."

Laidley looked about him uncertainly: then he said in a hoarse whisper, "Virginie Morôt!"

The captain sprang to his feet: "My wife? No, no! for God's sake!"

The light was swiftly drawn back into the cabinet and extinguished. After several minutes the voice was heard again: "The spirit summoned is present. But it has not the force to resume a material body unless the need is urgent. You must state the question you would have answered."

"I must see Virginie here, in bodily presence, before I'll accept any answer," said Laidley obstinately. "I'll have no hocus-pocus by mediums or raps. If the dead know anything, she knows why I need her. I have had money to which she had a—well, a claim. I've not spent it, perhaps, in the best way. I have a mind now to atone for my mistake by leaving it to a charity where I know it will do great good."

An amazed whistle broke through the darkness from the corner where the judge sat. The captain caught Laidley's shoulder. "William," he whispered, "surely you forget Jane."

Laidley shook him off. "The money is my own," he said loudly, "to do with as I choose. But if Virginie can return from the dead, she shall decide for me."

"It's enough to bring her back," muttered the judge. "Do you hear that?" thumping Waring's knee—"that miserable shrimp swindling her child in order to buy God's good-will for himself!"

There was a prolonged silence. At last a voice was heard: "She will appear to you."

The organ rolled heavily, low soft thunders of music rose and fell, a faint yellowish vapor stole out from under the cabinet and filled the darkness with a visible haze. Captain Swendon stumbled to his feet and went back to his daughter: "I can't bear it, child! I can't bear it!" dropping into a chair.

She took his hand in her own, which were quite cool, and stroked and kissed it. But she did not speak nor take her eyes from the door of the cabinet.

It opened. Within sat Miriam, immovable, her eyes closed. Beside her stood a shadowy luminous figure covered with a filmy veil. It moved forward into the room. So thick was the vapor that the figure itself appeared but a shade.[4]

Laidley stooped forward, his hands on his knees, his lips apart, his eyes dilated with terror.

The veil slowly fell from the face of the spirit, and revealed, indistinctly as the negative of a photograph, a small thin woman with eager, restless eyes, and black hair rolled in puffs high on the head in the fashion of many years ago.

"Virginie!" gasped Laidley.

The captain shuddered, and hid his face. His daughter, with a quick step backward, threw aside the curtains and flung open the shutters. The broad daylight streamed in.

Combe sprang toward her with an oath.

The young girl held back the curtain steadily. "We need fresh air," she said smiling resolutely in his face.

The rush of air, the daylight, the cheerful voice wakened the room as out of a vision of death. The men started to their feet; there was a tumult of voices and laughter; the materialized soul staggered back to reach the cabinet. The whole of the cheap trickery was bared: her hair was an ill-fitting wig, the chalk lay in patches on her face, the vapor of Hades was only salt burning in a dish: the boards removed from the window showed her snug hiding-place inside.

Dr. Dehr's fury made itself heard above the confusion: "You have brought Spiritualism into disrepute by your infernal imposture!" clutching the poor wretch by the shoulder, while another intemperate disciple called loudly for the police. The woman began to sob, but did not utter a word.

"Let her go, doctor," said Mr. Waring, coming up. "We paid to see a farce, and it was really a very nice bit of acting. This poor girl was hired, no doubt: she is only earning her living."

"What has she done?" cried Dehr. "Spiritualism in Philadelphia never has attracted the class of investigators that are here to-day, and she—" shaking her viciously—"she's an impostor!"

"Damnation! she's a woman!" wrenching his hand from her. She gave Waring a keen furtive glance, and drew quickly aside. While some of the seekers after truth demanded their five dollars back with New England obstinacy, and Combe chattered and screeched at them, she stood in the middle of the room, immovable, her sombre sallow face set, her tawdry stage-properties about her—the crown of false black hair, the sweeping drapery, the smoking dish with fumes of ghastly vapor.

Mr. Waring went up to a short, broadly-built man in gray who had been seated in the background during the séance. "I did not know that you were in town or here, Mr. Neckart," he said with a certain marked respect. "That is not an unpicturesque figure, I think. She would serve as a study of Night, now—a stormy, muggy town-night, full of ooze and slime."[5] Mr. Waring's manner and rhetoric were uneasy and deferential. Mr. Neckart was a power in a region quite outside of the little fastidious gossiping club of men and women whom he was wont to call the World.

"Your Night, apparently, has little relish for the morning," he said.

The woman's threatening eyes, in fact, were fixed on the tall fair girl, the captain's daughter, who stood in the window, busied with buttoning her father's overcoat and pinning his empty sleeve to his breast. She was looking up at him, and talking: the wind stirred her loose pale-gold hair; behind her branches of white roses from a vine outside thrust themselves in at the window: the birds chirped in the rustling maples beyond.

"What a wonderful effect of light and color!" said Waring, who had lounged through studios and galleries enough to enable him to parcel out the world into so many bits of palette and brush-work. "Observe the atmosphere of sunshine and youth. Cabanel might paint the girl's face for the Dawn. Eyes of that profound blue appear to hold the light latent."[6]

"There seems to be unusual candor in them," said Mr. Neckart, glancing carelessly at Jane again, and drawing on his gloves. "A lack of shrewdness remarkable in an American woman."

"The Swendons are Swedes by descent, you know. A little phlegm, a lack of passion, is to be expected, eh? Now, my own taste prefers the American type—features animated by a nimbler brain; as there, for example," looking toward Miss Fleming. "Ugly beyond apology. But there is a subtle attraction in it."

"No doubt you are right. I really know very little about women," indifferently. He nodded good-evening, glancing at his watch as he went out.

The captain was conscious of some malignant influence at his back, and turning, saw the woman, who had gradually approached, and now stood still. He hastily stepped between her and his daughter: "Good God! Stand back, Jane! This woman is following you."

"She looks as if she had the evil eye. But they are very fine eyes," said the young girl, inspecting her quietly, as if she had been a toad that stood suddenly upright in her way.[7]

"I owe you an ill turn, and I shall pay it," said the woman with a tragic wave of the arms. "I had a way to support myself and my boy for a year, and you have taken it from me."

"It was such a very poor way! Such a shabby farce! And it was my mother that—" She stopped, a slight tremor on the fair, quiet face.

"Oh, I shall pay you!" The woman gathered her cheap finery about her and swept from the room.

In the confusion Judge Rhodes had sought out Laidley, full of righteous wrath on behalf of his friend the captain, against this limp fellow who was going to enter heaven with a paltering apology for dishonesty on his lips. Laidley, however, was reclining in the easy-chair with his eyes closed, and the closed eyes gave so startling an appearance of death to the face that the judge was thrown back in his headlong charge. "Why, why, William! I'm sorry to see you looking so under the weather," he said kindly.

Laidley's eyes began to blink: he smiled miserably: "It's too late to throw the blame on the weather, judge. Though I'm going back to Aiken next week. I came North too soon."

"This affair has turned out a more palpable humbug than I expected," trying to approach the point at issue by a gentle roundabout ascent. "I wish Van Ness had been here—Pliny Van Ness. There's a man whose advice I seek since I came to Philadelphia on all important matters. A man whose integrity, justice—God bless me, William! You must know Pliny Van Ness. Why don't you take his counsel, instead of meddling with these wretched mediums? Raising the dead to tell you what to do? Bah! If you had asked me, now—"

Laidley had drawn himself up in the chair, his watery eyes gathering a faint eagerness: "Sit down. Here. I wish to speak to you, judge. Nobody will hear us."

"Certainly. As you ask me now—I know the whole case. Don't try to talk: it only makes you cough. You want to say that the property—"

"I want to say nothing about the property. My will was made last week. I am determined to throw my means into that channel where it will best contribute to God's service. He will not scorn a late repentance. But Van Ness—it was about Van Ness I wanted to talk to you."

"If your will was made last week, why did you try to bring back poor dead Virginie to advise you?"

"I don't know," said Laidley, coughing nervously—"I don't know. I thought she would confirm me—I—I want to be just to her daughter, God knows!"

"What is your idea of justice?"

"Why this—this," eagerly, catching the judge's red, fat hand in his cold fingers. "Jane will be a woman whom Van Ness would be apt to approve. I know he's fastidious. But she's very delicate and fair—as fine a bit of human flesh as I ever saw. As for mind, she has none. A mere child. He could mould her—mould her. Eh? I think I could throw out an inducement which would lead him to look favorably on her—when she's of a marriageable age, that is. If the girl were married to such a man as Van Ness, surely she would be well placed for life. Nobody could blame me for not making an heiress of her."

"Jane? Van Ness?" said the judge thoughtfully. "Well, Van Ness is a man whom any woman in the country should be proud to marry. But he is impregnable to that sort of thing. And Jane is but a child, as you say. The scheme seems to me utterly unfeasible, Laidley. Besides, what has it to do with her claims on you?"

"It has everything to do with them. I give her instead of money a home and husband such as no money can buy. They must be brought together, judge. You must do it. I have a word to say to Van Ness that will open his eyes to her merits. I will plant the seed, as I might say. It will grow fast enough."

The judge was silent as he helped Laidley, still talking eagerly, down the stairs and into his carriage. The whole fantastic scheme was, as he saw, the cowardly device of the dying man to appease his conscience. That this poor creature should have any power to influence Van Ness, the purest and strongest of men, was a mere bit of braggadocio, which surely did not deceive even Laidley himself.

But what could he do? To stab with reproach, even to argue with this nerveless, worn-out man, flaccid in mind and body, seemed to the kindly old fellow as cruel as to torture a dying fish or other cold-blooded creature of whose condition or capacity for suffering he could have no just idea.

PART 2

Chapter 3

Captain Swendon, with the majority of his sex, was never less a hero than when at home. Brute force, *od*, backbone, whatever you call the resistant power which keeps a man erect among other men, weakens under the coddling of feminine fingers and the smoke of conjugal incense. The aching tooth, the gnawing passion or the religious problem that strikes across his life like a blank wall, all of which he pooh-poohs out of sight in the street, master him indoors. A woman puts on her noblest virtues with the fireside slippers, but to a man they are a chance for remorse, for repining, for turning God's mighty judgments on himself into a small drizzling shower of miseries for his wife and the children. Give the same man his boots and the fresh air, and he will go to the stake gallantly.

The captain, pacing up and down the garden-alleys that night, thinking of the blow which would fall on his daughter in Laidley's threatened disposal of his property, was not altogether unheroic. There was nothing mean in the big gaunt figure with its uncertain strides, or in the high-featured, mild-eyed face: neither was there anything mean in his wrath. It was all directed against himself. His Swedish blood had infused a gentle laziness into his temper, and he had forgiven Laidley long ago for his lifelong swindle, as no American with English grandfathers would have done.

"It's Will's nature," he said now. "Will's a coward and desperately ill. He wants to pay his way into heaven, and I can't blame him. But *I*—I'm an incompetent fool! I can't even pay my girl's way on earth!" The captain's life, in fact, was a long ague of feverish conceit and chills of humility. Yesterday he was an inventor who would benefit the world: to-day he was fit for nothing but to dig clams. Going up and down the lonely walk, he summed up all the capital he had had to make his fortune in the world's market—the education, the opportunities, the great inventions that all fell just short of their aim. For himself, he did not want money. His workbench, his iron bed, a bowl of Jane's soup, a fishing-rod and a tramp into the hills now and then with the girl,—if he had millions they could buy him nothing better. But she—Why should she not be as other women? Why could he not work for her as other fathers—?

He raised his right arm, and the empty sleeve fell back from the stump, which burned and throbbed impotently. There was will enough in it to conquer the whole world for her. There was that aching love which mothers feel in his breast for her, as though his heart were physically wrenched.

But at breakfast the next morning, while quite as ready to die for her, he nagged and scolded incessantly, and threw the blame of their ill-luck on her, his voice sounding like the clatter of a brass kettle: "Omelette? No—no omelette for me. I am quite content to breakfast on dry bread and coffee. It is time we practiced economy. I'll make out a system for you, Jane. A system, and I desire you to follow it."

Jane laughed and helped him to cherries, and then devoted herself in earnest to her own breakfast. She never argued with anybody, and had that impregnable good-humor which so often passes for lack of feeling. Little griefs, either her own or those of other people, dwindled out of notice in the atmosphere about her, like mosquitoes buzzing in a large sun-lighted room.

"We certainly must practice economy. God knows where to-morrow's meals may come from!"

"Jane's hens are in good laying condition, and there are the cherries on the tree," said Miss Fleming tartly. She did not like Jane nor any other woman, but she usually fought for her sex against men in a mannish way—for the pleasure of fighting for the weaker party.

"Hens? Yes, and but for the whim of renting this tumble-down house with its great gardens out on the suburb, we could have had snug rooms in some business street, where I could have earned our bread and butter."

"It was your whim, captain. Why, she has kept up the table out of the garden, and you know it. Don't interfere with the child. She can turn a penny to the best advantage. Her ability is of the most practical kind."

The captain did not like her tone. He glanced uneasily at Jane, who ate her cherries in calm unconsciousness.

"I might as well stick pins in the divine cow Audhumbla!"[1] Miss Fleming said to herself every day. This child, as she called her, irritated her, just as a machine did, or an animal, or any other creature whose motive-power she could by no means comprehend. She was herself a mass of vitalized nerves, all of which centred in that secret I, Cornelia Fleming, over whose hopes, nature and chances she brooded night and day. This other woman, who simply grew in her place, concerning herself no more about her own mind, body or future than the larch yonder did about its roots or leaves, and who took praise and blame as indifferently as the tree, the sun or rain, roused in her a feeling of active dislike. She called Jane stolid to other people, but she was by no means satisfied that she was stolid. She was often sorry that she had brought herself measurably under the protection of Captain Swendon and his daughter by renting two of the rooms in their house, though she had planned and manoeuvred a long time to accomplish that end. When Miss Fleming came up to town to join the art-class at the Academy, she was exceedingly careful not to join also the emancipated lonely sisterhood, who set social laws at defiance. She might live alone, but it must be under the roof of conventionally correct people. She abjured the whole tribe of literary and artistic adventurers who haunted the studios and lecture-halls. She wrote home to her old mother that the Swendons, descended from the leaders of the first Swedish settlers, that family of Svens from whom Penn bought the land for his village of Philadelphia, had possessed culture and social rank, if no money, for centuries. Miss Fleming found for herself a lodging-place under their roof, with very much the motive of the low-born blackbird burrowing in the high, bare nest of the osprey.

She was on her way to the Academy—now, and touched her hat jauntily and shook loose her flowing-sleeve as she said good-bye with a lingering look at the captain, to which he did not reply.

The cold ague of despair was on him: he combed his grizzled beard with his fingers, stared at the carpet and saw nobody. "Yes, I ought to have rented two small rooms up town, and found work that would pay. I'll do it now," he grumbled.

Jane had uncovered a long table heaped with tools, glue-pots, drawing-materials, models in wood, in paper, in clay, with others finely draughted on large sheets of Bristol board. The captain preserved his failures as sacredly as a Chinese the dead bodies of his ancestors. She took up one of these models and studied it thoughtfully: "Very well, father. I could go on with the business, I suppose."

The captain burst into a laugh: "Absurd! Though," relapsing into anxiety, "this is, as you say, really my business. But I could easily find a place as professor of Latin and Greek in some Western college which would support us."

"Now, I don't quite understand the action of this screw, A, B," meditatively, "It interferes with the force of the piston, in my judgment."

"Impossible!" hurrying over to the table. "I'll explain that in a moment, Jane. Why, that screw is the finest idea in the machine. It's the meaning, in fact. It all hinges on that."

In five minutes his smoking-cap was pushed back, his spectacles on his hooked nose, and he was lost in the depths of valves, gauges and levers.

Jane took the place of a dozen lost hands. She made the models, she draughted them, she worked with carpenter's tools, needles, pencils, clay, by turns, and was both swift and skillful. She had been at this daily work, indeed, since the time her father had lost his arm. Now and then, being really nothing but a child in years, she clasped her hands over her head and yawned when he was not looking, or, when she was sent to the fire for the glue, sat down on the floor and began a rough-and-tumble romp with the dog, or while she was at work, sang scraps of songs into which the captain threw a fine rolling bass.

The morning was warm: the fire had burned down low in the grate, and both windows were wide open. The wind which entered, though raw, had a breath of spring in it. The scraggy plum trees outside were covered with deep pink blossoms, yellow dandelions blazed up out of the grass, and even in the muddy walks: a half-frozen bee buzzed among them feebly for a while, and then lost his way into the room and fell with a thump on the table.

Jane dropped her tools, and put out her finger for him to crawl upon. "Now you are too early afoot: you're greedy, you fellow," she said. "You are in too great a hurry to be rich. Haven't you a comfortable house? And plenty of honey?" She carried him to the window and set him in the sun on the sill. "He'll fall in some puddle and be frozen to death; and serve him right! I hate your early birds and ants and bees, always at work."

"It is work you hate, Jenny. Now tack this strip in place, child, and then paste on the muslin. We must finish this before night, and there is more than a day's work on it."

Jane tacked and measured diligently a while, and then dropped her elbows on the table and rested her chin on her palms. Her face was just in front of her father's. "I was thinking—"

"Yes."

"I mean that I saw in the paper this morning that there was a school of blackfish on the coast, the largest for years. I suppose the Lantrims will be out for them?"

"No doubt. The old captain wrote to me that he had bought Sutphen's Tuckerton skiff."

"Aha? You did not tell me that. What else did he say?"

"Oh, nothing. 'Crabs would be scarce this season; and couldn't we come down?' The larks were beginning to rise in the marshes."

Jane nodded thoughtfully: "A Tuckerton skiff? Now, I'm surprised at that, father. I should prefer something heavier—a yawl, say—for coming in on that beach. Well—The wind must be dead sou'-west to-day. It would bring the spray right up into your face if you were lying on the sand."

She was silent for some time, looking steadily out of doors.

The captain glanced uneasily once or twice at the dark blue eyes and at a ray of sunlight glistening in the loose yellow hair. "It is sou'-west. It really does begin to feel like summer," he said, dropping his pencil and fumbling for his tobacco.

Jane brought his pipe and lighted it for him. "I am dreadfully tired!" stretching her arm out, pushing up the sleeve, and looking at it as if it had done a day's ploughing. "Now, I suppose the men are all out in their boats by this time, but a person could easily rig Lantrim's little sloop and join them; or we could camp on the marshes all day. The scent of the pines would be heavy in this damp wind."

The captain nodded gravely and puffed in silence a while: "It's no use, Jane," taking the pipe from his mouth. "I haven't a penny."

She sprang up, ran to a writing-desk and took out a glove-box. In it were a pair of well-darned kid gloves and two tiny paper packages. She laid them before him: "It's all in silver: this is for your summer hat, and that for my shoes. What do you say, father? We are in time for the eight-o'clock train. We should have nearly the whole day on the beach."

"Hat? What do I want with a hat? But your shoes are broken."

"They can be patched," with a gasp of delight. "Here! clear away the work, father, while I put up a basket of dinner." She stopped by the window, looking out: "Somebody is coming through the apple trees: I smell a cigar. Now, remember, nothing must detain you. We can't break our engagement."

The visitor came in sight from under the apple trees—a sombre, heavy man in gray, the editor Neckart, to whom Mr. Waring had criticised the Swendons with such freedom the night before. Mr. Neckart had known the captain years ago. When he was a boy, too poor to pay for schooling, he used to go to the captain at night for help in his Greek or mathematics. Swendon had always preferred the companionship of younger men than himself, and was never without a "following" of clever, unruly schoolboys, whom he was as ready to help when they were lazy, as to tip with silver half-dollars—when he had them. Some of them had brought young Neckart to the captain, knowing nothing about him, except that he was miserably poor, with a desire for knowledge which they thought insane enough. Now that Neckart was a man, living in New York, and with very different problems to work from those of Euclid, he had but little intercourse with the slow, easy-going captain. They met occasionally, when Neckart came to Philadelphia, at the club or at dinner somewhere, when there would be a few minutes' hasty gossip about the old pranks of the boys—White, who died in California, or Porter, who was now in the Senate—and then a shake of the hand and good-bye, Neckart usually wondering to himself, as they parted, how soon that fellow Laidley would cease to cumber the earth and the captain would have his own and wear a decent coat again and the bits of gaudy jewelry in which he used so to delight.

The old man hurried down the garden-walk now to meet him, and wrung his hand heartily: "Bruce! is it possible? You have not crossed my threshold since the old Epictetus days."[2]

"No, and I interrupt you now? You are going out? I only called for a few words on business."

"Plenty of time, plenty of time! My little girl and I were going to run down to the shore to vagabondize for a day.—Jane, this is my old friend Mr. Neckart.—We have plenty of time in which to catch the train. Sit down, Bruce."

Mr. Neckart did not sit down, however. He found some difficulty now in putting his business into a few concise words. He had heard Laidley's avowal the night before that he proposed to leave the captain penniless. All his boyish regard for the old man woke in force. His boyish feelings were apt to waken and clog Mr. Neckart's strait-lined path to success. He did not sentimentalize about his old teacher, but he set aside half an hour in which to look in on him and see what could be done for him. Anything could be done in half an hour by a man who chose to work hard enough.

He expected to find the captain totally disheartened by this blow, but here he was making ready for a day's fooling on the beach; for the captain, finding that, his visitor did not promptly broach the subject of his errand, went on with his preparations.

So it happened that they fell into a brief silence. The old man by the fire screwed his rod as though rods were the business of life: the young girl sat by the window, a white-covered lunch-basket on the floor beside her, sewing strings, on a wide-rimmed hat which she meant to wear. Her yellow hair was bound loosely about her head, fastened by a band of black velvet: it made a faint shadow about the calm, delicate face. The dog sat at her feet, his head on her knee, watching her intently. She took her stitches slowly and with care, stopping now and then to put her hand on Bruno's muzzle and nod at him significantly about the fun they were going to have presently. It was a quiet, pretty, picture.

Now, silence or leisurely calm of any kind was rare in Mr. Neckart's daily life. He was the controller of a great journal: he was a leading politician. He had been making his own way, and dragging and goading slower men along, since he had left his cradle. Even his own party found the indomitable energy of this dwarfish giant intolerable sometimes. But his own action did not satisfy him. He had held his finger so long on the world's pulse that affairs in New York or Washington seemed but small matters. He liked to feel that they and he were linked by a thousand sympathies to the chances and changes of every country on the globe. A famine in India or an insurrection in Turkey were not mere newspaper items to him, but significant movements of the outer levers and pulleys of the great machine, part of which he was.

It is the straining horse that is always loaded, and there was no man in the party from whom such work was exacted as from Neckart. The night before he had received a deputation of French Communists proposing emigration: this morning he was to meet in secret caucus the leaders who would decide on the next candidate for the Presidency. So it went on day after day. To fall suddenly into this little room, among people to whom a day's fishing or sauntering with a dog through salt marshes was the object of life, startled him.

For years, too, people who talked to Neckart, though in but a street greeting, invariably recognized his power to help or harm them. If they had no favors to ask, they bore themselves deferentially, as to a power that could grant favors. To the captain he was still the boy Bruce, a good fellow, though dull in Greek: to the girl, intent on her holiday, he saw that he was an unwelcome guest, who would interfere with her journey. The jar of falling to the common level was sudden, yet oddly pleasant.

The captain, to fill up the time, began to discuss the different makes of fishing-rods. Mr. Neckart was used to give ten minutes each to men seeking interviews: their words had to be sharp as arrows, and driven straight home to the bull's eye of the matter to command his attention. Yet he listened to this lazy talk. The damp wind drove the perfume of the apple-blossoms in at the open window: the sunlight touched the glistening rings of hair on Jane's throat. How slow-moving and calm the girl was! He was quite sure that the blood had flowed leisurely in the veins under that pearly skin ever since she was born. None of that true American vim, sparkle, pushing energy here which he admired in his countrywomen.

"I really don't understand the new kinds of tackle," he said to Captain Swendon: "I have not had a rod in my hand for fifteen years."

"No. Of course not. You have other work to do. But Jane and I run down to the shore whenever we have money—I mean whenever we can manage to leave home. She knows every fisherman's hut from Henlopen to Barnegat. No better place to go for a breath of salt air than Sutphen's Point. You can troll with him all day, or dig for roots in the pine woods, or sleep on the beach in the sun."

Neckart smiled and glanced at his watch. At nine the committee would meet. Sun? Sleeping on the beach? He was a stout, strongly-built man, with muscles like steel, but, like most Americans who have urged their way relentlessly up, his brain before middle age gave signs of disease. As any other creature would, when overdriven for years it revolted, and failed in its work now and then. Night after night he lay sleepless, conscious only of a dull vacuity at the base of the brain; and by day, when some crisis demanded his most vigilant, keenest thought, thought suddenly blurred into momentary stupor. Any man who over-works his brain will understand how it was with him, and why, for physical reasons, this glimpse of absolute quiet and rest should touch his nerves as the taste of cordial would a fainting man. A sudden vision opened before him of yellow, silent sands, and dusky stretches of solemn pines, and the monotonous dash of the green sea all day, all night long. No doubt there were "old Sutphens" there, whole generations of people, outside of the living world, sleeping and sunning themselves. It was like a glimpse into some newly-discovered, silent, sunlit Hades.

Mr. Neckart put back his watch in his pocket, and looked irresolutely at the captain. The foolish, kindly old face belonged to his boyhood—to the time when his shoes were patched and his feet chilblained, but all the world was waiting for him to be a man to do him honor. If he could sit for an hour with the old man on the beach, would it bring the boyish feeling back again? He was conscious of a purposeless temptation—unreasonable as that which he had felt at the edge of a precipice to throw himself over. Nonsense! The committee would be waiting; there were appointments for every hour of his stay in Philadelphia; there was the leading article on the situation which nobody but he could write, that must go to his paper by the next mail.

He took up his hat: "It is time for you to catch the train, captain. Will you take me with you?"

Captain Swendon looked at him hastily: "The very best thing you can do, Bruce! Just what I should advise.—Jane, go on before with Bruno. Mr. Neckart and I will follow."

Mr. Neckart was annoyed. He had forgotten that the girl was to go, and had thought of the captain as his only companion. But she walked far in front of them, through the apple trees, and down the quiet street, engrossed with the dog. She probably would not be in his way.

Chapter 4

Down on the coast the world suddenly broadened and lifted into larger spaces. In lieu of eight-feet strips of pavement to walk on, there were the gray sweeps of sand, and great marshes stained with patches of color in emerald and brown, rolling off into the hazy background: instead of the brick and wooden boxes wherein we shut ourselves up with bad air in town, there were the vast uncovered plain of the sea, shapeless ramparts of fog incessantly rising and fading, an horizon which retreated as you searched for it into opening sunlit space, refusing to shut you in. The very boats and ships in which these people lived were winged, ready for flight into some yet farther region.

"Are you glad to come out of doors, Bruno? I am," said Miss Swendon to her dog as she stood looking at the sea; and then they sauntered away together.

Her father and Mr. Neckart went down to the mouth of the Inlet, where some fishermen were patching a boat which they had drawn up on a heap of mussel-shells. One or two crabbers, standing on the bow of their little skiffs and poling them along the edge of the water by the handles of their nets, had stopped to watch the job, which was being done with rusty nails and a bit of barnacle-moulded iron from a wreck instead of a hammer. When the iron and nails broke they all sat down and talked the matter over, with any other subject which happened to be lying loosely about on the fallow fields of their minds. When Captain Swendon came up they shook hands gravely with him, and made room for him on the bottom of an up-turned, worm-eaten scow. They were all captains as well as he, and he was hail, fellow! well met! with them as with everybody.

Mr. Neckart, who was formally introduced, nodded curtly, but did not sit down.

"A good day for the perch, Sutphen," said the captain, handing round a bundle of cigars.

"Yaas."

"But you ought to have been on the banks by daylight." Mr. Neckart's sharp, irritable voice jarred somehow on the quiet sunshine.

"Yaas. But I lent my boat last week, and this here one's out of repair.—Give me more of them nails, David."

"The boat could have been mended at night, and ready for use," in the tone which a teacher might use to idle boys.—"It is singular, Captain Swendon," turning his back on the men as on so many mud-turtles, "that the sea-air begets improvident habits in all coast-people. You cannot account for it rationally, but it is a fact. Along the whole immediate shore-line of Europe you find the same traits. Unreadiness, torpor of mind and body.—Ah! Captain Swendon and I wish to hire a boat for the day," turning to the fishermen again. "Can any of you men furnish us with one?"

Sutphen lighted his cigar leisurely: "We always manage to provide Captain Swendon with a boat when he wants it. We kin obleege him," with a slight stress on the pronoun.

"At what rates?" sharply.

"Waal, we kin talk of rates when the day's over. The captain and us won't disagree, I reckon."

"I never do business in that way. Bring out your boat and put a price on it."

"Come, Neckart," said the captain, rising hastily, "we will walk up the beach a bit.—I'll see you about the boat presently, Sutphen.—You don't know these fellows, Bruce," when they had passed out of hearing and found a seat in the thin salt grass. "They are not used to being dealt with in such a prompt, drill-major fashion."

"I deal with all men alike. Order and promptness have been necessary to me in every step of my way. I must have them from others. I pay to a penny, and I exact to a penny. It is not the money I want: it is discipline in the people about me. They must move as if they were drilled if they move to further my ends."

The captain took his cigar out of his mouth and turned blankly on him: "'Further your ends?' But, Bruce?—"

Neckart laughed: "Oh, no doubt they were created with some other object in view than to serve my purposes. But that is the cognizance which I take of them. Really, captain, if you were in public life, and saw with what eagerness masses of men follow feeble leaders who know the trick of piping to them, and how willing they are to be manipulated, you would soon come to look upon the American public simply as a machine ready for your own use when you had the skill to work it."

The captain's cigar went out in his fingers as he sat staring with dull perplexity at Neckart. There was a certain nobility in the carriage of the powerful figure and black shaggy head, an occasional fire in the deep-set eyes, a humor in the fine smile, which argued a different order of man from this scheming, selfish politician.

"I can't place you at all, Bruce. Now, I should have thought you would have been a reformer—worked for humanity—that line, you know. You were a sensitive lad, like a girl."

"I am quite too warm-hearted a fellow to be a philanthropist," laughed Neckart. "The philanthropists I know work for principles, liberty, education and the like: they don't care a damn for the individual Tom and Jerry. The chances are, that your reformer is a cold-blooded tyrant at home: he makes a god of his one idea: his god makes him nervous, ill-conditioned—the last man in the world to choose for a friend or a husband."

"You amaze me! I should have said that they were the wisest and purest of men. Next to clergymen, of course. I don't go to church myself, but I respect the cloth. But speaking of yourself, Bruce, you were a most affectionate little fellow. Do you remember how you referred every new idea to your mother? I recollect you told me once that you read your lessons in your school classics to her to amuse her. You must have cleaned the translation sometimes to make it fit for her ear."

"Yes."

"And I remember, too," regardless of the sudden silence which had fallen on his companion, "how you watched my wife making a cap one day—she had nice fingers in such work, Virginie—and how you saved your money to buy lace and ribbon for her to make your mother a cap;

and how anxiously you sat watching every stitch as it went in, and carried it off triumphantly when it was done."

"I remember quite well. Mrs. Swendon was very kind to me in the matter."

The captain did not reply: he glanced at Neckart with sudden alarm. What was it that he had heard of Bruce's mother? Some wretched story that came out at the time of her death: had she committed a crime or gone mad? He could not recall it, but something in the silence of his companion told him that he had blundered. He began to smoke violently in contrition of soul, and remained silent, while Neckart lay still in the sand, his hands clasped behind his head, looking at the surf.

It was not the surf he saw.

It was that little silly cap which he had held on his boy's chapped fist delighted and proud. Twenty years ago! He had earned the money to buy it by work after the other boys in the shop had gone home. He could see the very pattern now that was worked in the lace, and the ribbon—a pale blue, just the color of his mother's eyes. He had carried it home in the evening, and smoothed the gray hair over the gentle little face, and tied it on her before he would let her go to the glass. She was just as pleased as he, and kissed him with her arms tight about his neck and the tears in her eyes. An hour afterward he had found her tearing it into bits with an idiotic laugh. A little later—

He shut his eyes, as if to keep out some real sight before him.

It seemed to him as if his whole boyhood had been made up of just such nights as this one which he remembered.

It was not often that Neckart looked back at that early time. He was neither morbid nor addicted to self-torture. He had carefully walled up this miserable background of youth from his busy, cheerful, wide-awake life. Why should he go back to it? Something, however, in the air to-day, in the moan of the sea through the sunlight, brought it all before him, more real than the stretch of water and sand.

The captain smoked out his cigar and began to talk. Gaps of silence were so much wasted time in the world; and besides, he owed a duty to Bruce. Here was a man going headlong to the devil by the road of ambition, a sweet, high nature becoming soured and tainted, all for the lack of honest direction from somebody of age and experience.

When Neckart roused himself enough to understand, the captain was in the full swing of his dictatorial oration. "I don't want to intrude with my opinion. But no man should live for himself," he said. "Now, if my scissors had turned out as I expected, I should have been worth a million to-day. I'd have spent a good share of it—let me see—on churches, I think. Small churches—at corners in place of grogshops. Pure Gothic, say—"

"Stained glass and gargoyles instead of whiskey? You must bid higher for souls in back alleys than that, captain."

"Well, schools, then—colleges, asylums, soup-houses. I tell you, Bruce, if I had your opportunities, if I could work political machinery, I'd lift this festering mass below us up—at least to civilization and Christianity."

"I thought you meant me," laughing. "Go on."

"Of course I can't give you detailed advice. Take me on pistons and screws, and I'm at home; but I know only the broad outlines of political economy. My view," ponderously, "is purely philosophic. Our politics need reform, sir. An honest man who would come to the front just now would save the country. The masses would follow him to honesty. The Americans are a just people by instinct. I tell you, sir, if I had your chances—Talk to Pliny Van Ness, Bruce. There's a keen man of the world, who is as pure and lofty in his notions as an enthusiastic woman. He has a scheme just now for bettering the condition of the children of the dangerous classes of Pennsylvania. I wish you knew Van Ness."[1]

"I've seen him;" adding, after a moment's hesitation, "He is as upright a man, I believe, as you say—the very man to be inspired with your heroic rage for reform, and to carry it into effect. I am not the same kind of material."

"Bruce, you belie yourself. I knew you as a boy—"

"Then you knew an ordinary, not bad sort of a fellow, captain, but no hero. I have had one or two qualities which have pushed me up—a skill—craft with using words, as you have with tools, for instance, an inflexibility of purpose, a certain tact in influencing large bodies of men. I have never had any affection for them. I have two or three stanch friends. Other men and women are part of the world's furniture to me. Nothing more."

"But the power which these qualities have gained for you? How do you mean to use it?"

"You press me closely," with an amused scrutiny of the captain's monitorial face. "I shall use it, just now, to make money. That is the thing of which I have had the least in the world, and which has yielded me most substantial pleasure. When I am a rich man I can command knowledge, power and whatever else I covet." His eye kindled at the last words. There was a darkened background in his thoughts, to which Neckart, with all his easy frankness, admitted no man.

The captain studied him with perplexity: then his face lightened: "I have it! You must marry! A wife and children are the very influences you need to soften and broaden your aims. Yes, I know I'm speaking plainly. But—have you never thought of it?"

Mr. Neckart did not reply for a few moments. "It is impossible that I should ever marry," he said gravely. "There is an obstacle which would make it simply criminal in me. I never think of it."

The captain colored: "I beg your pardon, Bruce. I did not know—"

"You have not intruded: you have not hurt me in the least," laying his hand for an instant on the captain's knee. "It is not a matter about which I have any soreness of feeling. The obstacle arose from circumstances: I am not in any sense guilty."

Captain Swendon nodded and occupied himself with rebuckling his shoes. He could neither answer to the purpose nor rid his face of the shocked alarm visible in it. To have been told that Neckart was dying would have startled him less, and seemed not so pitiable to him as to know that he was shut out for life from love and marriage.

Neckart read his thoughts. "There's a difference in men," he said, concealing a smile. "It would not suit you, captain, to go through life as an anchorite or a Catholic priest, but it really agrees with me very well.[2] I am not a domestic man by taste, nor susceptible to woman's influence. I have met a few women, of course, beautiful, and with the intellect and wealth which would make them desirable wives; and I have no doubt if I had been differently situated I should have loved and married. But it never cost me a second thought to pass them by."

"But this obstacle—it may some day be removed?" ventured the captain.

Mr. Neckart's features settled into the hard lines again. "Not while I live," he said.

If there was one quality in himself on which the captain could build with confidence, it was his keen insight into other men. He read Neckart's life as an open book. "Bruce is married already," he said to himself. "He was precisely the kind of lad to be taken in by some creature that is now a secret burden on him. Drinks or chews opium, I've no doubt, or has gone to the devil with one jump. Tut! tut! He would not be divorced. I know what his opinion is on that head. But she'll die: that sort of women never live long.—It will all come right, Bruce," he said aloud. "There's more ruling of eternal justice in all of our lives than we give God credit for. But this matter astonishes me. I've heard of your intimacy with certain women in Washington—leaders of society. I always thought of you as a marrying man."

"Because I cannot marry I have the more right to accept whatever entertainment or friendship women can give me," falling into his ordinary easy tone. "I have the keenest appreciation for an ambitious woman who has intellect and culture, and is alive with energy and coquetry. I know such women. They seem to be full of subtle flame. Certainly, I would make a friend of such a one. Why not? I would marry her if I could."

A moment after he looked up the beach, and seeing the captain's daughter, smiled to think what an absolute contrast she was to this ideal live, brilliant woman. She was sitting on a log, the dog asleep at her feet, her hands clasped about her knees, looking out to sea, and he could swear she had sat there motionless as the stretch of gray sand about her for an hour. Such torpidity revolted Neckart. Neither did it appease him that the nobly-cut, dim-lighted face, the mass of yellowish hair rolling down from its black band, the coarse brown dress which hung about her in thick folds, all gave him pleasure. In the moment he had met her first he had felt an odd repulsion to this girl. The women with whom he had fraternized were akin to himself: Jane, child as she was, was antagonistic. He felt for her the same kind of irritated dislike as that which Miss Fleming gave to her, and which people of active brains are apt to give to any creature whose animus is totally different from their own.

What did the girl sit there for, thinking her own thoughts? Young women at her time of life blushed and fluttered and plumed themselves when a man came near who was of the right age to love and marry. And so they ought, so they ought! Neckart was used to see women of any age plume themselves when he was in sight. It was simple admission of his position. They knew their own capital of beauty or wit, and showed him the best of every point, just as a pheasant turns every golden feather to the sun when a passer-by comes near. He liked these radiant, self-asserting women, to be sure, very much as he did the silly fowl or a Skye terrier conscious of its beauty in every hair. But beauty was so much wasted material on this daughter of Swendon's, who did not seem to know she had it.

Besides, Mr. Neckart had always been thrown into contact with women who had careers and aims. Each one of them wished she had been born a man, and did what she could to snatch a man's prerogatives. One wrote, another painted, a third sang; this one strove for political power in the lobbies of Congress, that for money, the majority for husbands: they were wits, littérateurs, society women. But for a young girl to jog on from year to year striving neither for knowledge nor lovers, making her world of the whims and wants of a weak-minded old man, composedly building up every day models which she knew would prove failures to-morrow,—here was a most inane life.

Any eye which had grown used to the flash and flutter of brilliant tropical birds in a cage would be apt to find the little dull-breasted swallow sitting motionless by her nest a very insipid subject of study. Probably no other man, as active and busy in the world as Neckart, would have wasted so much thought on a chance young girl sitting on a log. But women being forbidden fruit to him, he was morbidly curious about them all. Old Chrysostom, barred into his cave by an impassable line, was much more inquisitive about the princess asleep outside than if he had been a hearty young fellow free to go out and kiss and make love to her.[3]

Miss Swendon came up presently, the dog marching alongside. "Father," she said, "you are spending the whole day with Mr. Neckart. You have not told Sutphen the town news. I am afraid the old man will be hurt."

"That's a fact: I'll go over directly. You will like to be alone a while, Neckart, at any rate.—Come, Jane."

Neckart rose: "You are not going over to those rough fellows, Miss Swendon? There are no women there."

Jane laughed. "*I* am a woman," with an arch little nod. "One queen-bee makes the whole hive proper, conventionally."

"Of course. But really those men are vulgar and fishy to such a degree—Nothing but a missionary spirit can take you to them?"

"On the contrary," gravely, "they are the best-bred men I know. Their talk is fuller of adventure and sincerity than any book I ever read."

"Still, stay with me. I have feelings to consider as well as Sutphen."

"Very well.—I will come over presently, father. Tell the little boys to make a fire clear enough to broil the fish for dinner." She sat down and called Bruno to her feet. There was a grave, childish simplicity in her motions which was a new study to Neckart.

"I believe," watching her keenly, "you would rather have gone. Sutphen would have been a better companion than I?"

"I don't know as yet. I have never tried you. I do know Ichabod."

"Or perhaps the truer courtesy would be to leave you alone with the sea? You were making a picture of it in your mind a while ago?"

"No," knitting her brows. "I could not do that. I know people who look at the sea or mountains or sky as so much canvas and gamboge and burnt umber and bits of effect. They are very tiresome."

"You have imagination rather than fancy, then? You hear the secret words in that everlasting moan yonder? You know what the mountains say to you at nightfall?" Neckart vaguely remembered the jargon of sentimental novels, the heroines of which always keep their heads on Nature's breast. He did not mean to chaff any woman, but he would gladly have proved this one sentimental and weak to explain his strong antipathy to her.

"No, I never thought of those things. But one grows tired in town—

housekeeping, models and all of it. My work is very light, but I do not like to work at all. And here—the beach is silent and the sky blue and the sea rolls—rolls all day long: it is like coming home after one has been out on the streets."

"About as keen comprehension of Nature as the tree yonder," thought Neckart contemptuously. But, after all, the tree was warmed, and its sap ran stronger, and it grew and broadened in the sun and air; and that was more than he could say of painter or poet.

He lay at her feet, leaning on his elbow, for an hour or more. He had meant to gauge her intellect, experience and character in a few minutes. It was a recreation which had sometimes amused him when with women. As soon as his curiosity was satisfied he was done with them. But the discoveries he had made in those pretty little dwellings innocently opening their doors to wandering hearts of marriageable men! The miserable shams inside, the traps, the dark rooms full of all uncleanness! To-day he forgot his system of exploration. He began to feel the physical effect of coming from close streets and striving work into this vast open space—the drowsiness which men experience on high mountains or by the sea, and which has a subtle, lasting enchantment in it. The damp wind bent and whitened the stretches of salt grass in the meadows behind him; brown clouds swept from west to east overhead in endless procession; the great dun-colered plane of the sea rose and fell steadily: for the rest, except the shrill pipe of a fishhawk perched on a dead tree by its nest, there was silence. He spoke to Jane now and then, but for the most part forgot her. She had fallen into the motionless quiet which seemed habitual to her. Some of the brilliant women he knew would have dug holes in the sand, or chattered gossip, or interpreted to him with much intellectual force the meaning of land and sky, or have taken their last love-affair or other private little misery to give words to the complaint of the sea. This girl seemed only a part of the shore, as much as sea or sand. The sun warmed, the air blew on her as on them: if they gave her anything besides, she too kept their secret.

Occasionally Neckart roused himself to talk briefly to her, and noticed then a blunt directness in her speech that would have appalled an ordinary hearer. It was her habit and choice to say nothing, but if pushed to the wall what was there that she would not say?

The dog, lying at her feet watching him steadily, did not give up to him the secret of its own being or its opinion of himself; but if it once did speak it would do both, and with no white lies in the words either. "The girl is like her dog," thought Neckart.

She rose at last, and went across the sands to her father. Neckart was soon conscious of an uneasy change in everything about him. The atmosphere of sunlit rest was broken. The clouds only meant rain, the sand was sand, and the sea but a wet swash of water: he began to look at his watch and think of the trains. The influence that had quieted him so unaccountably had been in the girl, then? He shut his eyes and tried to recall the erect figure, the fall of yellow hair, the clear Scandinavian face. He felt the same strong repulsion from her, yet in their brief interview she had certainly affected him uncontrollably—brought him back to old boyish ways of thinking. It was perhaps, he thought, because he was unused to such absolutely honest women.

He sauntered up the beach, and in five minutes wondered how he had based such magniloquent ideas on a child out for a holiday. The fishermen on this solitary beach apparently made a holiday whenever Swendon and Jane came, and humored the latter in all her vagaries. No doubt they would have preferred to eat properly in their own kitchens, but the cloth was spread on the sand beside the fire. The captain, with the perspiration streaming, was broiling ham at the end of a long stick; Sutphen cleaned the crabs; Lantrim's wife cooked the perch, and Jane herself was making the coffee.

"Don't speak to me: I'm counting," as Mr. Neckart stopped beside her. "Five, six, seven. You can't trifle when you make coffee," peering into the pot with the gravity of a judge on the bench.

The smell of the broiling ham in the salt air suddenly brought back to Neckart a day when he had gone fishing with his mother in the old place in Delaware. How happy and hungry they were!

"Give me your stick, captain. You are burning up," he said, sitting down on the log beside him.

"You've been on this beach afore, sir?" said Sutphen, who was his neighbor, and felt it his duty to play host.

"Never but once, when the Argyle went ashore."[4]

"You were here fur the Treasury Department?"

"Yes. Did you know anything about that case?" eying him with sudden interest. "It was a muddled account that was sent up to Washington."

"Likely. Yes, I knew. I've been in the wracking and life-saving service thirty years come June."

When Jane came to that side of the fire twenty minutes later, none of the crabs were cleaned, and the ham and stick burned black together while Neckart held them in the fire.

"I ought not to have allowed two men to sit together: I might have known they would gossip," she said.

Mr. Neckart had just made up his mind that Sutphen and the two Lantrims were as shrewd, common-sensed witnesses as he had ever examined. He was hungry too, and as they ate together he borrowed Sutphen's clamp-knife, and told some capital stories, and handed about his cigars when they had all finished.

"I misjudged that black-a-vised fellow," said Ichabod to Lantrim. "He's consid'able of a man."

Lantrim nodded ponderously. One story or slow monologue followed another—of shipwrecks, frequent on that murderous coast, of rescues by wreckers, of "vyages" down the coast or to India, Africa, with plenty of sailors' superstition in it all. Neckart lay on his back smoking, his hands under his head. It seemed as if he were the boy he was on that day's fishing long ago. His blood quickened and heated at these tales of adventure, just as it used to do when he pored over La Pérouse or the *History of Great Navigators*.[5] The afternoon was darkening, raw and cold; their fire was a mere ruddy speck in the indistinct solitudes; a wall of gray mist moved down the marshes toward them.

Jane, he noticed, was uneasy, watching her father anxiously after the dinner was over, until Sutphen proposed to have some music and begged the captain to sing. Then she was quite happy, sat closer to him, taking his hand, and as his cracked voice piped manfully out some ancient drinking-song she nodded complacently and beat the time softly with his hand upon his arm.

Mr. Neckart watched her furtively through his half-shut eyes. She was wrapped in her cloak, her head rose in clear relief against the background of fog. The men and their wives, he saw, looked upon her as a child, a straightforward little girl, with whom they had fished or cooked crabs for years: very different from the ladies who came down in summer, and were a fearfully and wonderfully made species of human being. Neckart would have analyzed these women at a glance as easily as he could impale a butterfly on a pin: why should he watch Jane as though she were the Sphinx? The dark-blue eyes that met his now and then were the most frank and friendly in the world, but the naked truth in them irritated him as though it had been the gleam of a drawn sword. He sat erect, thinking that if there was anything repulsive to him in a woman, it was physical indolence, and a strength of any sort greater than his own.

Old Sutphen presently asked him if he too wouldn't give them a song. Now, Neckart never sang except when alone, as his voice was a very remarkable baritone, and he had no mind to make a reputation on that sort of capital. He could not afford to be known as a troubadour. But he sang now, a passionate love-song, of which, of course, he felt not a word: the air was full of fervor, with an occasional gay jibing monotone. The words in themselves meant nothing: the music meant that whatever of love or earnestness was in the world was a sham. The men nodded over their pipes, keeping time: Jane held her father's hand quiet in her own, looking straight before her.

"Thank you, sir. Very lively toon that," said Lantrim when it was ended.

"Kind o' murnful too," ventured his wife.

Jane, with the last note, rose and walked hastily down the beach, where the fog was heavy. She did not return. Mr. Neckart smiled: he could only guess the result of his experiment, but he did guess it.

"Miss Swendon did not ask me to sing again," he said to the captain.

"Well, no. The song hurt her somehow. Jane had always an unaccountable dislike to music," apologetically. "I'm exceedingly fond of it myself: it's a passion with me. I enjoy anything from an organ to a jewsharp. But she does not. When she was a baby it seemed to rouse her. She's a very quiet little body, you see.—Go, Bruno: bring your mistress back."

She came in a few minutes, as they were making ready to meet the train. She hurried to her father, caught his arm, and when they were seated in the train still held him close: "Stay with me, father. Mr. Neckart does not need you. Don't leave me alone again: *I* need you."

"But, dear child, that is hardly courteous. He is our guest."

"He need not have made himself a guest. He has spoiled our whole holiday. He has spoiled the whole dear old place for me," her eyes filling with tears. "I shall never hear the sea again without hearing that song in it."

"It was a very good song, I assure you, Jane. I do wish you had a better ear. Why, Bruce has a voice of remarkable compass. I fancied he struck a false note once, though."

"It was all false—false and cruel!" vehemently. "And why should he sing it there, where you and I have always had such good times?"

"I am astonished, Jane! But you never had any perception of character. Bruce is such a thoroughly good fellow, I fancied you would be friends."

"I never saw any one before whom I disliked so much," slowly, as if to collect her verdict with certainty. "He seems to me like so much unmitigated brute force."

"Tut! tut!" said the captain absently, looking out to see how the early wheat was coming on.

She touched his arm presently: "Father, you said you thought we should be good friends. I never had a man for a friend but you."

"Certainly not. Good Heavens! What are you thinking of?"

"Most girls do," gravely, her color rising. "Oh, I know all about the world. Miss Fleming told me that when she was my age she had a dozen chums—hearty, good fellows."

The captain hastily put his arm about her: "All very well for Cornelia Fleming, child. She's a middle-aged woman. But not for you."

"When I am middle-aged, then," looking up at him anxiously, "if I have a friend I know precisely what he will be. Of fair complexion, placid, truth-telling—"

"Yourself duplicated," laughed the captain. "But here is Mr. Neckart."

The two men took the seat in front of her, and as night came on and the lamps burned dimly, Jane wrapped her veil about her head and fell asleep. Mr. Neckart remembered at last the purpose of his visit in the morning.

"Surely something can be done to compel Laidley to leave the property to its rightful owners. Have you stated the case to him plainly?" he asked.

"I? State it? Now, Bruce, how could I? If I were not the one to be benefited by it, I'd put it to him forcibly enough. But as it is—No, I've not the moral courage for that."

"But for your daughter's sake—"

"I know. I've thought it all over. But Jane and I can keep on in the old way a little longer. Scanty and happy-go-lucky, but, on the whole, comfortable." He was silent a while, and then in a cautious whisper said, "I'll explain to you, Bruce. I might have made Jane's life easier if I had worked. I know that. I know our friends look on me as a lazy, selfish dog, a dead weight on the child. But—you are the first person to whom I have ever told this—I have had for many years a disorder, an ailment, which must in any case make my life a short one. Confinement and continued exertion would bring on a crisis at once. My physician told me that five years ago. Now you know why I have indulged myself. I still hoped some of the infernal patents—" He choked, and turned to look out of the window.

"But your danger is another reason why you should not be kept out of your property."

"Of course. But it's my luck."

"Does your daughter know this story?"

"No. Don't tell her, for God's sake!"

Nothing more was said until the train rolled into the station.

"Come, Jane, child," the captain called briskly. She rose and took his arm.

Mr. Neckart took leave of them under the flaring lamps outside. "You have left all the life and color of your face down in the salt air, Miss Swendon," he said. "You will not mark this holiday with a white stone, I fear."

49

"No," she said, waiting until he was gone before she spoke again.—
"We shall go to Cousin Will's now, father. I wish to say good-night to
him."

"Very well, my dear. I'll leave you to read to him while I run round
to see if any letters have come. I feel confident somebody will answer
my advertisement about the scissors."

Chapter 5

A luxurious apartment, of which the most salient features were excess of heat and color. A glowing fire burned in the grate. Persian rugs, richly-tinted curtains, tiger and leopard skins, light and gilding on every side, threw into more miserable contrast Laidley's pinched, pallid face as he stood in the midst. His back was to the fire, his claw-like hands behind him, opening and shutting mechanically as if to grasp the heat, his pale eyes blinking through his eye-glasses on Jane standing before him.

"Do I understand what you say?" in a tone of blank amazement. "That you, a child, come here to a dying man to assert your claim to his property! It is incredible that you came of your own free will. Who sent you?"

"Nobody, Cousin Will. It seemed to me the thing I ought to do. I do wish you would sit down," anxiously. "You are not able to stand."

He sank into a chair: "Bring me some wine."

She brought the wine, tucked the leopard skins about him, wiped his forehead tenderly, placed a cushion beneath his feet. He shivered, closed his eyes for a moment, then fixed them on her: "Now go on."

She did go on without the slightest hesitation, without even a flush of color, quick as her blood was to come and go when she was moved. The thing she had to do evidently seemed to her exceedingly simple and easy: "I knew you did not see the matter just as it is, or there would be no difficulty about it. No one else seemed willing to speak to you, and so I came myself."

He put out his hand toward the wine: she set it within his reach, and resumed her place, one arm resting on the mantel-shelf, looking down at him. There was only that sorrowful pity in her face with which any large-hearted, healthy woman would look at a diseased, dying man.

"I don't deny," he said, coughing feebly, "that at first sight you have a crude, illegal claim on my property—"

"My father—not I," throwing out her hand hastily.

"But even your claim admits of argument—argument," staring into the fire. "Yet what if I should meet Virginie Morôt yonder, and she should tax me with having wronged her child?" looking about him with a sudden turn.

A tricky girl could have gained her point now on the instant. But Jane, dull and straightforward as usual, knelt quickly down and took his fingers in her own cool, strong hands, as if she were dealing with a nervous child.

"Put my mother out of the question. She is not going to blame you for doing what seems to you just. I want you to see that it is not just. It is of the living, not the dead, you ought to think."

"Give me that medicine, can't you? My blood is like fire. Oh, you stand there," after he had swallowed it, "with your dogged, calm way of putting the question, as if it were a matter of a new gown. Hush!" as she began to speak. "You are but a child. You're not even a clever child. How can you understand the relations of a dying man to his Maker? It has been shown to me how with this money I could make peace with— with Him. The way has been opened for me to give it to the poor and the churches. Why, the rich man was commanded to 'sell all that he had and give to the poor, and he should have treasure in heaven.' The place is marked in the Bible there."[1] His hands worked feebly together, and he looked from side to side, avoiding the face in front with its steady dark eyes. "Why should I take from the poor to give to your father?"

"Because it is not yours to take or give."

He waited for her to go on, but she said no more. "I haven't forgotten you, Jane. I've planned for you as your father never would have done. There's good-fortune waiting for you which any woman would envy you. Go now—go!"

"I did not come to you with any claim of my own," the indignant lips trembling. "You shall not think so meanly of me as that. I told you why my father needs the money—all that he told to Mr. Neckart. Surely, you don't understand?"

"Oh, I understand your father very well," smiling dryly. It suited him just now to consider the captain a shrewd humbug, and his mysterious ailment the last dodge to raise money and sympathy.

52

The man at that moment looked so ill, so small and spiteful, that Jane's heart gave a sudden wrench of pity. It was a cruel, brutal thing, she felt, in her to stop him on the edge of the grave and demand his money. She put her hand to his forehead: it was cold and clammy. "Don't wrong my father in this way," she said in a lower voice than before. "You have had our money all the time, and our life has been hard—hard. I never said that before, but it is true."

He looked at her now, his courage flickering up to meet the crisis: "I hear you. Go on!"

"My father's life depends upon your honesty. I only ask you to remember that."

"You use plain words. So shall I." He thrust his hand into a drawer of the table before him, drew out a folded paper and pushed it toward her: "There is your answer. That is my will. My property is left in the way it will do God service. You can read it if you choose."

"And my father—?"

"I have not left him a dollar."

She turned on him, silent, a moment: he cowered and evaded her eyes.

"You shall not wrong him. He shall not die for the want of the money if I can help it," in the same quiet voice. She took up the paper, passed him and laid it on the fire, then watched it shrivel and burn to ashes. He could not have detained her, any more than he could stay the scorching flame with his hand.

She threw her cloak about her without a word, and drew the hood over her head.

He pulled the bell violently: "You have only given me the trouble of preparing a second copy. It shall be identical with the first."

Old Dave, coming in, observed that Miss Swendon's very lips were without color. But as she went out of the room she halted to move a screen, so as to protect Laidley from the draught.

She met her father on the stairs. "Do not go up," she said. "David is with him, and I want you to take me home." . . .

Before daylight the next morning Captain Swendon was summoned by David to his master. A keen north-east wind had caused a sudden change in the weather, and Mr. Laidley had sunk rapidly, and was now scarcely conscious.

"It is only what I anticipated," said the physician, meeting the captain at the door. "Though if he had remained in the South he might have lingered until midsummer. Not longer."

The captain nursed the dying man anxiously all day, and when he was dead came home excited and haggard. It seemed to him by that time that one of the most lovable fellows in the world had gone out of it. He always was of that opinion at a funeral.

"Well, it's all over, Jane!" he cried, coming just at dusk into the room, where she stood at the window, her back turned toward him. "Yes. Poor Will! He was a good fellow years ago—witty, hospitable. You didn't know him in his prime. Your mother liked him. That is, well—" He sat down by the fire, staring at it with his owlish eyes, pulling off his old boots and soaked coat, for it was raining hard, and wondering a little that Jane had not a warm change of clothes ready for him as usual. But she did not move. "Yes," with a groan. "He knows the great secret now, poor fellow! I wish I'd been kinder to him. There's lots of things I might have done. But that damned money! I suppose it soured me."

Jane turned. "I am glad *I* did what was right to him," she said slowly.

The captain looked at her surprised. The shock had been too heavy on the child, he thought: her eyes were quite sunken in her white face. "Yes, yes. You were always a very nice, attentive little nurse. But when anybody dies one is apt to remember one's shortcomings to them, and wish for even an hour to set all right."

"I have done nothing to him which I would wish to set right," she said again, her lips moving with difficulty.

Her father did not answer. But she was so unused to speak of herself in any way that he observed her persistence now as peculiar.

PART 3

Chapter 6

A year after Laidley's death, Judge Rhodes, being in New York, breakfasted with Mr. Neckart. He noticed that the editor had grown lean and sallow. "And God knows he had no good looks to spare," smoothing down his own white beard over his comfortable paunch. Something, too, of that easy frankness which had made Neckart so popular was gone; no topic interested him; his eye was secretive and irritable: he spoke and moved under the constant pressure of self-control. The judge, as he watered his claret, eyed the dark face opposite to him critically. "Now, I never," he thought, "saw a sign of ill-temper or cruelty in that man. Yet I have a queer fancy that if the reins were once taken off he could not master himself again. It must be devilishly uncomfortable, holding one's self in in that way," the last morsel of quail sliding down his throat unctuously, "*I* can let myself out without danger."

"Why, you eat nothing! The campaign's been too much for you, Mr. Neckart," he said aloud. "You've run down terribly in the last year. Always the way. You young men make too many spurts in the first heat, and break down before the middle of the race. Well, that's our American policy. But the American physique won't stand it."

"Do you only mean that I have broken down physically, or do you see any change in my work? The leading articles are mine, you know. Don't be afraid to be frank."

"Well, now that you ask me—Your articles are more forcible lately, more popular: they bring down the galleries, eh? But it's a sledge-hammer force, it's vehemence, d'ye see? There's a lack of that moderation, that repressed power, in which was your real strength. You asked me to be frank?"

"Yes. And I knew just what you would say. Well, what must be, is!" with a gesture which dismissed the subject.

"Nonsense! It's your nervous system that needs toning, that's all. If our side goes in, get a foreign mission—some warm, lazy place on the Mediterranean, say. Rest a few years, and when you come home take an easier pace for the rest of your life. Lord bless you, boy! I've been through it all. When I was a young fellow—mere bundle of nerves, high-strung, sir—high-strung! Ambition, love! Constitution wouldn't stand it!—Bit of the steak, John, rare.—Joe Rhodes, I said, either come down to the jog-trot level or die. So here I am! Good for forty years yet, please God! When you are my age you may be just what I am, if you choose."

Neckart's eye twinkled: "Try the birds, judge."

He made an effort after that to resume his old careless manner, and the judge had tact enough to drop the subject. But he was not deceived. "There's more here than meets the eye," he said shrewdly to himself. "Neckart has had a blow that has made him stagger. He has worked like a horse in a treadmill. But he has the constitution to stand it. Functions in healthy condition—tremendous vital power. Either hereditary disease is at work, or some morbid passion, or he would not have given way."

He urged him to eat with tender solicitude, even gave him his famous recipe for a salad. No matter what our sympathy, our help for each other can seldom come any closer than skin or stomach, after all.

"By the way," he said presently, "I hear that Swendon has bought a place up the Hudson. Can you tell me anything about him?"

"I meet him everywhere," said Neckart. "The old man is failing fast. But he takes life just as he always did—like a boy let loose for the holidays."

"And his daughter?"

"She never comes into town: she is not a woman of society."

"I remember the little Swede was no favorite of yours," noticing a certain reserve in Neckart's tone. "But I had an object in asking for her. Of course you would not be likely to know much about them: they are out of your line."

"I have met the captain and his daughter several times during the year," said Neckart. "They were camping on the Maine coast last summer, and I stumbled into their tent one day. Miss Swendon fancied her father would grow strong on a diet of fish of his own catching. When the cold weather set in she took him to St. Augustine. I ran against him by the old fort the very morning I arrived, and in the spring we met at Omaha, and made the overland trip to California together. There is no kind of air and no kind of amusement which she has not tried, since she had the means, to give the old man his health back again. To no purpose, however."

"Very odd!" the judge nodded mysteriously. "Very odd indeed about that property! Laidley told me the very night before he died that he had made a will leaving it in charity. Now, Jane inherited by virtue of a will made two years before. No other forthcoming. I suppose remorse seized him *in articulo mortis*.[1] There was a curious thing occurred in that last interview of mine with Laidley.—How can I see Swendon?" interrupting himself. "Where is their house?"

Mr. Neckart hesitated a moment: "I am going there this evening to dine and spend the night, and I will take you with me. It will be a surprise which the captain will like."

"The very thing! Precisely! The truth is, Neckart—light a cigar—the truth is," lowering his voice and leaning over the table, "Laidley exacted a half promise from me that night which troubles me. The fellow died forthwith, you see, and so clenched it on me. He had a plan for Miss Swendon's future, and asked me to forward it. I thought he was going to cheat the girl, and paid little attention to it. But he did the clean thing after all, and then died promptly. I must say Laidley acted in a much more decent and gentlemanlike way than I expected. So, now I feel as if I owed it to the fellow to keep my word."

Mr. Neckart nodded. He asked no questions, but scanned the judge's flabby face narrowly. Rhodes lifted one leg on to the other knee and nursed it. It was his confidential attitude.

"It's a delicate matter, you see. Van Ness is concerned."

"Van Ness, the antiquarian?"

"Oh, he's more than that! You don't suppose a man of his breadth of intellect confines himself to old bricks and dry bones? Why, God bless you! Pliny Van Ness is the final authority in Philadelphia on new singers or pictures or cracked teapots or great religious or philanthropic reforms. If he were taken from it, the underpinnings of that town would be knocked away, and it would fall flat."

"Last fall, I think, I heard he had a plan for enforcing compulsory education in Pennsylvania?"

"Well, yes. I don't know why that didn't pass. It died out. Van Ness was trying, too, to establish a grand scheme for the benefit of the mining population. But somehow I haven't heard of that lately. Oh he's a great man, sir! When I hear him talk half an hour it quite lifts me up to purer air. I always say when I come away, 'Joe Rhodes, you're a selfish scoundrel! A selfish scoundrel!'"

The judge smoked in silence a few minutes. "Yes," he resumed thoughtfully, "it was about Van Ness. Poor Laidley had that reverence for him which men of his calibre are apt to have for a character of perfect excellence, and in his anxiety for Jane he planned that a marriage should be brought about between them. I was to inaugurate the matter—bring them together. Easily, naturally, you understand? The sort of thing that is done every day. I've seen excellent matches made in Virginia by a little quiet management of friends."

"Yes. It is done every day." Mr. Neckart yesterday would have talked of the marriages of half the women he knew as "good matches" or "well managed" without knowing that he was vulgar in so doing. But now the whole idea struck him as loathsome and disgusting. Were women to be paraded before their buyers as in a slave-market? He looked at the poor judge babbling innocently as he might at some venal go-between in the markets of Cairo.

"Thinking the matter over," pursued the judge anxiously, "it has occurred to me that Laidley would not have been so confident of Van Ness's ultimate concurrence in the scheme unless Pliny had shown some prepossession in favor of the little girl."

"You think, then, the sultan is ready to throw the handkerchief?" dryly.

"Oh, that's a coarse way of putting it, Neckart. But, considered as a match, now, really, you know. Van Ness is—The idea that he was favorable to it was suggested to me again yesterday when he proposed that we should look up the captain and call upon him. He is not a man who usually makes advances."

"Is Mr. Van Ness in New York with you?"

"Yes, certainly. I thought you knew that."

"And you propose to take him out tonight?"

"Why, that seemed a good plan. Unless you have some objection?"

"What objection can I have? What does it matter to me?" He stooped to pat his dog, that sat upright watching his face.

"Surely, that is that savage wolf-hound of Miss Swendon's?"

"Yes. He divides his time between us." After a few minutes he said, "You seem to anticipate no difficulty in the way of your conquering hero? Yet Miss Swendon by no means belongs to the warm-blooded, susceptible order of women. This Van Ness, as I remember him, is a starved, insignificant-looking fellow."

"Oh, on the contrary! He has a very noble presence. Pliny is tall, with much dignity of carriage."

"Pompous, eh? 'I am Sir Oracle'?"[2]

"Nothing of the kind. Rather deprecating manner, with a calm face, beaming blue eyes, and abundant fair hair and beard. The very finest of Saxon types, in fact."

"Ah? But these reformers are apt to be underbred, irritable, with nasty peculiarities of habits and manner which they never have thought it worth while to cure. I suppose your friend is like his brethren?"

"Now, Neckart, just wait until you see Van Ness. You'll be charmed, or I've no judgment. Most men are, and all women," laughing significantly.

They rose at the moment. As they left the room Neckart caught sight in a mirror of his own dwarfed bulk and the massive head set in its black mane. He stopped and looked for an instant at himself fixedly, a thing which he had not done perhaps for years, and then walked on in silence beside the judge. When they parted in the street he wrote a line on a card and gave it to him.

"In case I am not able to go out on the same train with you, this is the route to the farm," he said.

He could scarcely be courteous. He was in a rage of indignation. Not, of course, that it mattered to him whether Jane married this or any other man whom she loved. She was only an acquaintance—more perhaps—

his little friend.[3] She must marry: he had thought of that often; and she would love—with a strength and fidelity beyond that of any woman he had ever known. He had often thought of that too. When the time came—years hence, perhaps—he would consult with her father as to the man. They must be satisfied that he would make her happy—they two. It must be a careful, cautious, slow matter. He might surely claim so much of a guardianship over her! He had studied her character very carefully, and appreciated it as a rare and delicate one; and he was very fond of the captain—very fond of the captain. But as for the plan of marriage— Mr. Neckart understood his own disgust at the judge, and accounted for it naturally. He had but little of the ordinary chivalric belief in woman's modesty and purity. Much knowledge of female lobbyists and literary tramps and champagne-tippling belles had shaken his faith, probably.

"But this girl is the most innocent, sincerest thing God ever made," he said. "She is clean in thought and body and word."

In those long days on the Maine coast, or by the sea-wall at St. Augustine, or crossing the interminable mountain-ranges or alkali deserts, he had had time to read this candid soul page by page: her clear skin and liquid eyes were not more transparent than her thoughts. All through that day's work a young noble figure moved like a shadow—a woman with the brave blue eyes, the ruddy lips, the grand unconsciousness of the great women of her race. The blood of Aslauga and Ingeborg was in her veins.[4] So strong was this feeling upon him, that always, when he was making ready to meet her, he bathed and arrayed himself as if he was going to take part in the rites of a church or some sacred place. "'So white, so fair, so sweet was she!'"[5] he sang softly to himself. And guzzling Rhodes, with his oily laugh and fat hands, meant to show her off, exhibit her fine points to this Admirable Crichton of morality, and persuade him to marry her![6] Was there any danger that she would love or marry him? She was undoubtedly dull in perception of character: had she not always made a demigod of the silly old captain? The finest vessels were always first to break themselves to pieces against some earthen pitcher.[7]

He made haste to take an early afternoon train. He would see his friends again before Rhodes arrived.

Chapter 7

The Hemlock Farm, the captain's new possession, was a great un-trimmed tract of farm and woodland on the Hudson, with a rough-hewn stone house, open-windowed and wide-doored, uncivilized and picturesque, set down hospitably in the midst of it. Mr. Neckart, strik-ing across the fields from the little station, caught glimpses through the forest for a mile or two of its walls and heavy chimneys stained with smoke and lichen. They seemed to grow out of the ground as naturally as the oaks and gray beeches.

It was a damp, cool day in June. Ragged patches of clouds were driven down across the tree-tops; the dark blue of the sky had yet a tinge of moist yellow in it after the night's rains; the wind was wet as it blew now and then gustily in Neckart's face. He jumped across a brush hedge overgrown with smilax and blackberry vines, and passed in under the hemlocks. They were dark and still. Outside, the sunshine flashed sometimes, pale and watery, and the blackberries in the hedge were getting rid of their white blossoms and reddening their green knobs, and a wild tiger-lily here and there blazed its answer to the summer; but the old hemlocks, just as Neckart knew them when a boy, kept si-lence and nodded thoughtfully together, meditating over their ancient secret. He walked more slowly. How long was it since he had left the office or sat in the club-room at breakfast with Rhodes's puffy face and unsavory talk?

Why, even the hedge with its sleepy hum of bees and yellow butter-flies seemed to be of the world, worldly here. He left it far behind. The aisles of the wood grew higher and more solemn, and slowly filled with pale-green light. The wind and rain last night had not reached these solitudes, yet he climbed over fallen trunks rank with soaked emerald moss and branching fungus yellow or red as coral. A lizard with bulging eyes of jet darted across his foot: now came the whir of a partridge from under the dead leaves, now the veery cut the air with its fine silver pipe.

Neckart stood still and drew long slow breaths. The life of the woods was like sleep to him; the air was marrowy, stimulating; he could feel himself growing quiet and stronger in it. A moment later he drew his breath deeper.

"She is coming!" A tall, erect girl, bareheaded, came noiselessly down between the gray trunks of the trees, her feet sinking at each step into the dead, ash-colored moss. Her color rose as she saw him, and her eyes lighted, but she put her finger on her lips. "You have frightened them," she whispered. "They have all gone into their houses."

"They—?"

"Hush-h!" She sat down on a fallen log and motioned him to a place beside her: then she waited, listening. There was a space of silence: presently a red squirrel came out overhead and darted along the limbs; the ragged bark of the tree in front of them was suddenly full of creeping things, busily hurrying up and down; the coffee-colored water of the brook at their feet began to glance with silvery flashes of minnows and wagtails; out of a miniature hill came a long procession of ants; they marched, deployed, disappeared, and came again; monster spiders, like lumps of glittering enamel, swung in the air by invisible threads; two black beetles rose to view by Neckart's foot, rolling a white ball twice as big as themselves toward a flicker of clear sunshine on the grass.

"They are taking the babies for a sunbath," whispered Jane.

The muffled hammering of a woodpecker, building its nest, came from a hollow tree at a little distance. A flock of kingbirds dashed boisterously through the underbrush. The pewees began their pitiful cry of "Lost! lost!" A scarlet tanager sat like a sentinel on a dead branch and challenged them with a sharp single note. The whole air grew full of that strenuous, mysterious wood-sound which is next to silence—the voice and movement of millions of living things too small for sight. It rose to a full orchestra as the two human listeners sat motionless, though only a few notes were familiar to Neckart—the tic-tic of the grasshoppers, the low monotone of countless unseen springs escaping under the grass, the lone call of the thrush, a single minor note from a golden bugle. But it was not the grasshoppers or thrush to which he listened breathlessly: it was the soft breathing of the young girl beside him, as she sat attentive, a quiet delight in her face, her blue eyes gathering soft lustre. Nature, when she and the world were young, might have looked with such motherly tenderness on all her living things. Her large nervous hands were clasped about her knees: the yellow hair glistened close beside him, and as her full bosom rose and fell he could hear her heart beat in the silence.

He stood up quickly with a shiver: "Shall we go to the house?"

She rose: "Yes, if you will. They are learning to know me now. I come here every day. There is a partridge lives under that bush, and he came out and actually let me see him drum once, and yesterday I found a blacksnake attacking a bluebird's nest in time to help fight the battle."

They had reached the hedge: Neckart held apart the thorny bushes, but did not give her his hand to help her through, as he would have done to any other woman. He was always scant in personal courtesies to her.

She looked back at the woods: "Yes, there they all live and keep house, and marry and quarrel and die. It does not concern them at all what man you make President, Mr. Neckart. It is very hard to make their acquaintance. I think they ought to know their friends at sight."

"I don't know. I know two human beings," said Neckart gravely, "who, when they first met, felt a strong mutual antipathy, and now they—"

She turned, looking keenly at him.

"They are good friends. Miss Swendon," looking into her eyes.

"Yes. There could not be any better," putting out her hand frankly. He held it but an instant, as he might have done a boy's when offered to him; but as she turned away a soft lovely color dyed her throat and face.

"There is so much wild mint growing here," she said incoherently, stooping to gather it, "and pennyroyal, and a plenty of sweet basil. I am going to have an herb- and seed-room, and give out the seeds to Twiss myself next spring. I have not told you any of the news. Father has slept every night without a tonic. Don't you think his color is better? Did you see him yesterday?" anxiously.

"Oh, it is better without doubt."

"I am quite sure, now, we did the very wisest thing in coming here. The house is on an elevation, you see—above any chance of malaria—and then the warm moisture from the river—just what he needs. And the going to town—Do you often meet him in town? Is he enjoying himself? Did it strike you that he was improving until I suggested it?"

"Why, it was only to-day," said Neckart, "that I told Judge Rhodes how I met Captain Swendon everywhere—at the club—"

"Yes. *I* urged him to join the club," her face beaming.

"Couldn't have been a wiser move.—At the club, at dinners, at the theatre, meeting old friends, taking in new life everywhere, and making new life for everybody. Why, to see him on Broadway waving his hat and calling 'Hillo!' to somebody across the street puts even the cab-horses in good humor."

She laughed: "I knew it, I knew it! And here on rainy days he has so much to do. He is trying every one of his patents in the house or grounds. I am fitting up a billiard-room to surprise him on his birthday. But come and I'll show you some of the patents at work. And I have never showed you the barn or the orchard. Father will not be at home until evening. He expected to meet you on the train. We can go exploring all the afternoon."

They crossed the meadow to the barn, Jane explaining that the former owner of the Hemlocks had lived for years in Europe, and left house and land to run into their present overgrown decay. "Farmer and gardeners worry about new fences and repairs, but I will not have even the dead leaves cleared from the paths. I remember you said once you liked to hear them crisp under your feet," sliding her own feet among them.

There was nothing in the idle, purposeless afternoon which any practical man or woman would have thought worthy of an hour's remembrance; yet it stood out for ever after, above all of Bruce Neckart's life, as some fair tableland lifted from the fogs near to the sun.

They went into the house, examined patent hinges and locks, and explored the vacant rooms and mysterious garrets filled with lumber. She sat down by an old spinning-wheel, turning it and singing a scrap of Gretchen's song, while the light from the dormer window touched her white arched throat and yellow hair. They went to the stables, and the old Scotch hostler brought out the horses and talked with Neckart of the mysteries of flanks and strains of blood, while Jane looked on shyly, standing with the dog in the wide door.

"Maybe I shall know them as well as I do you some day, Bruno," she said gravely to him. "But I shall never like them as well. That wouldn't be possible: they're strangers." The dog nuzzled his head into her hand and marched steadily beside her. Then she took Neckart and Bruno over a little hill to a spring-house, into which you went through a mossy door across a sparkling little brook. She went inside and brought out a bowl of yellow cream, all of them watching the kitchen windows guiltily as she did it; and then they went on aimlessly across the stepping-stones in the brook up through the field of young corn until they skirted the brush hedge again, when Bruno left them in pursuit of ground-squirrels. There was a bank running along the river-shore, topped with nodding ferns and purple iron-weed, and brown with the soft, feathery tops of the mouse-ear. The bank was on one side, the water on the other, swift, dark, mobile, throwing back now a still belt of sunshine, now gloomy woods, now the yellow shadows of low-driven clouds. They walked with the river, not against it. The wind blew damp in their faces. Since Neckart had talked so confidently of her father's improvement, Jane had been gay and light-hearted as a child, with a nervous quaver now and then in her voice as if a word would bring the tears. She looked at him thoughtfully as they walked on.

"You ought to go to California again," she said abruptly.

"I can take tonics at home, if you mean that I need them."

"Yes. You are more worn and haggard than when we left Omaha. Every day of the journey I used to see how the wrinkles left your forehead, and your eye cleared and your voice changed. It was the mountain-air. There is no tonic for you like the mountain-air."

Neckart shifted his hat uneasily, and turned to look at the river as though the frank blue eyes anxiously inspecting his face hurt him.

"I was harassed and perplexed then as to the policy which I should adopt for the paper in a certain political question. My grim looks were no doubt owing to that. You decided the question for me."

"I? Why, I know nothing of politics."

"No. But the choice offered me was between right and financial ruin on one side, and a fortune and neutrality on the other. It would be impossible," in a tone which suddenly became careless and matter of fact, "for any man to come in contact with a nature as absolutely honest as yours, Miss Swendon, and not be influenced by it. I do not think I spoke to you at all of this question, yet it seemed to me that you dictated every step of my course. I never have told you of my affairs since, yet every day I take your advice on them. It is always different from that of my political friends, because it is simply the broad truth and common sense. I follow it." He turned to her with one of his rare smiles and an odd break in his controlled voice. "I hold your hand in mine every step of my way."

She did not smile in return. She was standing still in the path, as though she had been stopped by a blow. "Honest? *I* honest?" she said.

The dog jumped up on her breast to go on with his romp. She pushed him down, looking straight into Neckart's amazed face.

"You may have made mistakes: everybody is liable to do that," he stammered. "But as for sincerity—"

She drew a long breath as if throwing off a burden: "No. I have been honest. You are not wrong about me there. I have made no mistakes." She turned and walked on quickly.

As he followed her he observed for the first time how steady was her step and how close set the finely-cut jaws. His own mouth, by the way, was coarser, but more facile: it spoke when silent: the chin was cleft and sensitive.

"When she once makes up her mind, the verdict of the whole world will not make her flinch," he thought with keen approval. The quality which he had that very day damned as mulish obstinacy in one of his clerks was infinitely alluring to him in this young girl. He came closer to her, watching her averted face, a passion of delight and longing gradually dulling all past resolves or reason.

If she would but turn her eyes on his face again searching for signs of trouble or illness! It was actually the first time in Neckart's life that a woman had taken any care of him. His mother had been a burden and charge on him since his boyhood. That single kindly glance had opened to him unknown possibilities of tenderness, of the touch of a woman's fingers, and all that came to other men through them.

But she walked on without speaking, her head sunk on her breast. She seemed to have forgotten that he was in the world.

At a bend in the road they met the captain. He was heated and agitated, and tried to hide it by tremendous hilarity. He welcomed Neckart boisterously, shaking hands with him again and again before he turned to Jane, who stood watching him with delighted eyes.

"How well you are looking this afternoon, father! Your cheeks are as red as a girl's!"

"Oh, I'm all right! Don't bother about me. Think of other people sometimes, child. Now, there's a matter I want to speak to you about, if I could only put it to you properly."

"I am ready. Put it directly, pointblank: that is the best way in delicate questions."

"Don't laugh. It's no laughing matter. It's the most serious business of my life, and I've only a few minutes to make you understand," mopping his hot forehead with his handkerchief. "The train will be due in half an hour."

"The train? Serious business? The commissioner of patents is coming?—"

"Damn the patents! I beg your pardon, Jane. But really—This is a request I have to make of you. A request of you from poor Will Laidley."

She drew back. The weight which she had a moment ago thrown off fell on her again. "A request of me?" she said slowly. "Whatever he asked me to do I shall do. I owe him at least so much."

"Of course! You owe him everything. You know he might have left us without a penny, as he thought of doing. Instead of which, there was not even a legacy to any charity."

"No. Every dollar of it came to me. I know."

"Oh, Will behaved most generously, nobly, to you, there's no doubt of it! And this plan of his shows such tender care of you. I never heard of it until to-day from Judge Rhodes. God forbid that I should influence you! But you would be sorry to thwart him in his grave."

"I will not thwart him again."

"If I could put it to you properly now!" The captain grew red and coughed. Mr. Neckart looked at him with fierce disgust. Was he so brutal as to talk to any woman of her marriage with a man whom she had never seen?

"You forget," he said coldly. "Miss Swendon owes no gratitude for money which was justly her own. William Laidley, too, was a weak, impure man—the very last who should be allowed to stretch his hand out of his grave to control any woman's life. You should not hamper her with any such gratitude."

"You cannot judge of this for me, Mr. Neckart," said Jane. "He has the right, especially when it concerns his money.—What is it he wished me to do?"

The captain stammered with embarrassment.

"Tut! tut! Money has nothing to do with it.—As for poor Will, Bruce, he had his good points. *De mortuis*—you know. I knew him in his prime. It's a trifle, after all," evading Neckart's eye, of which he had read the meaning. "But you are so apt, Jane, to take unreasonable prejudices against people. This is a friend of Will's, whom Judge Rhodes will bring out this evening. And it was your cousin's wish that he should be your friend also—adviser, eh? I've no head for business, you know, and you might refer knotty questions to him. Consult him about stocks, and the drainage of the stables, and this and that," glancing at Neckart for approval of his delicacy and cunning. "I only wanted to warn you not to take an antipathy to him, but I am clumsy—"

"Is that all?" putting her hand to her eyes for a minute as though they ached.—"Come, Bruno. It is time to dress for dinner."

"Yes, do, my dear. Haven't you any dress with frills and fal-lals, such as the ladies are wearing now? These clinging gowns do well enough for homefolks like me and Bruce, but—Something airy, gay, now. It's only as an adviser that Will recommended Mr. Van Ness to you, you understand? Your cousin consulted him of late years in all financial matters. I do suppose Van Ness—and Laidley too," turning to Neckart—"would think the child was flinging the money to the dogs, buying such a place as this to humor her old father's whims."

Jane halted, her hands on the dog's collar: "I will have no advice from Mr. Van Ness, father, as to my disposal of the money. It is mine. No man, dead or living, shall interfere with my use of it," she said in a low voice.

"Now I've prejudiced her against him," groaned the captain as soon as she was out of sight. "I saw you thought me coarse in urging this matter on her so abruptly, Bruce. But you do not understand. My time here is short—God knows how soon it may end—and I can't bear the thought of leaving the child alone. Van Ness is so pure a man—a Christian whom all the world reverences—What better can I hope than to see her his wife before I go?"

"His wife?"

"Yes. Is there any objection to him? Be frank, Bruce. It is nothing to you, but it's life and death to me. Van Ness told Judge Rhodes candidly this morning that he had watched Jane since she was a child, himself unknown, and that it was his hope their acquaintance would deepen into something warmer than friendship."

"Good God! what a model lover! Stands off watching for years— weighs her carefully in his scales. Item, so much amiability: item, so many pounds of healthy flesh; item, annual income so much. Then he steps in to inspect her a little closer, and if she prove satisfactory he will marry her."

"Bruce, you're unjust. Every man has not your sensitiveness. The way that Rhodes stated it there really was no indelicacy in it. Do you know any objection to Van Ness? Be candid. Have you any reason to urge against the marriage in case—?"

Mr. Neckart did not answer for a few moments. He had been smoking, but the cigar went out in his mouth. "No," he said at last. "I have no objection to urge to it. I have nothing to say. Go in, captain. The train is due now. I will follow you when I have finished my cigar."

Chapter 8

Miss Swendon, going up the wooded hill toward the house, raising her head, saw a man coming toward her down the narrow path. The low sunlight struck through the trees on his broad forehead and magnificent golden beard flowing full on his breast. He was in evening-dress; a topaz blazed on his snowy shirtfront; he walked meditatively, his hands clasped behind him; his eyes rested on her with beaming pleasure. She turned her head away, but saw him, without her eyes, advancing upon her—coming, it seemed to her, into her life.

Mr. Van Ness's personality indeed was too potent to admit of his slying unnoticed, like an ordinary human being, in and out of anybody's vision. You might look at him but for a moment, but his majestic port, the fineness of his linen, the very set of his high hat, his Christian benignity and grace, remained with you ever after, a possession of comfort and joy.

Jane knew him at a glance, though they had never met before. All of her life she had heard Aristides called the Just, and been a trifle bored by it.[1] Undoubtedly this was he. She was not petulant or bored now.

If we want a key to her feeling, we can find it in the fact that there was not a moment since she burned the will that she had not known that she was right in doing it, and that there was not a moment in which she had not remembered that in the judgment of the world she was a thief.

Here was the man sent by Laidley out of his grave to judge her, a man who was embodied Virtue and Honor—in the world's eye.

There was evidently no doubt in Mr. Van Ness's mind, either, as to who the slight erect woman might be who came slowly up the rocky path, one hand on the dog's collar, the folds of her blue dress falling about her like the drapery of an antique statue, the coils of yellow hair only held in place by a black velvet band. If he had been watching her growth for years, as he said, waiting for this supreme moment, he gave no sign of emotion now that it had arrived, except that the radiance in his protruding light eyes became more intense. I may as well say, once for all, that Mr. Van Ness never was known to yield to weak emotion, irritability or any of those vicious humors which beset other men. If he had done so it would have grievously wounded the faith of his disciples. He possibly had met these temptations in his cradle, as the infant Hercules the serpents, strangled them and left them dead there, so passing into a serene boyhood and victorious middle age.

Bruno at this moment caught sight of the stranger, and began to growl ominously. Now, the dog was an amiable, courteous dog ordinarily, but subject, like his mistress, to irrational antipathies, and, like her, with a large reserve of untamed blood to support his prejudices. He stopped, dropped his head between his fore legs, his eyeballs reddened, he barked a short, sharp warning. Miss Swendon knew the signs: she had seen them once before. She caught him by the collar, looking straight at the exceptionally handsome man with the underbred blaze of yellow on his shirtfront: "Down! down, sir!—You had better go back," to Mr. Van Ness. "I beg of you to go back."

"No, no," gently, and still advancing. "Poor fellow!—Let me catch his eye, Miss Swendon."

It was something in the eye, however, which maddened the dog: he shook in every limb; his lips were drawn back; the sharp teeth glistened.

Jane threw herself on her knees, her arms about his throat: she motioned Van Ness back with her head, but the enraged animal threw her off as he would a wisp of straw, and sprang straight at his throat. Van Ness, though a heavily-built man, staggered back; but he caught the dog about the throat with both hands, and held him as in a vise. The red eyeballs and panting tongue were close to his face. Next, Bruno struck with his paw at one of the white soft hands, and tore a great gash in it, from which the blood gushed; but the pleasant smile did not leave the lips of his antagonist.

"Now, Miss Swendon," he said gently, "I think you can soothe him. I will hold him quiet to listen to reason."

Jane came to him, and in a few moments had the beast subdued and lying panting at her feet, his bloodshot eye still fixed on Van Ness. She was pale and trembling, offered her handkerchief to tie up the wounded hand, and was humble in her apologies; but Van Ness knew all the while that her sympathies were with the dog. Judge Rhodes had heard the scuffle, and arrived now, out of breath, and violent in his abuse of poor Bruno.

"Why you keep such an ill-conditioned beast, Jane, I cannot understand," he cried as he swabbed and tied the wound.

Mr. Van Ness beamed down unruffled on the stout little man: "You are always unjust to dogs, Rhodes. Now, I should say that our friend Bruno was one of the Brahmin caste—fine-natured and well-bred as a rule.[2] Liable to mistakes, perhaps.—I am right, Miss Swendon?" and he beamed down in his turn on Jane, who sat on the bank, stroking the dog's muzzle as it lay on her knee. She forced a smile which proved a failure, said that he was right, and that she must hurry before them to the house. She stopped as soon as she was out of sight to hug the dog with a sob: "But we are not wild beasts, are we, Bruno?"

She felt the dog's insane desire to tear off this amiability, this cloying gentleness of the newcomer, and find what was beneath. It was just as it used to be long ago when prim, polite little misses came to play with her—white, pink-eyed poodles consorting with a big Newfoundland. She used to feel clumsy and worsted beside them, possessed by the devil too to scare and disgust them. Yet she knew herself more right than they all the time.

When she sat at the head of the dinner-table an hour or two later, soft silken drapery having taken the place of the soft woollen, and her usual calm good temper on the surface instead of pallor and tears, her secret mood was very much the same. Mr. Neckart sat apart from her: he spoke little, and that only to the captain, who was eager about the political question of the day. Judge Rhodes, dropping his voice, poured into her ear eulogiums on Van Ness.

"Did you see him smiling down on that brute? Now, how did he know but he had given him the hydrophobia?"[3]

"I appreciated the self-control," smiling. "So did Bruno. It drove him mad."

"Self-control? I tell you, it's superhuman! I've thought sometimes it was a divine power sustaining him. Why, I saw that man at his mother's deathbed. She lay in his arms, and he sang to her—hymns, you know—sang to her in a clear, unbroken voice until her spirit had passed out of hearing. I couldn't have done it, even for a stranger."

"I am sure you could not," said Miss Swendon.

"He sinks self out of sight wholly, you see. Now, he had a dog once—a hound like yours—brought him up. It was touching to see them together—the devotion of the poor brute. Well, he sold him, and gave the hundred dollars to his State Home for Children. He could not afford such a luxury as the dog's love, he said, while these poor wretches needed so much."

"But my dog," said Miss Swendon quite distinctly, "is more to me than all the wretches in Pennsylvania."

There was an awkward silence.

Mr. Van Ness turned his handsome face on her with a benign nod: "How natural and beautiful that is! Her dog and her babe and her lover are more to a woman than all the outside world. So they ought to be! Love is like air: when it is confined it only fills a given space, but give it escape and it spreads over all God's creation. The day is not far distant when young, fair women will freely give themselves to the work of raising the dangerous classes."[4]

"Well, I don't know about that," said Rhodes. "I'm growing hopeless. What with ignorance and whiskey and conceit, the dangerous classes even here are too heavily handicapped to make any running. They will need two or three lives after this, it seems to me, to bring them up to a fair starting-point."

"That's a fact!" cried the captain. "Now, there are beggars. My plan is to give to 'em all, and so be on the safe side; but the organized charities tell us they are all impostors; and then every day some organized charity turns out a swindle! What is a man to do?"

"To do? Give himself up, I suppose, to the cause of the poor and the Lord, as this man has done!" cried the judge earnestly, touching Van Ness on the shoulder, who shook his head and smiled—a sad, deprecating smile.

"Don't look for wages of any sort, then. If a man wants to be suspected by the rich and abused by the poor, let him take up my work," he said a moment after, meeting Neckart's eye with a frank laugh.

"No doubt you are right," said Mr. Neckart gravely. "I never tried it."

They were rising from the table at the moment. As they passed through the hall, Mr. Neckart halted beside a window in which grew some house-plants. Jane came directly to him. She had fallen of late into the habit of consulting him in all her plans, as they both knew very well that she was not at all a capable woman—according to the New England idea: she lacked acuteness and knowledge of facts and all the fashionable aptitudes. She had not even cognizance enough of Wagner or cloisonné or old andirons to put her *en rapport* with her times.[5]

It was a daily matter for her to appeal to Neckart to help her ignorance here or there, yet when he heard the soft rustle of her skirts beside him he grew perceptibly colder and stiffer, waiting without a smile for her to speak.

"I have brought my mind, as usual, to have it made up," she began gayly, growing instantly sober when she caught his glance. "What do I want with this ready-made Mentor? Do you think I need a financial adviser?"

"I have no doubt you will find Mr. Van Ness both shrewd and honest in that capacity, if you choose to consult him."

"Why should I? I suppose the money is invested properly. I draw the dividends regularly, and I have no use for money but one. I mean to make my father's life happy with it, and I know how to do that. Nobody can teach me. What have I to do with this reformer and his State Home?"

Mr. Neckart had been in the habit of looking down on her in her occasional outbursts with an amused indulgence as from an immeasurable difference of years. He was looking down at her now with unsmiling and, as she thought, unfriendly eyes; but she was suddenly, for the first time, conscious of how young he actually was, and how near to her in many unworded, fathomless ways. She drew back within the narrow limits of the window, and was silent.

He withdrew his eyes from her with an effort, and did not immediately answer. When he did, it was in a cool business tone. "I do not know what relation Mr. Van Ness may hold to you hereafter, if any," he said. "But he seems to me thoroughly honest and manly. He is the first professed reformer I ever saw who was not either subservient or aggressive to me, as a newspaper-man who did not ride his hobby."

"I do not see him with your eyes," she said with a shrug. "Bruno's, rather."

Neckart laughed. After the manner of men, he had judged the man who was crossing his life with calm common sense and justice, but he was quite satisfied that the woman with neither should condemn him.

The late clear twilight lingered with a haze of red in the sky, although the sun had been down for an hour or more. Jane stood irresolutely in the window. Through the bushes she could see the stoop where her father and the judge sat smoking, Mr. Van Ness beside them, his benign, sheep-like gaze wandering slowly around in search of her.

"Of course he does not smoke!" she said. "He has not a single weakness on which one can hang a liking; and he has actually taken father's own chair!" which by the way she had cushioned herself years ago, when it and two small stools furnished their shabby room. No wonder that she and the captain looked upon it as a sacred relic.

The window where they stood was shaded on the outside by privet and althea bushes: it opened to the ground, and a sandy little footpath ran directly to the river, where her boat was moored. Usually, while the captain took his after-dinner nap, she rowed along the shore, and Neckart, when he was there, would sit in the stern reading or scribbling his next leader, but oftener leaning back, his hands clasped behind his head, listening with half-closed eyes to her chatter. It is significant to note the occasion on which a silent woman has a *flux de bouche*.[6] The necessity for talking was upon Jane at this moment. There were twenty things which she must tell Mr. Neckart to-night—how the shoemaker Twiss, who used to live—or starve—in the alley back of their garden, was here as head-gardener; and how capitally that consumptive sempstress, Nichols, managed the dairy and was growing quite fat at the work; and how that boy in the stable, whom Neckart had brought from the printing-office, where he was going headlong to the devil, had really turned out the best of fellows. The truth was, that there were very few people who had been kind to Jane or the captain in the days when they were all hungry together whom Neckart had not met at the farm, either as visitors or settled in fat sinecures of office. He had arranged the business part of their removal, indeed, in many cases. But he was in no mood for consultation to-night—answered briefly when she spoke to him: his face, hard and inflexible, was turned toward the river. "His mind is filled with some matter of state—that Navy appropriation bill, I suppose," she thought, looking at him deferentially.[7] Her little affairs and thoughts fell back on her as if they had struck against iron.

She never wanted sympathy or advice from others: sometimes there were whole days in which, her father being gone, she scarcely spoke a word. But now, at the necessity for silence, her heart sunk with a miserable emptiness, her throat choked, hot wretched tears came up into her eyes. She had thought all the week of this day, and she had kept the best of all she had to tell until this evening. She thought, of course, they would go out in the boat, and now his mind was full of the Navy appropriation bill!

She pulled the white threads from the ragged cactus leaves beside her, looking at him sometimes from under her lashes. "I think I will go out on the river," she said timidly.

"Shall I push out the boat? The water will drift you without rowing," going promptly before her down the path. He took up the little anchor, wiped the seat of the bateau with the sponge, and held out his hand to help her in. She seated herself and took the oars. Surely he was coming? He never had allowed her to go alone. No: he waited with one hand on the stern, and then pushed her off, taking off his hat as the boat darted out into the current and her oars struck the water.

It was the bill: no doubt it was the bill! She knew he had been sent for to Washington on business concerning it. Of course he was a statesman, and it was quite right that the government and the country should have the benefit of his best thoughts. But what if this bill and other bills should always fill his mind, and leave no room there for—for the poor little affairs of his friends? "What would father do then?"

The oars rested motionless in the rowlocks. Her eyes were dry, but there was a breathless stricture on her breast, as though an iron hand had clenched her and for the moment crushed the life back.

Chapter 9

Mr. Neckart, standing back in the shadow of the scrubby althea-bushes, his hands clasped behind him and his eyes following the skiff as it drifted down the river in the twilight, compelled himself to argue the matter out according to the rulings of common sense, just as he would the appropriation bill.

He had been coming too close of late to this little girl in a brotherly way—of course in a brotherly way. He must stand farther off. She must marry. He had always looked forward to her marrying, and the time, in all probability, had come now. Van Ness was a manly, strong fellow: her father would urge it, and Jane would soon be won. For Neckart, with the majority of men, regarded amiability and high-colored, beefy good looks in his own sex as the irresistible attractions in a woman's eyes.

"They both have youth and personal attractions and culture—everything to make a marriage suitable. I can find no objection to it," proceeded his most reasonable meditation.

"But I can never see it!"

He had not spoken, but it seemed to him as if he had cried out. Then he laughed to think what an egregious ass he was. What was this yellow-haired girl in the boat to him more than any other of the millions of women with whom the world was filled? Nothing. They all were nothing to him.

He turned his back on the river and struck into one of the dusky alleys of the garden, pacing up and down below the old plum trees. He whistled to himself, and ran his hand through his shaggy hair as if to be rid of some cobwebs in his brain. As he brushed against the branches a bird fluttered out of its nest and chirped angrily. Why, women and their love and their homes could no more come into his life than that silly robin or her brood! Two years ago this inexorable necessity did not even give him a moment's chagrin. The newspaper, his army of followers, the policy of the country,—these made life big and full enough. If he wanted little selfish pleasures, there was his arm-chair and open fire, his shelf of old books, or a dinner at Delmonico's with some clever fellow, or a dash to Europe, or across the continent, to pry into the background against which other clever fellows, whether white or yellow or black, lived and worked. He would go back to the office to-night; he could hear the engine puffing at the station now, making ready for the next train; he could finish the evening with his old friends, the books; he could order a dinner to-morrow that would satisfy even his palate,—and he used to be an epicure. He ought to go. He would go.

He walked up the open path leading to the house. Then he stopped, turned and struck directly through the trees and bushes to the river-side. The boat was at some distance: he called once or twice for her to come and take him on board before she heard him. His voice sounded hoarse and strange to himself: he did not know himself in what he did. As for the world, there was nothing in it but that boat yonder which shot through the water, and the woman with eager face rowing swiftly toward him.

There was not a Wall-street banker or a politician among Neckart's confrères who would not have looked upon him as insane for the moment. This dull wisp of a woman to blot out all business, power, place, from his life? But, after all, there is no insanity so practical or long-lived. Why does A bull and bear the market, or B sell himself and his party, but for the sake of some ugly, faded woman and the common-place children she has borne him? They are not thought worth notice by anybody but himself, but he ignores honesty, death, God himself, for them his life long. A plodding, shrewd fellow too, probably not a whit heroic.

Neckart was tramping along the common road which all of us know, but it seemed to him that he was breaking ground in a new world full of misty splendors and untried action. When he called to her his breath failed him, as it used to do when he was a boy wild with excitement. The sand under his feet, the brambles on the bank, the overarching sky, were not the same they were an hour ago. When the boat darted up to the shore, rocking as she held it fast with the oar, it seemed strange to him that she should speak in her ordinary tone. Did she not know?

She stood up in the bow steadying the skiff as he sprang into it. His hand touched her fingers for an instant, and she noticed that it shrank from hers.

"Did my father call me?"

"No: I wanted to talk to you alone."

She pushed from shore and dipped her oars: in a moment they were out in the current. It was a rippling belt of steely blue, the banks making indistinguishable ramparts of shadow on either side. Overhead was the soft starless twilight of June, through which a nighthawk flapped heavily and vanished. When it was gone they were alone. Could she not understand that they were alone? In this wide dark world that there were only they two, a man and a woman?

He could not distinguish her face, and her figure was but a light dark outline like a silhouette against the air. But the power of her womanhood was upon him, a something which Neckart had never felt before—a terrible, pure passion.

"Give me the oars," he said. "Let me help you," reaching forward to take them. His hand rested on hers accidentally: he did not remove it. *Now* did she understand? His mouth was closed. It seemed to him as if words were poor to say what was in his blood, in his soul, in the water, the air, the very ground.

She was startled, and turned to him wondering. The moon, rising higher, showed him the childish, sensitive mouth, the dark eyes heavy with tears, for she had been crying. What was that which gleamed through them, half answering him, frightened at itself? It seemed to him in this brief pause that they had been waiting all their lives for this word—he to speak and she to hear.

"Jane!" He took her hand in both of his and held it close, and then he threw it from him, drawing back: "My God! I had forgotten."

"Forgotten?" She closed her eyes once or twice, bewildered, as if suddenly wakened from sleep. "You are in trouble," she said anxiously. "Can I help you?"

The question brought him to sober reason sharply enough. It was precisely the frank, tender tone which she would use to her father; and the truth was, that the girl to herself did not yet distinguish between her father and this friend. A moment before a strange emotion had touched her. But it had passed like a warm gust of summer. There was not a seven-year old child in the city yonder who did not know more about love than Jane. She had never heard servants or schoolmates chatter about it; novels had bored her; the captain, whatever he had left undone, had kept the air pure and cold about her as for a very nun.

"What is this trouble, Mr. Neckart? You have been ill for months, I know. Can I—? Or perhaps father—"

She leaned forward, the oars suspended in her hands, her lips apart, attentive and eager.

He leaned over the edge of the skiff and wet his forehead and eyes, forcing a careless laugh: "One moment, Miss Swendon, and I will explain to you," adding presently, precisely in the manner with which he would have discussed the weather, "We men each have our skeleton to hide, according to popular belief, and mine is no worse than the rest. It is the most practical of facts. Only I am apt to forget it, and then, when it meets me unawares, it is as grim as death."

She nodded, watching him intently as if he were physically ill: she would not let the oars strike on the water, lest the noise might jar on him. All kinds of wild plans for helping him filled her brain. If the trouble were anything which money could help, there was plenty of that, thank God! If it was political difficulty—bills maybe—she could not even understand it. If God had only not made her so stupid! the humble tears rising slowly to her eyes.

Mr. Neckart did not see them. He was careful not to look at her as he spoke, and hurried on with his explanation, as if it were business of small importance. But she was not deceived by that. "I never have talked of this matter, and least of all should I have told it to you. I can bear the trouble when it comes without difficulty. The most ordinary men meet disaster coolly which they know is inevitable. Commonplace fellows who are born with scrofula or consumption march along with them to early death cheerfully. They make no tragedy out of it. There is no reason why I should complain of my lifelong companion." His tone was harder than he had ever used in speaking to Jane before.

"I have never told you of my mother?"

"No," eagerly, hastening to spare him pain. "But I have heard of her from Cornelia Fleming, who was your neighbor in Delaware. I know all that she suffered. You need not tell me."

"She was the last of the Davidge family. There was not one of them for generations who had not inherited disease of the brain. They were either epileptics from youth, or became, as she did, incurably insane. The disease invariably manifested itself in that way after middle age, and from that time they were helpless burdens to their children. Yet there was not a Davidge who refrained from marriage, so entailing the curse on another generation. It would have been more righteous to have put a pistol to their heads and have blown out their brains."

His manner was quiet and cold. Jane made no answer.

"Naturally, I have studied the pathology of insanity closely. I know that I have inherited the disease. The symptoms within the last six months are unmistakable. I know that in five or ten years at the outside I shall be of no more use in the world than any other mindless animal. But I will have no woman, nor child, suffer for me."

When he ceased to speak the silence and the night fell oppressively on them. The boat had drifted down to the edge of the bank and grounded. The moonlight showed her to him sitting in the bow of the boat facing him, her hands clasped on her knees. She was so near that if he but opened his arms he could take her to his breast. Yet he knew that she was separated from him now as though death itself lay between.

"I have known this necessity which lay upon me for years, Miss Swendon," he said quietly, but leaning forward to watch her immovable face. "It is my duty to isolate myself as other men need not do. The more dear"—his voice failed suddenly, but he recovered himself in a moment and went on—"the more dear a woman is to me, the more I must shut her out of my sight. I can never try to win her nor marry her."

Was the girl stone? Had she not even common human sympathy for him?

"You understand why I do this?"

"Yes, I understand."

"And you think I am right?"

She looked up at him with her usual blunt directness: "You are altogether right. An honest man could not do otherwise." Her chin fell on her breast again. Not a moan, not a breath of regret, at the blow which struck them apart. Weaker women would have cried a little at parting from a dog who had been sometimes a companion. This cool-blooded Swede gave her verdict on the right and wrong of the matter as though it had been a sale of goods, and there was the end of it! All the long-latent passion in Neckart's nature revolted and flamed into life. He moved restlessly, watching her sit there stony and immovable. He would have flung away life, as men used to do against the dumb Sphinx, to tear from her some word of pity or life.

The boat rocked in the shallow water. She rose to leave it. Neckart mechanically held out his hand to help her jump ashore. She held it tightly, and when she stood beside him on the grass took it in both her own: "No. You ought never to marry. You ought to hold yourself apart from the world. These strange people would only irritate and wear you out. Now you can give yourself entirely to us. We are your nearest friends. You shall give up the paper and politics: it is the work and anxiety that are telling on your brain. You shall live here with father, in the quiet and country air. I will take care of you both." She stroked his hand as a mother might that of her dying child, trying to believe that it was not growing cold. For a year the girl had fought death back from her father step by step. Now, her one friend, who with the old man filled all the world for her, was to be taken from her.

He seated her on a fallen log and pushed back the hair from her clammy forehead: "Child! child! you do not understand! All I have told you has gone for nothing!"

"I do understand. I can cure you both. Rest and the air—I am dull, but you don't know how good a nurse I can be for my own people," with a pitiful laugh.

He did not speak. The soft golden hair lay in his hand, warm and alive. He looked down at her. He could soon turn this childish affection into love: he could wrench her soul into his own. Why should he not take what God had set before him? All the other men of his race had done it.

One moment he stood irresolute. Then the hair dropped from his hand. "Jane," he said, as if reasoning with a child, "when I remember my mother first she was a pretty, tender little woman, with hardly a thought outside of her boy. For years before she died I was forced to fasten her as one does a wild beast, that she might not kill me. Do you understand what that was to me? Do you think I can bring the misery I knew in those years to any woman? My wife shall never have it to bear."

"But you can have no wife!" she cried. "You said you dared not marry! *I* can bear the misery. You will come to us—us. Those women in Washington of whom you tell me—how could they know what you need? I have nobody but you and father."

She felt herself so young and strong! Death, a most horrible and certain death, was creeping upon him. In her agony of pity she held his hand to her wet, burning cheeks.

"Jane, you drive me mad!" stooping over her trembling. "It is you—you that I dare not marry!"

She stood erect: "*I* marry you? I never thought of that," simply.

"You never thought of it?" with a queer uncertain laugh. "You never thought that I loved you?"

"That you loved me, Mr. Neckart? Me?" The blue innocent eyes that had been fixed on his suddenly filled with light; she dropped her face into her hands; her whole body burned with blushes, and she turned away.

Neckart slowly followed her. Jane's thoughts were always transparent as crystal: he had read in that one brief glance all the delight, the tender passion, whose first impulse was to escape from him.

"I have been a damned scoundrel!" he said to himself: "I have ruined her life!"

He was now thoroughly awake to what he had done—saw it as any other practical, honorable man would do, unbiased by his passion or his pity for himself. He walked silently beside her as she went up the steep path to the house.

As for Jane, she did not know that he was silent: she would scarcely have heard if he had spoken to her. She did not know what this was that had come to her, that had lifted her whole life upward as by a touch. She could not look at him. If she could only reach her father and hide from him, that he might never find her—never! She remembered how a minute ago she had held his hand to her face, and the hot flood of shame covered every other thought: the next she glanced shyly at him with a sweet pride;—he loved her, he would understand! The terrible story he had told her had passed out of her mind like a breath of smoke in sunshine. He loved her: she could keep him out of all danger. Even if she had remembered that she could never be his wife, it would not have troubled her. He loved her! She thought no more of marriage than the bird in its first song of dawn thinks of the barred lines and visible notes to which its music might somewhere be written down.

Neckart followed her up the steps and into the wide hall, carrying his hat behind him in his hand. The damp air wet his hair, and it hung lankly back from his haggard face. He felt physically ill. He had acted like a brute, a coward! This was the end of his stern resolve, his life-long self-denial!

A lamp burned at the foot of the wide staircase. He paused beside it: she had gone up a step or two, and halted, her hand on the rail, looking down. "Goodnight!" she said shyly.

The light shone full on the pink glow in her cheeks, the loose hair glistening like a golden mist, the half-frightened, half-triumphant gleam shot down from the blue eyes.

He did not answer her.

The delicate virgin bloom of this love which he had coveted so madly an hour ago scarcely stirred his heart now with pleasure. A man can-not live all the time on the heights of emotion or of religion; the air is too rarefied up there for healthy lungs; he comes down punctually to the ordinary levels of his saner self; and Neckart, on his ordinary level, was an exceedingly practical, honest man. He knew that he had brought irreparable injury to this girl, and that it was his duty now to make amends as best he could.

PART 4

Chapter 10

Miss Fleming arrived that evening while Jane was on the water. She was in the habit of coming out to the Hemlock Farm for a day's holiday, and went directly to her own room as though she were at home. When she stepped presently out on the porch, where the gentlemen had gone to smoke, a soft black silk showing every line of her supple figure, glimpses of the rounded arms revealed with every movement of the loose sleeves, one or two thick green leaves in her light hair—ugly, quiet, friendly—they all felt more at home than they had done before. There was a pitcher of punch by the captain's elbow: she tasted it, threw in a dash of liquor, poured him out a glass and sat down beside him, and he felt that a gap was comfortably filled.

"You have turned your back on Philadelphia, they tell me, Miss Fleming," complained Judge Rhodes. "New York sucks in all the young blood of the country—the talent and energy."

"Oh, I came simply to sell my wares. New York is my market, but Philadelphia will always be home to me," in her peculiar pathetic voice. "I left good friends there," with one of her bewildering glances straight into the judge's beady eyes, at which his flabby face was suffused with heat.

"You do not forget your friends, that's certain," he said, lowering his voice. "That was a delicate compliment, sending my portrait back to the Exhibition. I felt it very much, I assure you."

Cornelia bowed silently. Neither she nor the judge said anything about the round-numbered cheque which he had sent her for it. In the moonlight they preferred to let the affair stand on a sentimental basis.

Mr. Van Ness meanwhile eyed Miss Fleming's pose and rounded figure with a watery gleam of complacency.

"An exceptional woman," was his verdict. He turned the conversation to art, and asked innumerable questions with a profound humility. Cornelia replied eagerly, until the fact crept out from the judge that there was not an aesthetic dogma nor a gallery in the world with which he was not familiar. Then to pottery, in which field his modesty was as profound, until the judge pushed him, as it were, to a corner, when he acknowledged himself the possessor of a few "nice bits."

"I have some old Etruscan pieces which I should like you to see, Miss Fleming," with his mild, deprecating cough, "and a bit of Capo di Monte, and the only real specimen of Henri Deux in the country."[1]

"I must see them," emphatically. "Where are your cabinets?"

"Oh, nowhere," with a shrug. "My poor little specimens have never been unpacked since I returned to this country. They are boxed up in a friend's cellar."

"God bless me, Cornelia!" cried the captain in a muffled tone, "how could Mr. Van Ness spend his time koo-tooing to cracked pots? He has, as I may say, the future of Pennsylvania in his hand. When I think what he is doing for the friendless children—thousands of 'em—" The punch had heated the captain's zeal to the point where words failed him.[2]

After that the friendless children swept lighter subjects out of sight. Mr. Van Ness, whose humility in this light rose to saintly heights, had all the statistics of the Bureaux of Charity at his tongue's end. He had studied the Dangerous Classes in every obscure corner of the world. He could give you the *status quo* of any given tribe in India just as easily as the time-table on the new railway in Egypt. No wonder that he could tell you in a breath the percentage of orphans, deserted minors, children of vicious parents, in his own State, and the amount *per capita* required to civilize and Christianize them. As he talked of this matter his eyes became suffused with tears. The great Home for these helpless wards of the State he described at length, from its situation on a high table-land of the Alleghanies and the dimensions of the immense buildings down to the employments of the children and the capacity of the laundry—a perfect Arcadia with all the modern improvements, where Crime was to be transformed wholesale into Virtue.

"Where is this institution?" asked Miss Fleming. "It is strange I never heard of it."

"Oh, it is not built as yet: we have not raised the funds," Mr. Van Ness replied with a smothered sigh.

The judge patted one foot and looked at him compassionately. It was a devilishly queer ambition to be the savior of those dirty little wretches in the back alleys. But if a man had given himself up, body and soul, to such a pursuit, it was hard measure that he must be thwarted in it.

Miss Fleming also bent soft sympathetic eyes on her new friend. The Home was not built, eh? Not a brick laid? She wondered whether that box with the priceless treasures existed in his friend's cellar or in his brain: she wondered whether he had not seen those pictures of the old masters in photographs, or whether he had travelled in Japan and the obscure corners of the earth in the flesh or in books. There was more than the wonted necessity upon her to establish sympathetic relations with this new man: she had never seen a finer presence: the beard and brow quite lifted his masculinity into aesthetic regions; she caught glimpses, too, of an unfamiliar mongrel species of intellect with which she would relish Platonic relations. Yet with this glow upon her she regarded the reformer's noble face and benignant blond beard doubtfully, thinking how she used to stick pins in brilliant bubbles when she was a child, and nothing would be left but a patch of dirty water.[3]

"Jane is out on the river, as usual?" she asked presently.

"Yes," said her father: "Mr. Neckart is with her. Neither of them will ever stay under a roof if they can help it. They ought to have a dash of Indian blood in their veins to account for such vagabondizing."

"Is Bruce Neckart here?" with a change in her tone which made the captain look up at her involuntarily.

"Yes."

"I thought he was in Washington: I did not expect to meet him."

The judge puffed uneasily at his cigar. He was a family man, with a stout wife and married son. He did not meet Miss Fleming once a year, but he felt a vague jealousy of Neckart.

"By the way, you must be old acquaintances?" he said abruptly. "Both from Delaware? Kent county?"

"Oh yes," with a shrill womanish laugh, very different from her usual sweet boyish ha! ha! "Many's the day we rowed on the bay or dredged for oysters together, dirty and ragged and happy. There is not very much difference in our ages," seeing his look of surprise. "I look younger than I am, and Bruce has grown old fast. At least, so I hear. I have not seen him for years."

She was silent after that, and preoccupied as her admirers had never seen her, and presently, hearing Jane's and Neckart's steps on the path, she rose hastily and bade them good-night. They each shook hands with her, that being one of the sacred rites in the Platonic friendships so much in vogue now-a-days among clever men and women. Mr. Van Ness offered his hand last, and Cornelia smiled cordially as she took it. But it was clammy and soft. She rubbed her fingers with a shudder of disgust as she hurried up to her own room. There she walked straight to her glass and turned up the lamp beside it, looking long and fixedly at her face. She knew with exactness the extent of its ugliness and its power.

"It is too late now even if it ever could have been," she said quietly, and put out the light. Then she went to the window. Mr. Neckart had left Jane inside, and, not joining the other men, turned back to the garden. She saw the bulky dark figure as it passed under her window.

She stretched out her hands as if for a caress, with the palms pressed close. "Oh, Bruce!" she said under her breath. "Bruce!"

After he had passed out of sight she stood thinking over all the men who had made a comrade of her since she saw him last—how they had handled her fingers and looked into her eyes; how her every thought and fancy had grown common and unclean through much usage; how she had dragged out whatever maidenly feeling she had in the old times, and made capital of it to bring these companions to her who were neither lovers nor friends.

"When I could not have the food which I wanted, I took the husks which the swine did eat," she said, leaving the window, with a short laugh. "Well, I could not die of starvation."

Chapter 11

When Jane woke the next morning a bluebird was singing outside of the window: she tried to mimic him before she was out of bed, and sang scraps of songs to herself as she dressed. The captain heard her in his room below, but pretended to be asleep when she came down as usual to lay out his clothes, for, although she insisted that her father should have Dave as a valet, she left him but little to do.

Watching her from under the covers, the captain saw that she had left off the black snood and tied her hair with a band of rose-colored ribbon. Her lips were ruddy and her eyes alight: once or twice she laughed to herself.

"What high day or holiday is it, Jane?"

"Oh, every day is a high day now!" running to kiss him. "I was just thinking how comfortable money is, and how glad I am that we have it," glancing about delighted at his luxurious toilet appointments before the low wood-fire. Then she spread out his dressing-gown and velvet smoking-cap, and eyed with her head on one side the fine shirt and its costly studs.

"Do you remember the rag-carpet in your room which we thought such a triumph? and the old tin shaving-cup? Now, my lord, look out upon your estate!" opening the window. "Your musicians have come to waken you, and your servitors stand without," as Buff tapped at the door with hot water.

"He is as comfortable as a baby wrapped in lamb's wool," she thought as she ran down the stairs. "And this air is so pure and the sun so bright! Oh, he must grow strong here! Anybody would be cured here— anybody!"

The captain followed her to the barn-yard. It was one of her inexorable prescriptions for him that he should drink a glass of warm milk-punch before breakfast, and smell the cow's breath during the operation. She was milking the white cow herself, while the pseudo sempstress, Nichols, waited with the goblet, and the bandy-legged shoemaker, Twiss, stood on guard, eyeing Brindle's horns suspiciously.

"Now the glass! These are the strippings. Oh you'll soon learn, Betty! You'll make butter as well as you used to make dresses badly."

The little widow and Twiss laughed, as they always did at Jane's weak jokes, and took the punch to the captain. She was the finest wit of her day in their eyes. The hostler's boy ran down from the stable to speak to her. She thought he had as innocent a face as she had ever seen. No doubt he would have gone to perdition if Neckart had not rescued him. She stopped to talk to him with beaming eyes, and meeting Betty's toddling baby took it up and tossed it in the air, and then walked on, carrying the soft little thing in her arms. The farm was like the Happy Valley this morning![1] God was so good to her! She could warm and comfort all these people. Then she turned into the woods and sat down on a fallen log. It was the place where they had stopped to rest yesterday, Neckart lying at her feet. There was the imprint still in the dead moss where his arm had lain. She looked guiltily about, and then laid her hand in the broken moss with a quick passionate touch. The baby caught her chin in its fingers. She hugged it to her breast, and kissed it again and again. From the hemlock overhead a tanager suddenly flashed up into the air with a shrill peal of song. Jane looked up, her face and throat dyed crimson. Did he know? She glanced down at the grass, at the friendly trees all alive with rustling and chirping. The sky overhead was so deep and warm a blue to-day. It seemed as if they all knew that he loved her.

The captain found Mr. Neckart standing on the stoop listening to some sound that came up from the woods.

"It is Jane singing," he said. "You would not hear her once in a year. Hereditary gift! In the old Swedish annals we read of the remarkable voices of the Svens."

"I never heard her sing before." Yet he had known at once that it was she. It was the most joyous of songs, but there was a foreboding pathos in the voice which moved him as no other sound had ever done.

"You are not going before breakfast?" cried the captain.

"Yes, and I shall not be able to come again for a long time. Say to Miss Swendon—But no. I will go and bid her good-bye."

He met her as she was crossing the plank thrown across the brook, and they stopped by the little hand-rail, not looking directly at each other: "I came to bid you good-morning."

"Do you take the early train, then?"

"Yes." He did not mean to tell her that he would not come again. The more ordinary their parting the sooner she would forget it and him. He had thought the matter out during the night, and being a man who was apt to underrate himself, was convinced that the feeling which she had betrayed was but that transient flush of preference which any very young and innocent girl is apt to give to the first man of whom she makes a companion.

"There is nothing in me likely to win enduring love from her. A more intellectual woman, indeed—" He had gone over the argument again and again. When he was out of sight her fancy would soon turn to this new lover, so much better suited to her in every respect. For himself— But he had no right to think of himself. He struck that thought down fiercely again as they stood together on the bridge. No more right than he would have, were he dead, to drag down this young creature into his grave.

He patted the child on the head as it clung to her dress, and talked of the chance of more rain with perfect correctness and civility; and when Jane managed to raise her eyes to his face she found it grave and preoccupied, as it usually was over the morning papers. He saw Van Ness coming smiling to meet her.

"It is time for me to go," he said, his eyes passing slowly over her: then with a hasty bow, not touching her hand, he struck through the woods to the station, thinking as he went how she was standing then on the bridge in the sunshine, with the man whom she would marry beside her. She looked after him, her eyes full of still, deep content. He loved her. She had forgotten everything else.

"A perfect morning, Miss Swendon," said Mr. Van Ness, stroking his magnificent golden beard. "You see just this deep azure sky above the

Sandwich Islands. Now, I remember watching such a dawn on Mauna Loa. Ah-h, *you* would have appreciated that. Our friend has gone, eh? Most active, energetic man! I heard him tell your father he should not return soon again."

"Not return?" stopping in her slow walk.

"No. It really must be impossible for an editor to spare time often for visits to even such an Arcadia as this.[2] No stockmarket or political news in Arcadia, eh?" with a benevolent gurgle of a laugh. "Business! business! Miss Swendon. Ah, how it engrosses the majority of men!" shaking his head ponderously.

She said nothing. It was as if she had been suddenly wakened out of a dream in the crowd of a dusty marketplace. He had gone back to the world, to his real business and his real trouble. She, with her love and her intended cure for him, was a silly fool wandering in a fantastic Arcadia.

Miss Fleming was walking up and down on the porch as they came up, more carefully dressed than usual. The captain had just told her that Neckart had gone.

"Ah? I'm very sorry," carelessly. "I should have been glad to see him again. Though no doubt he has forgotten me."

She went forward to meet Jane with a smile, but a withered gray look under her eyes. "I have been making a tour of your principality," she said as they went in to breakfast. "I see you have brought out a colony of Philadelphia paupers. Twiss, and Betty, and the rest."

"They were not paupers," said Jane, taking her place behind the urn. "Did you see into what a great boy Top has grown? And Peter?" It gave her a warm glow at heart to remember these people just now. At least, there her care had not been fantastic or thrown away.

"I hardly expected you to take up the role of guardian angel. It requires study, after all, to play it successfully," pursued Cornelia with an amiable smile, cutting her butter viciously.—"Very young girls are apt to be impetuous in their charities, and damage more than they help," turning to the judge. "These poor people, for instance. Betty had her kinsfolk about her in Philadelphia, her church and her gossips. She complained bitterly to me this morning that she 'had no company here but the cows: Miss Swendon might as well have whisked her off into a haythen desart.'"

"She complained to you!" cried the captain. "Why, the trouble and money which Jane has given to that woman and her family! They were starving, I assure you!"

Jane listened at first with her usual quiet good-humor. Miss Fleming's waspish temper generally amused her, as it would have done a man (if he was not her husband). But she began to grow anxious.

"You really think Betty is not contented here?" her hand a little unsteady as she poured the cream into the cups.

"Contented? She seems miserable enough. Home is home, you know, if it is only a cellar and starvation. But perhaps"—with a shrug—"that class of Irish are never happy without a grievance. Now, Twiss, it appears to me, has just ground for complaint.—A shoemaker," turning to the judge a face beaming with fun, "whom this young lady has transported and set down in charge of gardens and hot-houses. He does not know a hoe from a mower, and he is too old to learn. He had a good trade: now he has nothing."

"But he could not live by his trade," cried Jane.

"Well, cobbling is looking up now. In any case, you have pauperized him."

"That's bad—bad! Now, in Virginia we used to feed everybody who came along!" said the judge, shaking his head. "But I've learned wisdom in the cities. Every bit of bread given to a beggar degrades human nature and rots society to the core."

"But suppose he is starving?" urged the captain. "The Good Samaritan wasn't afraid of pauperizing that poor devil on the road."[3]

"Let him starve. He will have preserved his self-respect. The Good Samaritan knew nothing of political economy, sir."

Jane left her breakfast untasted. She understood nothing about political economy, but she saw that she had done irreparable injury to these people whom she had tried to serve—God knew with what anxiety and tenderness of heart. In one case, at least, there had been no mistake.

"Did you see Phil?" she said, turning with brightening countenance to Miss Fleming. "We intend to have Phil educated. He is such a keen-witted little fellow."

Miss Fleming laughed outright now: "Mr. Neckart's protégé? Yes, I saw him. He has been stealing tobacco and money from Dave, it appears, ever since he came, and was found out this morning. There was a horrible row in the stable as I passed."

"Of course he stole!" said the judge triumphantly. "I tell you, the more efforts you make to reform the dangerous classes the more hardened you will grow. It's hopeless—hopeless!"

Her other listeners each promptly presented their theory. Like all intelligent Americans, they were provided with theories on every social problem, and were ready to hang it on an individual stable-boy or any other nail of a fact which might offer. Jane alone sat silent. She did not hear when her father spoke to her once or twice.

"You are disappointed," Mr. Van Ness's soft soothing voice murmured in her ear. "I know how these baffled efforts chill the heart. I will explain to you the machinery which I propose to bring to bear on these classes."

"I don't know anything about machinery or classes. Twiss and Betty were friends of mine, and I tried to help them, and have failed."

Miss Fleming, who was watching her furtively, saw her dull eyes raised presently and rest on the captain, who with a red face and bursts of laughter was telling one of his interminable stories.

"This girl," Cornelia said to herself, "has everything which I have not—beauty, wealth, Bruce Neckart's love. Yet she looks at that weak old man as if he were all that was left her in the world." She had put Jane before on the general basis of antipathy which she had to everything in the world that was not masculine, but the feeling had kindled since last night into active dislike.

When breakfast was over and their guests had gone to their rooms to make ready to meet the train, Jane decoyed the captain away to Bruno's kennel, where he was tied during Mr. Van Ness's stay. Once out of sight, she retied his cravat, arranged his white hair to her liking, stroked his sunken cheeks. Here was something actual and real. She knew now that she had never had anything that was truly her own but the kind foolish face looking down on her. She never would have anything more. Only an hour ago life had opened for her wide and fair as the dawn: now it had narrowed to this old hand in hers, to his breath, that came and went—O God, how feebly!

"You are looking stronger to-day, father. You are gaining every day. Oh that is quite certain! Very soon we shall have you as well and strong as you were at forty."

What if she had not had money this last year? He never could have lived through it. God had been kind to her—kind! She pressed his hand to her breast with a quick glance out to the bright sky. The captain saw her chin quivering. His own thoughts ran partly in the same line as hers.

"Oh, I'm gaining, no doubt of it. Though I never could have pulled through this year if we had had to live in the old way. God bless Will Laidley for leaving the money as he did!"

"It was not his to leave otherwise!" she cried indignantly.

"Tut, tut, Jane! Of course it was his. By every law. He could have flung it away where he chose; and he had a perfect right to do it."

It was not God who had been kind to her, then: it was only that she had stolen the money?

"Come, Jenny: we must go back to the house."

"In a moment, father. Go on: I will follow you."

She walked up and down the tan-bark path for a while. She was sure of nothing. Wherever she had done what seemed to her right and natural, she was barred and checked by the world's laws and experience. She had brought these starving wretches out of a hell upon earth into this paradise, and even they laughed at her want of wisdom: the very money which was her own in the sight of God, and which had lengthened her father's life, ought to be given back today to the poor, its rightful owners. If there was any other cause for her to fight blindly against the narrow matter-of-fact routine which ruled her life, she did not name it even to herself.

Looking toward the house, she saw her father escorting their guests to the gate, where the carriage waited, David resplendent on the box. The captain walked with a feeble kind of swagger: his voice came back to her in weak gusts of laughter. She laid her hand on a tree, glancing about her with a firm sense of possession. "The property is mine," she said, "and I'll keep it as long as he lives, if all the paupers in the United States were starving at the gates!"

Chapter 12

Mr. Van Ness returned to the Hemlock Farm at stated periods during the summer. He had, to be plain, sat down before Jane's heart to besiege it with the same ponderous benign calm with which he ate an egg or talked of death. There was a bronze image of Buddha in the hall at the Farm, the gaze of the god fixed with ineffable content, as it had been for ages, on his own stomach.

Jane went up to it one day after an hour's talk with Mr. Van Ness. "This creature maddens me," she said. "I always want to break it into pieces to see it alter."

Little Mr. Waring, who had come with Van Ness, hurried up as a connoisseur in bronzes, adjusting his eye-glasses. "Why, it is faultless, Miss Swendon!" he cried.

"That is precisely what makes it intolerable."

Much of Jane's large, easy good-humor was gone by this time. She had grown thin, was eager, restless, uncertain of what she ought or ought not to do, even in trifles.

Mr. Waring and Judge Rhodes were both at the Farm now. They ran over to New York every week or two. Phil Waring was not a marrying man, but it was part of his duty as a leader in society to be intimate with every important heiress or beauty in the two cities. Out of sincere compassion to Jane's stupendous ignorance he would sit for hours stroking his moustache, his elbows on his knees, his feet on a rung of the chair, dribbling information as to the nice effects in the Water-Color Exhibition, or miraculous "finds" of Spode or Wedgwood in old junk-shops, or the most authentic information as to why the Palfreys had no cards to Mrs. Livingstone's kettledrums, while Jane listened with a quizzical gleam in her eyes, as she did to the little bantam hen outside cackling and strutting over its new egg.

"We must have you in society this winter," he urged. "It is a duty you owe in your position. You have no choice about it."

"You are right, Mr. Waring," called the captain from the corner where he sat with Judge Rhodes. "The child must have friends in her own class." He dropped his voice again: "The truth is, Rhodes, she has no ties like other girls. Her dog and two or three old women and some children—that is all she knows of life. It's enough while she has me. But I shall not be here long, now. Not many months."

The eyes of the two men met.

"Does she know?" asked the judge after a while.

"No." The captain's gaunt features worked: he trotted his foot to some tune, looking down from the window and whistling under his breath. "It was for this I sent for you," he added presently. "If I could only see her settled, married, before I go! She is no more fit to be left alone in the world than Bruno."

The judge shook his head in gloomy assent. His own opinion was that Jane would follow her own instincts in a doglike fashion if her father was out of the way, and God only knew where they would lead her! He had brought his own girls, Rose and Netty, with him to visit her, in order that she might have a domestic feminine influence upon her. They found, accidentally, that she did not know a word of any catechism, and, terrified, loaned her religious novels to convert her: she took them graciously, but never cut the leaves. There were to them even more heathenish indications in her hoopless straight skirts: the good little creatures zealously cut and trimmed a dress for her from the very last patterns. She put it on, and straightway went through bog and brake with Bruno for mushrooms, coming back with it in tatters. They chattered in their thin falsetto voices the last Culpepper gossip into her patient ear—the story of Rosey's balls at Old Point, and Netty's lovers, all of whom were "splendid matches until impohverished by the war." She listened to their chirping with amused eyes, tapping them, when they were through, approvingly on the head as though they were clever canaries. The girls told their father that they "feared her principles leaned toward infidelity, and that it was never safe to be intimate with these original women," and had gone home the next day, not waiting for the judge. They washed their hands of her, and gloved them again, but he still felt responsible for her. After he left the captain he went to her, fatherly interest radiant in every feature: "Mr. Waring is right, Jane. It is high time that you were taking your part in society. Your father wishes it."

"I will do whatever he wishes," quietly.—"You did not know us when we lived in the old house in Southwark, Mr. Waring. We invented our patents then. Sometimes we could afford to go to the gallery at the theatre when the play was good. Father and the newsboys would lead the clapping. And we went once a year in our patched shoes a-fishing for a holiday. Those were good times."

"Perfect child of Nature!" telegraphed Mr. Waring uneasily to the judge. "How Mrs. Wilde will rejoice in you, Miss Swendon! Nature is her specialty. She is coming to call this morning.—Miss Swendon," turning anxiously to the judge, "can have no better sponsor in society than Mrs. Wilde. She only can give the accolade to all aspirants. No amount of money will force an entrance at her doors. There must be blood—blood. 'Swendon?' she said when I spoke to her about this call. 'The Swedish Svens? I remember. Queen Christina's gallant lieutenant was her great-grandfather.[1] Good stock. None better. The girl must belong to our circle.' So, now it is all settled!" rubbing his hands and smiling.

"Jane is careless," said the captain eagerly. "People of the best fashion have called, and she has not even left cards. Her dress too—Now a Paris gown, fringes and—"

The three men looked at her at that with a sudden imbecile despair, at which she laughed and went out.

The captain found her presently down by the boat in which she had heard Neckart's story. She bailed it out and cleaned it carefully every day, but she had never gone on the river in it since that night.

"Father," stepping ashore, "what have I done that I must be turned into another woman?"

"Now, Jenny, making models and crabbing were well enough for you as a child. But, as Waring justly observes, the society to which you belong is inexorable in its rules for a woman."

She flung out her arms impatiently, and then clasped them above her head. It seemed as if a thousand fine clammy webs were being spun about her.

"If you had any especial talent, as Waring says—if you were artistic or musical, or concerned in some asylum-work—you could take your own path, independent of society. But—"looking down at her anxiously.

"I understand. I don't know what I was made for."

It was the first time in her life that she had been driven in to consider herself. She stood grave and intent, saying nothing for some time. Every other woman had some definite aim. The whole world was marching by, keeping step to a neat, orderly little tune. They made calls, they gave alms, they dressed, all of the same fashion.

"Why not be like other people?" her father was saying, making a burden to her thought.

"I don't know why," drearily.

"What would you have, Jenny?" taking her hand in his.

"Father, I never loved but one or two people in the world. You and Bruno and—not many others. I can do nothing outside of them."

"Nonsense! You cannot be a law to yourself, child. God knows I want to see you happy!" his voice breaking.[2] "But," straightening his eye-glasses, "Waring says, very justly, you are out of the groove which all other girls are in." He stopped inquiringly, but she did not answer. She was a strongly-built woman in mind and body, and just then she felt her strength. The blood rushed in a swift current through her veins. Why should she be hampered with these thousand meaningless, sham duties? She was fit for but one purpose—to serve two men whom she loved. Her father was ill, and he pushed her from him into Society; and Bruce Neckart was alone, and with a worse fate than death creeping on him, and he—

"Why does not Mr. Neckart come to us?" she asked abruptly. "It is months since I have seen him."

"His health is failing. There is some trouble of the brain threatened. I hear that he is going to give up the paper, and is settling up his business to go to Europe." Her question startled him: he watched her with a new keen suspicion.

"If this must come on him, why should he not come here to bear it? I can nurse you both. Surely, that is as good work as returning calls or learning to dress in Parisian style," with a short laugh.

The captain's face gathered intelligence as he listened. He knew her secret now. For a moment he felt a wrench of pity for her. But love, with the captain, had been a sentimental fever ending in a cold ague: he had experienced light heats and chills of it many a time since. This wild fancy of the girl's would speedily burn itself out if judiciously damped. He would at once take the matter in hand.

"Neckart," he said deliberately, eying her to gauge the effect of his words, "is a man of sense and knowledge of the world. He knows his condition, and in the little time left to him he attends to his business and important political affairs, instead of nursing a romantic friendship which cannot serve him, and would only compromise you."

"Compromise me? I don't understand you, father."

"A woman could not render such service as you offer except to her betrothed lover or husband."

"Why, he would understand."

"But Society, child—"

"Oh, Society!" with a laugh. "But you do not remember!" clasping her hands on his shoulder. "If this thing comes upon him—he has looked forward to it all his life—he has nobody. He is quite alone."

"At least," impatiently, "you will not be involved. I did not understand before why Bruce had deserted us lately. I see now that he has acted very properly. It was not his fault nor yours—this flirtation—preference— or whatever you may choose to call it. But Bruce knows the world, and knows just how long-lived such fancies are, and he intends that it shall be no hinderance to your marriage—making an excellent match."

"I marry? Make an excellent match?"

"Yes. Certainly. What else should you do? Don't look in that way, my darling. It frightens me. I'm not strong. It is not death that is coming to you, but a good husband. You need not turn so white."

"And Mr. Neckart planned this for *me*?"

"N-no. I can't say 'planned,' to be accurate. But he agreed in our plan. Why, Bruce has common sense. He knows it is the way of the world that a woman should marry, and he will be much happier to know that you are the wife of a good man—good and good-looking too. Much more presentable than Bruce, poor fellow!"

The captain watched her closely as he gave this home-thrust. How a woman could turn from that magnificent, devout reformer to any lean, irascible politician! Her foot was on the edge of the little skiff. She pushed it into the water. While he sat in the boat there that night, with the moonlight white about them, while he told her that he loved her, he had been planning this good match for her! There was no such thing as love, then, in the world? Or truth? But there was Society and common sense and the inexorable rules of propriety. Bruce Neckart represented to her Strength itself, and he submitted to these rules cheerfully. He was happy to think of her as the wife of a good, presentable man!

When she had thought of him as going alone with his terrible burden away from her into the wilderness, true to her until the last breath of reason was gone, there had been a thrill of delight in the intolerable pain. But planning, like finical little Waring, that she should fall snugly into a fashionable set, Parisian gowns, a suitable marriage!

Jane had not the womanish faculty of thinning every fact or thought that came to her into tears or talk. Neckart had gone out of her life. She accepted the fact at once, without argument. What the loss imported to her would assuredly be known only to her own narrow, one-sided mind, and the God who had given it to her.

"Shall we go to the house, father? Can't you laugh again, and look like yourself? Why, I will give myself up, body and soul, to Society or Philanthropy—anything you choose—rather than see you so shaken." She hung on his arm as they went up the path, talking incessantly, and laughing more, as even the captain felt, than the jokes would warrant. The moment was favorable for introducing the subject he had at heart.

"The last train brought out a dozen men to consult Mr. Van Ness," he began—"deputations from church and charitable organizations. 'Pon my soul, I don't know what Christianity in this country would do without that man!"

"It would wear a very different face," absently.

"I went with Rhodes to a great revival-meeting in town one night lately, and Van Ness, of course, was called up on the platform. Rhodes thought he looked like one of the apostles in modern dress; and all the ladies near me said that his face beamed with heavenly light. It would have made anybody devout to look at him. Are you listening?" glancing at her abstracted face. "You certainly think him remarkably handsome? As to his nose, now?"

"I don't suppose anybody could find fault with his nose," smiling.

"Nor with his manner?"

"Nor with his manner."

"And yet you are not friends, eh?" holding his breath for her answer.

"No," carelessly. "Mr. Van Ness and I could not be friends."

"Why? why?"

"How could I tell?" with a shrug, and looking at Bruno, who was fighting a cat just then without cause.

The captain looked and sighed. It was of no use, he thought, to try to account for the prejudices or likings of any of the lower animals.

Mr. Waring met them at the moment in an anxious flutter: "Mrs. Wilde is here. She is coming down the path."

Mrs. Wilde was a small, plump old lady with a sober, tranquil face framed in soft puffs of white hair; her dress never rustled or brought itself into any notice; her language never fell uneasily out of its quiet gait; when she spoke to you, you felt that something genuine and happy dominated you for the moment.

"I followed Mr. Waring here," holding out her hand. "One makes acquaintance so much more quickly out of doors. I must begin ours by asking for your arm, Miss Swendon. I am fat and scant o' breath, and apt to forget it."

Jane drew the puffy hand eagerly through her arm. She would have liked to say outright how welcome the motherly presence and the honest voice were to her just then.

Mrs. Wilde dismissed the captain and Mr. Waring, and the two women sat down in the arbor, and at once were at ease and at home with each other. Bruno came up, eyed and smelled the newcomer, and snuggled down on her skirts to go to sleep.

"He vouches for me," she said nodding. "You must take me at his valuation."

"He makes no mistakes."

"Nor do you, I suspect. That reminds me, Miss Swendon. I brought a friend with me, and now that I have seen you I mean to bespeak your good-will for her. She needs just such healthy influence as yours would be."

"Is she ill?"

"Only in mind. One of those morbid women who must make a drama out of their lives, and prefer to make it a tragedy. A Madame Trebizoff, an Englishwoman who married a Russian prince. She is a widow now, with large means—came to New York a few months ago, and has had much court paid to her. But her nature makes her always a very lonely woman." She spoke hastily as the trailing of heavy skirts approached on the grass. "Here she is, poor thing! Be good to her," she whispered before presenting her in form. Madame Trebizoff was draped in black, with a good deal of lace about her head and an artificial yellow rose at her throat. Jane went up to her with outstretched hand, but when the sallow face turned full on her she stopped short, looked at it a moment, and then bowed without a word.

"It is the materialized spirit!" But she did not speak, for in a moment she remembered that she had once taken the bread from the wretched woman's mouth. She would not do it again.

Chapter 13

Mr. Van Ness came beaming down through the lilacs to the arbor, and was received with much reverence by Mrs. Wilde. She was a devout woman, and Pliny Van Ness's name was in all the churches. They all sauntered back to luncheon presently, Mrs. Wilde and Jane going before, while Mr. Van Ness and the Russian princess walked more slowly through the woods, the foreigner talking with animation and many gestures of American trees, while the reformer listened benignly, ineffable calm in his smiling eyes.

"You followed me here purposely, Charlotte?" he said gently as she dilated eloquently on our autumnal foliage.

"No. I did not know that you were in New York. But I meant to call upon you soon. I have had no money from you since last August."

"Somebody, apparently, has filled my place as your banker," his placid eye sweeping over the costly dress and be-diamonded fingers.

"What is that to you?" with a sudden shrill passion. "Once you would have cared, Pliny. But that was years ago."

"Yes. Many years ago," buttoning his glove carefully. "A Russian princess, eh?" after a short pause. "You are playing higher than ordinary, Charlotte. You'll find it dangerous. I should advise you to keep to begging letters or the role of medium or literary tramp."

"One class is as ready to be humbugged as the other. Who knows that better than you?"

"In the religious and charitable work to which I have given up my life," deliberately measuring his words, "there are few impostors to be met. We usually detect fraud, with God's help, and do not suffer from it, therefore."

She stopped short, looking at him with blank amazement. Then walked on with a shrug: "Absolutely! He expects me to believe in him! He believes in himself! Can imposture go further than that?"

Mrs. Wilde, in the distance, caught sight of the two figures as they passed through a belt of sunlight, and smiled contentedly.

"I am so glad to bring poor madame under direct religious influence! Mr. Van Ness is speaking to her with great earnestness, I perceive."

The Princess Trebizoff scanned the great reformer as they walked, appraising him, from the measured solemn step to his calm humility of eye. She would have relished a passionate scene with him. After terrapin and champagne, there was nothing she relished so much as emotion and tears. But they had played up to each other so often! The tragedy in their relation had grown terribly stale! You could not, she felt, make Hamlet's inky cloak out of dyed cotton.[1] But he would serve as audience.

"I'm growing very tired of good society," talking rapidly as usual. "Now, you always enjoyed a dead level, Pliny."

"Yes. There's no Bohemian blood in my veins. I was designed for respectability."

"So? I mean Ted shall be respectable," with sudden earnestness. "He is in a Presbyterian college. I should be glad if he'd go into the ministry. Yes, I should. Provided he had a call from God. I'll have no sham professions from Ted," her black eyes sparkling. "You did not ask for the boy. In your weighty affairs doubtless you forgot there was such a human being."

"No, indeed. In what institution have you placed Thaddeus?"

"No matter. He's out of your influence, thank God! He never heard your name. But as for me, I think I'll drop this princess business soon," meditatively. "I began down town," with a fresh burst of vivacity. "On the boardinghouse keepers. Last December."

"You are Madame Varens! Is it possible?" turning to look at her. "The papers were filled with your exploits last winter."

"Precisely!" She had a joyous girlish laugh, infectious enough to draw a smile from Van Ness.

"You are really very clever, Charlotte," admiringly.

"I made a tour in the West just before that," excitedly, patting her hands together. "Agent for Orphans' Homes in the Gulf States. I wrote a letter of introduction from one or two bishops to the clergymen in their dioceses: that started me, and the clergy and press passed me through. What a mill of tea-drinkings and church-gossip I went through! But it was better fun than this."

Looking up, she happened to catch the cold, furtive glance with which he had listened, and kept her eye fixed on him curiously.

"Do you hate me so much as *that*?" she said with a long breath. "Well," frankly, "it must be intolerable to carry such a millstone about your neck as I am to you. You know I could pull you down any minute I chose," tossing her head and laughing maliciously. "No matter how high you had climbed. I often wonder, Pliny, why you do not rid your-self of me. It could be easily done."

The usually suave tone was harsh and hoarse as he began to speak. He coughed, and carefully modulated his voice before he said politely, "Yes. But it would involve exposure unless carefully managed. That is certain damnation. There is a chance of safety for the present in trust-ing to you. You were always good-natured, Charlotte. And," turning his watery eye full on her, "you loved me once."

"Possibly," coolly. "But last year's loves are as tedious reading as last year's newspapers. Better trust my good-nature. You show your shrewdness in that. I don't interfere with people. The world uses me very well. It's a hogshead that gives the best of wine—if you know how to tap it."

"You've tapped it with a will. You go through life perpetually drunk," he thought as she ran lightly before him up the steps. He habitually made such complacent moral reflections upon his companions to him-self, and took spiritual comfort in them.

The hall was wide and sunny, made homelike by low seats and grow-ing plants: it was occupied by half a dozen committee-men, who were waiting impatiently to see Mr. Van Ness. The princess seated herself, attentive, her head on one side like some bright-eyed tropical bird.

Van Ness, without even a glance toward her, took up his business of Christian financier. "Do not go, I beg," as the captain opened the inner door for Rhodes and the ladies to retire. "Our affairs are conducted in the eyes of the public. Sound integrity has no secrets to keep. That is our pride.—Ah, gentlemen?"

The captain was glad to stay. Surely, Jane would be impressed with the vast influence of this good man. Van Ness did not look at her once. But he saw nobody but her, and spoke directly to her ear.

Asylums, workingmen's homes, hospitals, in all of which he was a director, were brought up and dismissed with a few hopeful, earnest words. The vast system of organized charities through which the kindly wealthy class touch the poor beneath them was opened. Mrs. Wilde, a manager in many of them, joined in the discussion.

"What a useless creature I am!" thought Jane. "But the money," doggedly, "is mine, and I choose to give it to father if the whole world go hungry." She turned, however, from one representative of these asylums to the other with a baited look. Was it this one or that whom she had robbed?

"Now, as to Temperance City—*our* city?" demanded a puffy little man importantly. "You are the fountain-head of information there. We look to you, Mr. Van Ness."

"You shall have the annual report next week.—Temperance City," turning to Rhodes, his balmy gaze aimed straight over her head, "is a scheme to protect people of small means in the churches, especially women, from wrecking their little all in unwise investments. It is a town on the line of the Pacific Railroad. Lots are only sold to colonists who are teetotallers and members of some church. The stock is owned largely by the same class."

"Oh, almost altogether!" cried the little man enthusiastically. "Mr. Van Ness's name, as you will understand, gives it authority among all religious people. We distribute prospectuses at camp-meetings and at all sectarian seaside resorts. Shares go off this summer like hot cakes. There's nothing like religion, sir, to back up business enterprise. There's Stokes, for instance. His shoes are sold from New Jersey to Oregon on the strength of the hymns he has written."

"Yes," said the judge solemnly. "We used to keep religion too much in the chimney-corner—spoke of it with bated breath. But it's in trade now, sir. We hear every day of our Christian shoemakers and railway kings and statesmen. The world moves!"

"Moves? Oh there's no lever like religion!" gasped the little man. "No advertisement to equal it. And a good man ought to succeed! Are the swindlers to take all the fat of the land? Does not the good Book say, 'To the laborers belong the spoils'?"[2]

"But this is so charming to me!" cried the princess. "We foreigners have so few opportunities of looking into the workings of your politics and trade!"

Van Ness bowed respectfully.

"And the State Home for destitute children?" asked a raw-boned Scotch-Irish man. "We're interested in that here in New York. We've subscribed largely, as you're aware, Mr. Van Ness. May I ask when you wull begin the buildin'?"

"In the spring, I trust. If enough funds are collected."

"And hoo air the funds invested in the mean while?"

"Oh, in corner-lots in Temperance City."

The committee-men had hurried away to catch the next train: lunch was over, and Mr. Van Ness stood apart on the lawn under the drooping branches of a willow, when the princess tripped lightly out to him.

"You have an object in coming here? You had an object in bringing those men to-day and opening out your affairs. What is it?"

He regarded her composedly for a moment without answering: "You always erred, Charlotte, in ascribing your own skill in intrigue to me. It was a flattering mistake. What I am to others I am to myself."

She laughed, a merry, hearty laugh: "Yes, Pliny, because you are not satisfied with cheating the world and the God that made you into the belief that you are a Christian, but you parade in your godliness before yourself. There is not a spot within you sound enough for your real soul to lodge in. It is all like that," setting her foot viciously on a fallen apple. "Rotten to the core!"

A shadow of disgust passed over his handsome face. Van Ness had a fastidious taste. Her melodramatic poses had been familiar to him for years: they always had annoyed and bored him.

"What is it that brings you here? A woman?"

He hesitated a moment: "Yes."

"This yellow-haired girl? You mean to marry her?"

"I may marry her," cautiously.

Their eyes met. "I did not think you would push me so far," she said thoughtfully.

"It is to your interest not to interfere. You are mad, Charlotte. But you never lose sight of the dirty dollar in your madness."

"That is for Ted's sake," quietly. "I dislike that girl. She's so damnably clean! She's of the sort that would walk straight on and trample me under foot like a slug if she knew what I was. I owe her an old grudge, too. But that's nothing," laughing good-humoredly. "It was the most ridiculous scene! But it lost me a year's income. She nearly recognized me to-day. On the whole, I'll not interfere. Marry her. She deserves just such a punishment. By the way, there is my card. You can send the back payments that are due, to-morrow."

Van Ness received the card and command with a smile and bow, meant for the bystanders: "Of course, Charlotte, you understand that these payments must soon stop. I shall rid myself of any legal claims you have upon me before marrying another woman."

"Oh, I've no doubt you'll walk strictly according to law! You will not run the risk of a lawsuit, much less prosecution, even for Miss Swendon. You will have no trouble in gaining your freedom from me," shrilly.

"None whatever," stripping the leaves from a willow wand. She left him without a word, going to the house.

Mrs. Wilde had just summoned her carriage. "Where is the princess?" looking lazily around.

"Is Madame Trebizoff a guest in your house?" asked Jane suddenly. "Yes."

"I will call her. I have something to say to her."

She went to meet her with the grave motherly firmness with which she would have gone to give a scolding to black Buff or a lazy chambermaid. The princess, crossing the grass, slender, dark, sparkling, had no doubt of her own smouldering passionate hate against her. It was the proper thing for Hagar to hate Sarah.[3] Life was thin and insipid without great remorses, revenges, loves. The poor little creature was always aiming at them, and falling short. She was wondering now why Jane wore no jewelry. "Not an earring! Not a hoop on her finger! If I had her money!" glancing down at the blaze of rubies on her breast.

They met under a clump of lilacs.

"Stop one moment," said Jane, looking down at her not unkindly. "You must not let this go too far, you know."

"What do you mean?" The princess fixed her eye upon her, with a somewhat snaky light in it. Indeed, when she assumed that attitude toward Van Ness or any other man she could frighten and hold him at bay as if she had been a cobra about to strike. But the lithe dark body, the vivid color, the beady eye only reminded Jane oddly of a darting little lizard, and tempted her to laugh.

"No. You really must keep within bounds. Because I have my eye upon you. I can't let you cheat that good soul, who brought you here, to her damage."

The princess gasped and whitened as though a cold calm hand was laid on her miserable sham of a body.

"Do you know who I am?" stiffening herself into her idea of regal bearing.

"Not exactly. It does not matter in the least, either. I took your means of earning a living from you once, you told me, and I don't wish to do it again. I will not interfere as long as you hurt nobody."

The princess stared at her and burst into an hysteric laugh: "I believe, in my soul, you mean just what you say! You are the shrewdest or stupidest woman I ever saw! Do you sympathize with me? Do you feel for me?" tragically, "or are you trying to worm my secret from me?"

"Neither one nor the other," coolly. "I know your secret. You are no spirit and no princess. I shall pity you perhaps when you go to some honest work. Why," with sudden interest, "I can find steady work for you at once. A staymaker in the village told me the other day—"

"*I* make stays!"

They both laughed. Jane's chief thought probably was how bony and sickly this poor woman was: her own solid white limbs seemed selfish to her for the instant. She took the twitching, ringed fingers in her hand.

"Play out your own play," she said good-humoredly. "You will not hurt anybody very seriously, I fancy."

They walked in silence to the house.

The princess bent forward in the carriage-window as they drove away to look back at her. "I wish my son knew such women as that!" she cried.

"Son?" said the startled Mrs. Wilde. "You have not spoken before to me of your son, madame."

"I have always kept him under tutors—at Leipsic."

She leaned back as they drove through the sunshine, her filmy handkerchief to her painted eyes, seeing nothing but an ugly, honest-faced boy hard at work in a bare Presbyterian chapel. He would never know nor guess the life of shame which his mother led! Her tears were real now.

She even had wild, visionary thoughts of a confession, of staymaking, of so many dollars a week regularly. But she remembered the time when some fussy, good women had put her in charge of a fashionable Kindergarten. There was a fat salary! The house was luxurious: the teachers did the work. But one night she had broken the finical apparatus to pieces, left a heap of bonbons for the children, scrawled a verse of good-bye with chalk on the blackboard, and taken to the road again without a penny.

PART 5

Chapter 14

The Hemlock Farm was awake to its farthest worm-eaten old fence. Never since its trees grew or its grass was green had such a breath and stir of delight swept through them. The low October sun reddened the stubble-field and thrust lances of light through the darkening boles; a string band, hidden somewhere, as evening fell sent long wafts of music through meadow and woods; everywhere was the sound of children's voices—in the trees, in the hay-mow, down in the old-fashioned rose-garden, up in the dusty garrets. Boys and girls of every shape and size, from pale, gray-eyed midges to big, beefy hobbledehoys, beset the captain at every turn. With his one arm and his uniform, and his gusty delight in themselves, and the background of this marvellous old farm and nut trees, he was a hero belonging to the family of Signor Blitz or Kriss-Kringle.[1] In fact, this feast of feasts given by Miss Swendon yet lingers in the memory of its guests alongside of the enchanted garden of figs.

The feast had grown out of a word. Miss Swendon had talked of the nuts going to waste, and Mrs. Wilde of the hundreds of children she knew "who fancied nuts grew on a fruit-stand." Jane's face began to kindle. "Let us all go nutting with them," she said.

So it easily came to pass—with tremendous exertions, however, on the part of Judge Rhodes and the captain, whose ideas, vague and vast, of the necessary amount of cake and ice-cream doubled with each day.

"Our fear in Virginia always used to be that we should not have enough," said the judge in solemn consultation.

"When I was a boy I never did have enough," rejoined the captain.

The Twiss and Nichols children were put into their Sunday finery and turned out, their jealous mothers watching how the city children treated them, Betty's face red with delight as she announced to Jane that they were "paler and more delicate than any of 'em, and much better-looking." Buff and his father grumbled loudly how they "weren't goin' to let one of dem young debbils inter de stable;" but before the day was over even gray old Dave was at the top of every nut tree, shouting louder than any boy of ten. As for Jane, she was everywhere: she climbed trees and filled all the pockets, told no end of stories, laughed at the least jokes, and wiped away a hundred sobbing miseries.

"I did not know you were excitable," said Mrs. Wilde, meeting her suddenly with pink cheeks and shining eyes on her way to her father.

"I don't know. I never played with young people before. Did you ever know such a happy day?"

Mr. Van Ness came out in the afternoon, and stood in odd corners beaming down on the little folk. But she passed him without seeing him, as she might the bronze Buddha shining in the hall.

"Do you really think the children are having a good time, father?" hanging on his arm. "Have you been happy all day? Every minute?"

As the twilight deepened the moon came out yellow and round; a few Chinese lanterns were hung in the mossy crannies and projections of the old house; the carriages began to drive away with the happy children, who all came to say goodbye and cling about her with that wild fervor which children give to a new friend. Jane might be cold and slow with grown people, but she hugged these little folks as if she were mother to all of them, and ran to hug them again more closely, and could not keep the joyous tears down in her eyes as their soft kisses rained on her. Some of their mothers and friends had come to thank the beautiful young heiress for giving their children such a happy day, and they stayed, wandering about the queer old house and the illuminated grounds: they were the very people whose formal calls Jane had forgotten to return. But she did not think of that: she only saw that they were quiet, friendly folk, and that her father's face was glowing with hospitality and content. The band struck up a waltz, and some of the pretty girls began to dance on the grass. Jane stood apart watching them thoughtfully: her hands were folded together. This couple who floated past her now—surely they were lovers. What a magnificent young fellow he was! She caught the meaning of his eyes bent on the sweet fair face. She knew that little girl would be the best wife for him in the world. She was certain that she loved him dearly.

The yellow October twilight lingered warmly; even the cold moon glowed in the colored haze; the darkening woods, the shadowy house on the hill, the laughing dancers, the broad river at the foot of the slope, were softened into the mellow atmosphere of a dream. The music was faint, a single fine harmony often repeated.

The grave girl with the arched white throat who stood attentive and silent under a tree, a wolf-hound beside her, her gown of some soft creamy hue belted about her waist and falling in heavy silken folds, was to the visitors the most noticeable point in the picture. Mr. Van Ness, a few yards away, waited, hoping she would come to him. But Jane saw only the sky and the running water and the lovers who passed her by. "There are persons," said Mr. Van Ness suavely to the judge, "who are like children or animals. No intellectual poise. Good weather or a little amusement throws them completely off their balance."

The dog, which Jane held by the collar, began to pull and bark joyfully. There was a tall dark figure coming toward the group near her father. Jane trembled more than the dog.

"No, you must not bring him to us, Bruno: he doesn't wish to come."

He did not come. She could hear a word now and then. Everybody was hurrying to greet him. How had he been able to leave his post? Would this new platform save the country? And what would the Syndicate do in view of this last complication? She knew he was the leader of the Syndicate. Great leaders and the Syndicate and the country,—all these things were in company.

She crept back out of sight in the bushes. Bruno broke loose and ran toward him. She went down to the river.

In a moment Bruno came dashing back, crunching through the bushes. There was a steady step on the grass.

"Are you here, Miss Swendon?"

"Yes."

Any of the finical little ladies yonder, had they been in her place, would have met this lover who gave no sign of love with all the self-respect and dignity of womanhood. Not unwooed would they be won, yet every resentful word or tear that drove him back would have been alluring and maddening. Honest Jane went straight to him and gave him her hand. She could not keep the hot color from her face or the water from her eyes. She had told him once that she loved him. With her, done was done. Death itself, coming between, would not give her love back again.

Mr. Neckart took the frank hand and let it fall. "I came to you for this one evening," he said, "before—before I go. One evening surely can import nothing. It can make no difference to you."

Mr. Neckart was a fluent speaker in public: he had been used to talk to Jane by the hour with the lazy freedom of thinking aloud. Now, arguing perhaps against himself, he was awkward and stammered. He did not know what she answered, or if she answered at all.

They both fell into silence. For months Neckart had looked forward to this supreme moment of parting. He must see her once more. But she should not have a glimpse of his starved soul. He would act with perfect honorable propriety. A few friendly words, one look to carry with him until death,—that was all. He did not remember now that it was a supreme moment: it was only a deliciously happy one. What rare fine shades of meaning came out on her face each minute! The absurd downright sincerity of the girl too! Surely all these men must be mad with love of her! Where had she discovered that wonder of a dress? Did other women ever wear such garments? his eyes following the soft slopes.

As for the young woman in the creamy robe, she was filled with a great content. She did not once think of the actual insanity which had its hold upon him. She did not think of her dying father, or of Jane Swendon's crime, or of Jane Swendon at all. All her real life had dropped out of her memory. There was left the warm air and the happy day and the music, and this one living being beside her. His hand rested on the bough of an apple tree: she could see on his palm a peculiar red mark, a birth-mark, which she had often watched darken or fade. She never thought of Neckart without remembering it. But why she should settle into a great content at the sight of this mark, which was in no wise a beautiful or desirable thing, is not for us to say. It is certain that as soon as she saw it her hold on life became quite secure, and the world righted itself instantly.

The music deepened, it filled the night; warm air stirred all the trees; a robin chirped in its nest overhead. The lovers whom Jane had watched waltzed past them. Neckart and Jane looked after them. Then they turned to each other. After all, they were young: life that night throbbed high as it had never done before.

"Come with me," he said, and put his arm about her waist.

He had danced when he was a boy, and had since seen a thousand women waltz: it was to him nothing but music and a pleasant motion. But no boy or man had ever danced with Jane before or touched her. It was to her her wedding-day.

It lasted but for a moment. The music stopped and left them standing under the pines, the spicy smell strong in the air. When Neckart removed his hand he saw how bloodless and grave her face was.

"I ought not to have asked you to dance, Jane. But it will be something for me to remember as long as I live. And men are selfish."

"You do not mean to leave me—now?"

"My God! I don't know!"

In the shadow of the pines he could see the white face upturned to his. He took it between his hands. Why should he not take her to his breast and dare his fate? Nothing came between them but that shadow of honor.

He would obey it.

She would forget him: women were shallower than men. They always forgot. But for him there was only intolerable solitude to the end. He would meet it, although he had come back weakly to the forbidden fruit. He gloried in the consciousness that he was a most heroic martyr as he stooped and kissed her mouth again and again.

"Neckart!" called the captain.—"Somebody find Bruce. He has not a minute to spare."

Neckart released her. "I must make this train," he said. "I must go back to the office. You know that I go on the steamer that sails to-morrow."

Trains? Steamers? With these kisses on his lips?

"What line do you cross in, Bruce?" The captain had hurried down with the other men. "Where do you go first?" as they walked to the house.

"To France, and then to the East," buttoning his coat nervously, without a glance toward the stunned girl beside him.

"Be back in the spring, Mr. Neckart?" said a lisping young lady.

"Not for years. At least, that is my present intention."

The warmth, the happy day, music, love that had filled all earth and heaven but now, were gone. In their place the gaslight, trains, conventional talk of duty!

"Neckart"—she heard a whisper behind her—"goes to Russia and Turkey on secret business for the government."

The kindly old judge, seeing Jane's face, quietly gave her a chair and sheltered her from notice. If Neckart had waited on this girl, he was an infernal scoundrel, no matter what his political rank. He knew she was as good as betrothed to Van Ness.

Jane watched all these brilliant women flutter around Neckart, giving him messages to their friends abroad. His cloak was thrown loosely back from his broad shoulders: he bent to listen to them. She knew nothing of this world of theirs. She was like a poor limp rag of humanity, blown aside into a corner. She had her fantastic passion: all the world besides was orderly, moved in the grooves of common sense and duty.

Mr. Neckart looked at his watch: "I must really go now." He shook hands with Mrs. Wilde, giving a swift glance to the corner where Jane sat. Waring and his attendant young ladies closed in on him with more last words and purling laughter. He made his way through them.

"Good-bye! good-bye!" cried the captain, wringing his hand. "God bless you, Bruce! What is it? Jane? Oh, I'll make your adieux to her. You'll miss your train."

But he had reached her at last, and took her hand in his, all the world looking on: "Good-bye, Miss Swendon."

She could not say a word. They all followed him out, one pretty little girl taking off her slipper to throw after him. But Jane sat alone in the deserted room, looking at the door through which the heavy cloaked figure had disappeared.

Chapter 15

Jane was roused by a wild shriek from without. She thought at first it was an animal in an agony of pain or rage. The wind had closed the door, and she could not open it. She went round by a passage to reach the lawn. While she had been in the hall a scene fit for a melodrama was in progress without. The tiny black Russian landaulet with three ponies abreast which Madame Trebizoff usually drove stood a few paces back near the woods. In the centre of the open space, in the full light both of the moon and the lights from the house, stood the princess, black lace draping her tragically, rubies flaming in her jetty hair, and a blood-red poppy in her breast. She was turning from one group of men to another like a hunted animal: her voice, once let loose from the thin smooth level on which she held it, squeaked and chattered, and then fell into doglike growls and sobs. Mrs. Wilde stood between her and a burly man in gray.

"I assure you, sir, that there is no Madame Varens here. This is an English lady and my guest. My guest! You know who I am—Mrs. John Schuyler Wilde."

"Very sorry, Mrs. Wilde, to annoy you, or these ladies," turning to the group of frightened girls to whom the princess had flown for succor. She looked back from their midst like a furious crow from out of a covey of white doves. "I won't swear that her name's Varens. She's down in the description also as Mrs. Swift and Aurelia Lamb. Regular confidence-woman, madam. I didn't want to follow her in here. Nobody respects ladies as are ladies more than I do. Now, ma'am," turning to Charlotte, "you'd better come quietly. It's nothing serious. A few hundreds. Small operation for *you*. Not worth disturbing people of this class," nodding back over his right ear as he caught her by the arm.

"Class! What do you mean? This is *my* class!" shaking him back as if he had been a snake and tapping her breast as she lifted herself to her tiptoes. "*My* class! Do you hear? I am the Princess Trebizoff. I have witnesses.—Mr. Van Ness! Mr. Van Ness is here to speak for me."

"Pliny Van Ness?" said the awed detective. "If *he* vouches for you, ma'am—"

Mr. Van Ness, who had watched the arrest with much placidity, was suddenly left by the withdrawal of the crowd standing alone facing the detective and his prisoner. He stroked his blond beard and looked down at her with thoughtful compassion.

"Mr. Van Ness," she said shrilly, advancing a step, "I am in danger of a jail. Certify for me that I am—your friend, the woman whom I represent myself to be."

"Of course any friend of yours, Mr. Van Ness—I may be mistaken," interjected the officer.

"I am very sorry, officer," said the reformer, his mellow tones full of pain. "But this lady—"

"Do you refuse?" she shrieked. Then springing up to him and thrusting her face in his, she whispered, "For Ted's sake! I am your child's mother! If he should find me in jail!"

"I was about to say, officer," calmly pursued Mr. Van Ness, "that this lady is unknown to me except as a casual acquaintance. She may be a princess. She may be a thief. That is for you to settle. As for me—"And waving his white hands and shrugging his broad shoulders, he turned away.

The princess looked after him steadily a moment, then she turned to the men: "Are you going to see me hauled away to prison without a word? I am a woman! An Englishwoman! This is American justice!" She lifted herself again into her favorite attitude of malediction, shaking her fingers against the air as if scattering curses.

"Good gracious!" cried Mr. Waring. "Why! why! Surely I have seen that done before!—I say, judge! Don't you remember? The medium Combe? The spirit—"

"Come!" said the officer gruffly. "We've had enough of this. Your friends disown you, ma'am. I'll trouble you to step down to the hack—"

It was then that the poor princess gave the despairing shriek which Jane had heard. Eluding the officer's clutch, she darted across the open space and faced them, while she plunged her hand into her pocket and drew out a vial full of a dark liquid. There was a cry of horror as she put it to her lips, drained it and sank to the ground.

"Good God! She has taken poison!" cried the captain.

There were immediate shouts for a doctor, and frantic rushes out and back again on the part of Buff and Dave and the young men, who wanted to scatter the news, but were afraid something would happen while they were gone. Mrs. Wilde came up to her. "She really is an impostor, then?" holding out her trembling arms to take her.

"Oh, the worst kind! Dead-beat, confidence—as much lower as you can go. Don't touch her, ma'am. You'd better take them young ladies away too. This isn't the sort of thing for them to see."

"Certainly not," running off like a scared hen-partridge.—"Come, girls, I will take you home at once. This is a phase of life not fit for you to look into."

But she could not drive them farther than the porch, where they huddled, pale, all talking at once, looking back and declaring it was as exciting as any tragedy, and was the poor creature dead? and oh, to think they had all called on her!

By this time Jane was on her knees and had the princess in her arms. "Poor thing! poor thing!" she said. Her own heart was so bruised and sore that she might have sobbed over this other woman if she had had nothing else to do for her.

"Lay her down, miss, if you please. A doctor's been sent for. She's in the hands of medicine and the law."

"Father, where is your patent stomach-pump?"

"The very thing, Jane!" dashing into the house.

"May the Lord have mercy on her soul!" said Waring.

"Mr. Waring, are you there? Help me to carry her. Into my room."

"Somewhere else! Not there!" exclaimed the judge.

"These proceedings are very irregular!" blustered the officer. "Accordin' to New York law, the body shouldn't be touched until the coroner arrives."

"But is she dead?" interposed Mr. Van Ness, bringing the little procession to a full halt. "*Is* she dead? That is the question.—Allow me.

Lay her on this settee: one moment, Miss Swendon," prying one eyelid open and bending his ear to her heart with an air of judicial decision.

"Life," said the detective ponderously, "appears to have become extinct."

Jane pushed back the hair from the lean face. "Perhaps," she said, "she has a child," and then stooped and kissed her on the mouth.

Van Ness, at the word, paused and looked for a moment sharply from one woman to the other. Then with a sad smile he lifted the hand which clenched the vial tightly. It required a wrench to remove it. He uncorked it and put it to his tongue.

"Prussic acid!" said the detective. "Strong odor of peach-blossoms."

"Give me space one moment," said Van Ness excitedly. "There is a chance of saving her!—Stand back. Miss Swendon."

The officer and Jane drew back hastily. He stooped and whispered vehemently into the ear of the dead woman. She opened her eyes, sparkling and full of malice, stared at him doubtfully, then nodded. The captain, a physician and a dozen other aids arrived at the moment.

"You are too late," said Van Ness calmly, meeting them. "Madame Trebizoff had only swooned. She is willing to go with the officer.—Will you take my arm, Miss Swendon? You are faint, I am sure. As for the poison," lowering his voice as he bent toward her, "it was only sweetened water. The princess has taken it before."

Chapter 16

The steamer began to cut at last through the short curled waves, a bit of spray blown up on Neckart's mouth was salt, and, looking back, the great congregation of ships in the offing had dwindled to a few black spears of masts.

It was done, then! He had left all behind and cut loose, finally and for ever. He was glad that there was not a familiar face in the ship's company. The other passengers, looking critically at the well-known politician as he paced up and down, rated him as a keen, vigorous man in the maturity of power, wholly engrossed in affairs. He did not once think of the affairs of his own or any other country: he knew now but one fact—that the time was at hand when he must meet the fate to which he had looked forward so long, and that the sea must be between himself and Jane before that day came. But he was not likely to give any hint by appearance or words that this matter troubled him. There was a young mother with her first baby near him. God only knows what thoughts of Jane were in his mind as he looked at her. But he stopped to talk with her husband, who spoke to him about a shoal of porpoises; and afterward, when the captain inquired if health or pleasure took him from home, stated carelessly that it was a cerebral affection, and discussed the efficacy of some recommended bromide.

There was a lady sitting alone on the deck, a dark-green cloth dress belted neatly about a jimp figure, and cut short enough to show tight-laced boots: a close fur cap tied over her ears—an ugly little woman, but all alive and ready for action.

Something familiar in her carriage drew Neckart's eye to her a second time. She nodded and smiled: "You have quite forgotten me?"

"Miss Fleming! It is so many years since I saw you! Or ought I to say Miss Fleming?" looking about for her companion.

She laughed: "I am quite alone. On the ship, and everywhere else, for that matter. They are all gone, Mr. Neckart." She stopped abruptly and turned her head away. Cornelia never could speak of her mother without choking.

"I did not know," said Bruce gently. "It is long since I was at the homestead."

"Yes, there's nobody but me," she said presently with a nervous laugh. "I manage to support myself by art. It's poor support, and poorer art. But I have scraped together enough money to take me to Rome to make it better. With shawl-straps and a satchel American women can go anywhere, you know."

"You do not look like one of the modern Unas," glancing down.[1] There was, on the contrary, a singular degree of femininity in this woman: he remembered now how it used to impress him as a boy. In the crowds that had filled his later years Cornelia's face had faded completely out of his mind. It began to come up now out of his boyhood, not unpleasantly, but rather with much of the glamour of those early days clinging to it. Yet he was annoyed that any old remembrance was to be kept awake during the voyage. He had meant to make it a lapse of absolute forgetfulness, and after that—what? "A season of dreadful looking-for of judgment," he found himself repeating as he talked civilly to Cornelia about the color of the water. He rose at last, being under such a nervous strain that he could not keep still.

"I shall go and beg the captain to give me a seat next yours at table," he said smiling. "I must take an oversight of you."

"Pray do not," she said anxiously, laying her hand on his sleeve. "I will not be a charge on anybody. Why, I am as independent as any—female doctor! Just let me come and go without notice, and if ever you feel like talking to me, don't think of me as a young lady, but only as somebody whom you used to know when you were a boy."

Neckart bowed and smiled. There was something very cordial and sweet in the little speech. Was it genuine nature that dictated it or only fine tact? In any case, he was glad to be relieved of the duty of paying *petits soins* to any woman.[2] Of course he would not neglect the poor creature, who appeared to be very lonely, and, in spite of her grotesque little swagger, as ill able to stand alone as any woman he had ever seen. He glanced at the homely attractive face looking far out to sea when he turned in his walk. The second time he caught her looking at him with a sadness and hunger in her eyes that drove the blood to his heart like a blow. What was that which had happened between them when they were both children? A love-affair? Absurd! It was impossible that any sane woman could remember such folly. With every drop of blood tingling hot within him he turned down the deck and buried himself in the crowd in the cabin. Why had she never married? But what did that matter to him? He did not come near her at the table, nor join her during the rest of the day. But why had she never married? Could it have been the thought of him which had kept her aloof and solitary all her life?

Miss Fleming was one of the last to forsake the deck that night. She was a good sailor, and not likely to lose any time by sickness. "I can't afford to lose any time," she said to herself, her lips making a thin seam across her face, as she sat hour after hour waiting for him to return. "What I do must be done now or never." She had taken every penny she had in the world to pay for this fortnight in the ship with him.

"I shall succeed," rising, her thin cheeks pale, but her eyes like coals of fire. As she went through the cabin she scowled at the pretty young girls, who, like the birds in the fable, had a thousand lures of innocence and beauty and plumage. She was Reynard with his one trick— friendship and whatever she hid behind it.[3] "But I never failed yet," she said as she shut herself into the darkness of her state-room.

Chapter 17

The captain reported himself "under the weather" the day after the nutting frolic. His guests had all gone excepting Van Ness, who remained in New York, appearing at the farm every afternoon with a fresh invoice of diffusive sweetness and light. In a week the captain gave up his daily visit to the club, and one morning Jane found him in the work-room, busy again among the dusty models, with a gray pinched line about his jaws. She ran to put on her apron, and worked with him, jesting and laughing, but as soon as she could escape sent Dave to the doctor. The old gentleman came, chatted a while, and soon followed Jane out to the hall.

"Florida to-morrow? Southern California? No, not now. Let him have home comforts and good nursing this winter. Anything he wants to eat. Humor him as much as you choose."

Jane stood holding by the back of a chair: "You do not mean that there is danger?"

"I see no change in the symptoms," cautiously. "We'll try the new prescription a few days, and we shall see—we shall see."

Jane went back to her father and the models, and talked calmly of screws and pistons. If she could only take the shaking old gray head to her breast and cry her heart out! If she could lie down in the grave with him! They had been such friends all her life! He was the only friend she ever had. She got up and ran out of doors once or twice: her breath was leaving her: his face, with the strange change in it, drove her away. Outside, the ducks were wabbling in and out of the pond, the sun was shining, the chrysanthemums and crimson prince's feather were all in flower. Dave was currying a horse in the stable-yard and whistling a dancing tune. What a foolish fright she had been in! Everything in the world was going just as usual. When she went back, too, the captain was pulling out his patent scissors from a drawer, laughing, his face flushed. He never looked better in his life.

She never left him after that. She had a couch made for herself at his door, that she might hear the moment that he stirred in the night. She could see no change in him from day to day, but she watched everybody keenly who came near him, trying to read their opinion of him in their faces. She fancied there was a difference in the manner of even Dave and Buff to him—a forced jocularity, a peculiar tenderness of voice. Bruno, she observed, had deserted her altogether and kept close to his master.

It was at this time that Mr. Van Ness began to monopolize the house: the very air of it grew bland and decorous. He came early, and stayed until night. The captain treated him with reverential deference: Jane fell into the same habit. She was weak and suasible as a reed just now. She had lost all root and marrow out of her life. Every day her father dilated on Mr. Van Ness's virtues. She could not deny one of them. They began to fence her in as with smooth polished walls, with no breath inside. Bruno, alone inexorable, never allowed him to pass without a snap and growl, although he had yielded enough to the pressure of public opinion not to fly at his throat.

"Mr. Van Ness, my dear," said the captain one day, "has been good enough to look into the affairs of the farm. He says the income from it should be trebled. Ask his advice, Jane. Especially as to turnips. We failed there. What intellectual scope that man has! It grasps a vast theory one moment and the minutest detail the next."

"Yes, father." It mattered little to Jane who meddled with the farm now.

"Mr. Van Ness"—the next day—"was glancing over your bookshelves this morning, Jane. A course of reading such as he would dictate would be of immeasurable benefit to you."

"I know it," humbly. "I am shamefully ignorant."

"Why not put yourself wholly into his care, Jenny?" taking her hand tenderly. "He is one of the best of men."

"I believe he is," candidly.

At this moment the reformer came in sight on the lawn without, the full sunshine falling on him. They both looked at him.

"His intellect is of a high calibre, Jenny: he saw into that idea of mine for the gauge to-day in an instant."

Jane nodded dully.

"And as for looks—have you any fault to find with him, Jane?"

"No, none."

"Then, in God's name, why—" He checked himself. "Mr. Van Ness asked me to speak with you this afternoon. It's a very solemn matter, Jenny. It's for life. You know what I wish. Don't shove off your life's happiness for a prejudice of no more weight than so much fog. I think I'll lie down and sleep a while. Think the matter over. There he is outside. He wishes to talk to you of it now."

Jane lingered, tucked the cover over his feet again and again. She could not go out and talk to this man in cold blood of marriage. When she told him that it could not be, that she could not love him, what reason could she give? She had no reason. There was none. This husband waiting out on the gravel-path, and smiling in on her, was in every way admirable and lovable. But Bruno and old Dave were better comrades for her—nearer kinsfolk.

The captain opened his eyes drowsily: "You are going to read? That's right, Jenny."

She brought the book gladly, and Mr. Van Ness moved disappointed away. There were certain chapters in St. John which the old man himself had taught Jane. Her mother had little to do with the Bible, which she declared was full of Presbyterian bigotry, but the captain, who was at bottom a devout soul, had anxiously tried to give the child as soon as she could speak what he supposed to be the milk of the Word. Every day now she would hear him muttering to himself these passages from the Sermon on the Mount or in John's Gospel, and he would presently call on her to repeat them, explaining them to her as though she were still a child.[1]

"We got away from the Master as we grew older, Jenny: that was the mistake," he said now, stroking her hair as she kneeled by the bed. "I ought to have kept you close by Him. But you see the patents and the other worries—It's all been so hurried—I've hardly begun fairly. But we'll try and do what's right now. There's plenty of time before us."

"Oh, father!" She buried her head on his breast.

"If I've done wrong to any man, I'd like to have his forgiveness and to make restitution. Restitution"—the captain said, talking into the vague space which widened slowly about him every day. Jane, holding his shaking old hand, groped, as every other human soul in pain does, to find this Master.

She had but little faith then: like all other feelings, it would probably come slowly into her slow nature and abide there. But could He come close as her father said? She was so utterly alone! She would be glad to make restitution, though the money had been her own, if that would please Him. But restitution to whom?

"Go now: I want to sleep. Mr. Van Ness is waiting." She moved to the door: "Jenny, you'll say what is right to him. I trust you."

Mr. Van Ness did wait at the door of the conservatory. His white hand was held out, as if to lead her into perfume and light. Was it this which He would order her to do? Was it? The very touch of his hand seemed to her an indecency.

"Miss Swendon—" Van Ness began abruptly, in so rough and candid a tone that Jane looked at him startled and respectful—"you are prejudiced against me. I see that my manner impresses you as artificial. It is so, and I know it. I wish to account to you for that before I open my business to you." He passed his soft fingers slightly down the fold of his shirt, opened his thick red lips once or twice and shut them again, his eyes fixed on her own, probing, gauging her. "I must give you the keynote to my whole life," he resumed. "You were born among people of culture and gentle habits. I was a foundling, the child of vice, reared in it, fed by it, until I was old enough to stand by myself. Then I swore by God's help to leave it behind me for ever. I have struggled on this far. It has been hard work. That is all," with a long breath. "You know what I am now. I wanted you to know precisely what I have been."

It was unwomanly not to make a friendly sign to the man who had thus frankly humiliated himself before her. Jane forced herself to speak:

"You are very sincere—more sincere than is necessary. But I respect you for it."

135

"You can understand now why my manners and voice bear the evident marks of training. They both have an artificial twang which has prejudiced you against me. Am I right?"

"Possibly you are right," said downright Jane. "If it was only the manner and voice, I have been unjust to you."

He waved his hand with humble deprecation, and sighed audibly. Jane moved restlessly. No exhibition of character could be more noble or genuine: nothing could be more winning than the handsome blond head between her and the shelves of flowers. This senseless antipathy which she felt to both was that of an animal. She was ashamed of it, and stood smiling, her head bent with clumsy politeness, and the same look in her eyes which Bruno gave him.

"You will understand now, too," he continued gently, "why my interest in vicious and hungry children is so deep. I have been one of them. It is little for me to have given my life to help them."

"It must be a comfort to give your life to any certain work," cried Jane hotly. "It's very hard to reach middle age, as I have done, and find one's self fit for nothing! Nothing whatever!"

Mr. Van Ness did not at once reply. He scanned her curiously, as he might a tool about whose temper he was not certain, but which it was necessary for him to use.

"Your father has told you my reason for wishing to speak to you today?" he said abruptly.

Jane's head and very throat were scarlet: "Yes. But we will not talk at all of that matter, Mr. Van Ness," stammering with haste. "It is impossible, unnatural. You are more experienced than I: you must see that it is impossible more clearly than I do."

"In hoping," he resumed, after calmly dropping his light eyelashes while she spoke, politely attentive, "in anxiously striving, I may say, to gain you as my wife, I did not intend to give up the cause of the orphan and the fatherless."

"Oh you ought not to give it up! It would be really criminal! After you have gone so far! And I should be no help to you at all," she added breathlessly.

"But," with his light confusing gaze full on her, "you know, to speak plain English, that your father on his deathbed desires that you shall marry me?"

The blood came and rushed back from Jane's face, leaving it colorless.

"Why will you not grant this last wish?"

Why? There was no reason why she should not. She was dear to nobody else in the world than this old man—she was of use to nobody else. To nobody. She looked for some time directly into the shallow eyes facing her with aggressive complaisance. "I cannot do it," she said at last. She seemed to have grown stolid from head to foot.

"Why? What is this bar between us?" coming a step closer.

"How can I tell?" with a nervous shudder. "If I lived with you as your wife for years, you would be none the less a stranger to me."

"Miss Swendon," suddenly, and with the indulgent smile which he would have given to a child, "I will not accept such an answer. Take time. Consider the matter calmly. You speak rashly now. You have not a single reason to give for your decision."

"No," said Jane quietly. "But I shall not alter it."

"This woman," thought Van Ness, "is *all* mule." But he went on blandly: "In any other case the fact that you were possessed of large means and that I am almost penniless would have deterred me from approaching you in this way—"

"The money counts for nothing with me," quickly.

"I know that. I know that if you were my wife your generous nature would rejoice in giving it to me in furtherance of my great work. In fact—" He stopped, measured her again with the same hesitating inspection, and then, while Jane listened intently, proceeded: "To be quite candid, Miss Swendon, but for a sudden and most unexpected change in Mr. Laidley's disposition on the last day of his life, my Home for Friendless Children would have been made a certainty without your aid."

"What do you mean?"

"The will," deliberately, "which he made but a week before his death left his whole property intact to me as trustee for this charity. You know that he changed his mind and destroyed this will apparently in the very act of dying, and gave it to you. I am rejoiced that he did so: be assured of that. But if it should come back, after all, to the Home, and you with it as a helper, there would be a fine poetic justice in that, I think," with a pleased gurgle in his throat.

Mr. Van Ness had always regarded Jane as a young, insignificant-looking girl. But now, for some strange reason, she impressed him as a middle-aged, powerful woman.

"So you were the heir?"

"Yes. Or the Home, to be exact—the Home."

Jane raised her arms and clasped her hands over her head. She said at last: "The money is mine. It was mine when William Laidley gave it to you. I will keep it as long as my father lives. As soon as he is dead I shall give it to you. I shall be glad to give it up—glad." Her arms fell to her side: a great relief came slowly into her face.

At last the burden was to fall off. The way before her was simple and clear.

Mr. Van Ness laughed with keen amusement, but checked himself with an apologetic cough: "Forgive me, but really, Miss Swendon, you are so incredibly innocent! A mere baby in your knowledge of the world or ordinary customs. It would be impossible for you to make such a transfer. You could not give the estate, and I could not take it, unless upon one condition."[2]

"What is that?"

"That you give it as my wife."

"There is no other way," he resumed after a pause, finding that she made no reply. "Of course," with a bitter laugh, "I do not expect your zeal in behalf of the friendless children to tempt you to so repugnant a step as marriage with me. But that is the only way in which this property could be restored to them."

Still she was silent. A pot with a half-dead geranium was near her: she began to break off the yellow leaves and lay them in a neat little heap one by one. Did Van Ness suspect the truth? He stood erect, regarding her from calm heights of virtue. Presently he continued: "The property, as you say, is legally your own. The tenor of the will makes it so. But when I think of the starved bodies and souls of these poor children, and remember how little you value your great wealth, I feel that surely God meant it for them. It was some strange mistake that took it from them."

Jane did not meet his eye. She pushed open the little door, and went out hurriedly into the fresh air. Van Ness followed her. It is not probable that he had guessed her secret, but he certainly knew that for some reason this fact of the lost will had given him an inflexible hold upon the jaded, fluttering woman. He meant to press it with peremptory force.

The wind without was blowing keen and cold. Jane rallied in it. She turned to Van Ness with something of her ordinary courage. She was absolutely certain of her own honesty, and she hoped that God believed in it. What did it matter if by the laws of men and society she was a thief? It was some time before she caught the meaning of Van Ness's words. He was urging his cause with a surfeit of honeyed and long-conned phrases. He remembered as he talked how many women would receive any hint of courtship from him with delight, and the consciousness gave him a factitious dignity. He walked beside her down the path. Bruno, who leaped the barnyard fence to join her, marched on the other side, fixing a red suspicious eye on him.

"I have not made love to you as a younger man would do. I never have told you how different from every woman you are in my eyes. How attractive—how fair—" His eyes rested on hers for a full silent moment. She turned away with a shiver. "I never have told you how dear you are to me. But you must have seen it."

"No, I did not see it," said Jane bluntly. "But what has my beauty to do with the matter? Or your love? They do not alter you or me."

Even Van Ness was stunned by this calm delivery of fact. He recovered himself presently, and with a smile of hurt feeling gently replied, "Your antipathies are strong, Miss Swendon. Most women would cover them over courteously. But, do you know, I really like your honesty," pointing the tips of his fingers together mildly. "Yes, I do. Now I shall not urge myself personally on your notice any more. I did not seek an immediate marriage. I am willing that time should work for me. Promise me this," halting and suddenly facing her; "look at me as the representative of those poor friendless children whom I love so dearly, and whose inheritance you now enjoy." (He saw and took note of the sudden quailing of her whole bearing.) "You will give your wealth to them some day."

"God knows I shall be glad to do that."

"And yourself to me."

"Never!" she said quietly. But she smiled politely in his face. All the currents of her future life were ebbing from this half hour of time, and she knew it; yet that little taunt at her discourtesy had galled her sorely. Since she was a child she had felt herself and her rugged talk big and boorish and coarse-grained beside the polished complaisance of smaller women. When Van Ness, therefore, took her hand now, and, after kissing the thin fingers with his slow sultry glance, drew them within his arm and held them there close, she did not resist, and walked patiently beside him down the path. Van Ness's hand, as we have said, was unpleasantly cold and clammy.

Jane remembered a story in her primer of the little princess, who, having told a lie, was given over thereafter to the ownership of a frog. It sat on her plate, on her lap, on her bed, on her mouth as she tried to pray. It never left her. It was her master and owner.[3]

Chapter 18

As they turned into another path, Jane saw the boy Phil running toward the stables, and Betty came toward her, walking calmly, but twisting her sleeve into a rag with nervous fingers.

"My father!" cried Jane.

"Yes. He's awake, and he don't seem quite so peart as he was this morning. But it's nothing: don't you be scared, miss. I took the liberty of sending Phil for the doctor," panting after her as she ran.

Van Ness quickened his pace and followed.

The captain was in his arm-chair, wrapped in his flowered dressing-gown. Buff and Dave were busy over him, their black lips turning blue with fright.

"No, I'll not go to bed!" he cried testily. "What good will blankets and feathers be to me? It's death, you blockhead! But don't tell her—don't tell Miss Jane."

"Hyah she is, sah."

"Keep her out!—Oh, Jenny! Go, finish your walk. I—I'm very well, and I'd rather be alone a while. Dave will stay with me," looking helplessly up into her white face. Then he broke down and fumbled for her hand: "Oh, I'm going—I'm going, Jenny."

"No, no, father, you shall not go. It's just a passing pain. Swallow this," holding the gray head close to her breast. Her hand shook so that she could not put the spoon to his lips.

"I wish you would go away, child. It will worry you so. I never meant you to be with me when It came."

She could not answer. She laid him down, drenched his hands with camphor, seeing how blue and sunken they were. "His feet are like ice, Betty," she cried. "What shall I do? what shall I do?"

"I've got mustard draughts here, ma'am. Try and get him to take these drops."

"Yes, yes. Don't go out of the room, dear Betty! Don't leave him." She caught hold of this savior who was wise in mustard draughts and tonics. Why had she never learned such things in all her long, useless life? She would not look beyond the blue marks on his hands and the cold of his feet. She and Betty could fight them until the doctor came—just as the wrecked man sees only the floating logs and the raft, and will not look below at the unfathomable black sea waiting for him.

"'Pears to me, Miss Jane," said Dave presently in a pitying whisper, "as dat ar camphire on'y vexes him. His bref is mos' gone."

"Whah de debbil am dat doctor?" muttered Buff, going to the door, with a thrill of terror at his oath. For in the last moment the approach of an awful Power was felt in the commonplace little room. Yet the afternoon sunshine shone as before in the open door, the green curtains waved to and fro, a chicken came pecking up on to the wooden steps. The captain's feeble glance wandered to it.

"The gate of the poultry-yard is broken, Dave.—Remind me tomorrow, Jane—my new lock."

"De Lohd sabe us! Can't you take his mind off his patents, Miss Jane, an' Death jes' at hand?"

"I told Phil to bring the minister with the doctor," whispered Betty. She took the useless mustard away from the poor old feet and covered them reverently. They would never feel any touch again. Then she and Dave drew away from him, and stood back from the chair, leaving him alone with his child.

Jane knelt, holding him by the hand, looking into the dimming eyes. "Father!" she said. "You must not go. You shall not leave me! Father!"

The old man's soul, as always irresolute, halted at the call, going out to its long journey: "I will not leave you until I have taken care of you, Jenny," trying to smile at her.

"And how are you, my dear sir?" said a mellow voice behind her. "Feeling better, are we now—eh?"

"Van Ness? Yes." The captain's voice gathered a little of its old authority, and he struggled to rise. "Is it all settled? Have you promised to marry him, Jenny?"

"She will! she will!" replied Van Ness hastily. "It will be arranged as you wish, my dear sir."

"I must be sure of it," uneasily, with the restlessness of coming death and the old desire to control. "I cannot go until I see you his wife, Jane."

Jane held his hand immovable. She did not stir nor show any feeling more than the wooden plank on which she knelt.

There was a slight stir at the door. Doctor Knox came in with Mr. Lampret, the meek little Methodist minister from the village. The doctor went up to the captain, who waved him impatiently aside.

"Too late, doctor. Your occupation's gone. I have a matter to arrange, and—only a few minutes."

Jane raised her head, looking dully at the physician.

He shook his head. "There is no chance," he said. As he drew back he watched the girl, rather than the dying man. He was used to seeing women suffer, but he felt an unwonted pity for this friendless Jane.

The captain beckoned feebly to Mr. Lampret: "I'm glad to see you here.—Now—Van Ness—now. I can give her to you. I can die in peace."

Van Ness's color changed, perhaps for the first time in his life. He stood irresolute. He had not thought of immediate marriage with Jane. He scanned in that instant the danger involved in it—the probability that Charlotte would "make trouble"—the chance of buying her off. The actual risk involved was great enough to make even his ruddy face ghastly.

But if he allowed this chance to escape he would never regain his hold on her. Was this property twice to slip from his grasp? He took a step closer to her, and laid his hand on her arm.

"Will you consent?" he said.

She let fall her father's hand and stood up. She and Van Ness were a little apart from the others, so that his words were heard only by herself. There was absolute silence in the room, except for the breathing of the dying man.

Van Ness stooped closer to her: she could feel his warm clammy breath on her cheek. "You are very dear to me." Seeing that she shuddered, he changed his mode of attack to direct assault: "If you marry me you will restore the property—restore, you understand?—to the children to whom it belongs."

"Jenny," moaned her father, "are you ready? I cannot die in peace until this is done."

The clergyman took pity on the girl: something in her set, deep-lined face alarmed him: "Is there any reason why you do not wish to gratify your father's last wish?"

She did not answer. There was no reason but her hopeless passion for another man, whose wife she could never be. Yet it seemed to her that God was bidding her to be true to that true love at whatever cost.

"I infer," said the little man, turning to Van Ness, "that the marriage was arranged before, and is only hastened now by "-glancing at the captain—"circumstances."

"Yes, yes! Precisely!" suavely. "You may trust me. You may have heard my name before—Pliny Van Ness."

Mr. Lampret bowed deferentially: "The name is well known. Our church has reason—grateful," he murmured.—"My dear Miss Swendon, this is a hard trial—hard. A young girl would fain give herself away with joy and rejoicing. But as your father will not depart in peace, I see no reason why the ceremony should not immediately take place."

"Jane! Jane!" cried the captain shrilly, "why do you delay?"

There was no answer for a minute. Then there came into her face a sudden resolve. She turned and held out her hand to Van Ness: "I will marry you."

The words revived the captain. "Lift me up," he said to David.— "Closer, closer, Mr. Lampret! I can't hear very well." He listened eagerly until the last words of the marriage service were said. Then his head sank on his breast: "I'm always loth to interfere. But I am glad that is settled properly."

Van Ness turned to kiss his wife, but, without seeing him apparently, she went up to her father and put her lips to his. Van Ness followed her, as if to assert his rightful place, and, standing on the other side of the sofa, possessed himself of the captain's one hand, pressing it gently.

"He is sinking very fast," he said. "Let him rest in my arms."

She shivered, and held him tighter to her breast. When she would have stroked back the gray hair from his forehead, Van Ness's soft fingers were there with hers, soothing them: "Compose yourself. Our dear father will soon be gone."

"Jenny!"

"Yes, father."

"I'll hear you now—your chapter, you know. We ought to have read the Bible more. We forgot the Lord, we were so busy. But—but—" He lifted his hand, struggled to rise, his dim eyes lighting with sudden energy. "Jenny! He doesn't forget me now!"

"No, father, no!"

There was a long silence. Dave sobbed aloud. Mr. Van Ness cleared his throat composedly. "I will sing," he said. "A hymn would soothe his passage, probably; or shall I pray?"

Jane leaned forward: "Go away!"

"How? Eh?" aghast, and not sure he had comprehended the vehement whisper.

"Go. You shall not come between us in these last minutes. You have the money now. Go away!"

Van Ness wheeled instantly. He was plentiful in expedients for so slight an emergency as this. He beckoned the clergyman and doctor out of the room, and shut the door.

"It would be better to leave them alone, gentlemen. The relation between Captain Swendon and his—ah—Mrs. Van Ness—has always been singularly close and intimate. The presence of so many strangers oppresses them both."

"I readily understand that," rejoined Mr. Lampret eagerly, "as far as we are concerned. But do you return, my dear sir. Surely *you*—"

But Van Ness waved his hand lightly: "No, no! I am comparatively a stranger to the dear old man. In a few moments—when all is over—I shall return to support and console *her*."

"Delicate feeling there! Remarkably fine feeling, sir!" said the clergyman as he strolled with the doctor to his buggy, leaving Mr. Van Ness to the sanctity of his grief. "Going now? I shall remain until all is over. There appears to be a storm coming up," with a sad subjection of tone.

The gathering clouds darkened the room where the captain lay dying: the wind sobbed gustily through the open window. His feeble eyes were steady as they never had been in life: he nodded from time to time as Jane repeated the old verses which he had taught her when she was a little child.

"'Come unto Me.' That's good! It's all good.—Some water, Dave. What are you crying about, old fellow?—Yes, we'll read the Bible every day, Jenny. We'll begin all fresh. We've plenty of time—plenty of time—"

Dave, holding the water to his lips, took it quickly away and fell upon his knees.

"Oh, father! father!"

The darkness was heavy and the wind blew fiercely as this over-grown boy's soul went out to love and dogmatize and make mistakes elsewhere.

They let Jane lie a while upon his breast: she was as cold and motionless as the dead when they took her up.

"I'll go for her husband," said the sobbing old negro.

"No," said Betty shrewdly. "Let her alone a while. This is trouble enough, God knows, poor child!"

When Jane's senses came to her, and she looked about her intelligently, old Dave cried eagerly, "I'll fetch Mr. Van Ness: I'll fetch yoh husband, Miss Jenny."

She stood up quickly: "No. Let me be alone with my father a little while. Go out, please, and watch the door."

"Nobody shall come in," said Betty.

The room was nearly dark. She was alone with the dead for a long time. She stooped at last and kissed passionately the poor hand and face which had been close to her all her life.

"Good-bye!" she said. "Good-bye, father!"

When Mr. Van Ness and the clergyman entered the room later, they found Betty there, her lean visage half terrified and half defiant.

"Where is my wife?" said Van Ness with the sad authority becoming the master of this house of mourning.

"She—she begs that she may not be disturbed until to-morrow," said Betty with a scared look, behind her. "She's ill. The fact is, she's clean worn out with trouble."

"I can readily conceive that," said Mr. Lampret.

But Van Ness said nothing: he only glanced toward the still figure which lay upon the sofa covered with a white sheet, and turned away with a gloom and alarm on his benignant face quite new to it.

A couple of hours afterward, being alone, he met Betty coming out of Jane's apartment, and stopped her sternly:

"Mrs. Nichols, I must see my wife. If she is ill, my place is beside her."

For her answer Betty, with a gasp, threw open the door.

The room was vacant.

"Where is she?"

"As God sees me, I don't know. She bade me say this to you—That she had paid you the debt, and had gone where you would never find her."

Van Ness's smooth countenance scarcely evinced surprise. He went into the room and walked about it, and as he touched little articles of dress and the toilette which she had left scattered here and there, which were yet warm from her presence, the stout, bulky man could scarcely draw his breath. He stopped in front of the white pillow with the impress of her head on it, took up the velvet band which had fastened her hair, the knot half untied. So nearly within his hold—to escape!

"What is the money to me?" he muttered. "It is Jane that I want—*Jane.*"

Betty was standing at the door when he went out. She cowered back when she saw the sultry fire in his eyes.

"I don't know where she went. She only said as you would never find her, sir."

"I will find her," said Van Ness quietly.

PART 6

Chapter 19

The reason which Mr. Van Ness offered for Jane's disappearance, he protested, would suggest itself to everybody as the only possible one: her grief had deranged her, and she had wandered away bent on self-destruction. But the house was filled now with the friends of the captain, among them Judge Rhodes and Mrs. Wilde, and he read doubt and lurking suspicion on every face. The judge, it is true, directed the hurried searches through the grounds and the dragging of the lake.

"But I wish the captain had not pushed the marriage so hard. Drill-major to the last gasp. I was to blame in suggesting it at first," he said, point-blank to Van Ness.

"Suicide? Nothing of the kind," said Mrs. Wilde. "Jane is eccentric, as every thoroughly truthful woman is. But sane. One of the sanest people I know."

She summoned Betty, and the two women were closeted together for half an hour.

"You should have sent for me," she said when the story was ended. "The child should not have been left to the tender mercies of these men. Call him in."

When Van Ness appeared he saw that the old lady's eyes were red.

"You are going in pursuit of her? Mrs. Nichols has told me all," she said blandly.

"I shall search for her, undoubtedly. Her mind was evidently shaken. There is a bare chance that she may have gone on the train. But the river being so near and her grief so great, I fear the worst, Mrs. Wilde."

"No doubt, no doubt! But if you do follow her on the train—How was she dressed, Betty?"

"In gray. Black hat and gray feather," said Betty like a parrot.

"Thank you! That will be of assistance to me.—They are trying to help her escape," he thought as he went out, with a bow and melancholy smile. He had waited to talk with Mr. Lampret. He asked him for a certificate of the marriage.

"If my wife is living and wandering insane through the country, it will be necessary to prove my right to claim her."

To his surprise, the clergyman grew red and stammered, with a painful anxiety in his boyish face.

"I fear we were too hasty, Mr. Van Ness. Are you quite sure she consented freely to the marriage? There was no moral compulsion used?"

"There was none," coldly. "My marriage, as I believe, had in it all the elements of future happiness. Besides, that is hardly a question, it appears to me, for you to consider now. Whether suitable or not, the marriage was legal. When can you give me the certificate?"

Mr. Lampret did not speak for a moment. "I suppose it is irrevocable," he said with a long breath. "The making out of the certificate will involve a delay of a couple of hours."

"I shall wait for it," said Van Ness.

It was midnight before he left The Hemlocks and took the train into New York. There he had other work to do, which consumed an hour or two. He must lay plans to free himself from any hold which Charlotte had upon him. He had not courage to live, in even the rare delights to which he looked forward as Jane's husband, with that sword at his throat. He could find no trace of Charlotte. But he wakened up a lawyer (not the eminent counsel who systematized his vast benevolent schemes), and gave him full instructions and a blank cheque.

"I must have this connection closed at once. And at any price," he said as he left the door at one o'clock in the morning.

"To Desbrosses street ferry. In time to catch the Philadelphia express," he ordered the cabman.

He had not tried to find a clew to her in New York. She was unknown there—not likely to be recognized even by officials on the trains running up to The Hemlocks.

"She would try to escape from a place where she is a stranger. But it would cut her deeply to leave her father unburied," he argued shrewdly.

"She would go direct to their old home in Philadelphia, where the associations with him were strongest. She is full of such foolish notions!" He glowed with admiration of these warm affections, so becoming to a beautiful woman, as he leaned back in his seat in the car. Van Ness had indeed a keen appreciation of fine sentiments in books or in people. A noble thought fitly uttered or a pathetic strain of music would bring the tears to his eyes. All his friends will testify to-day that he is a man of most sensitive nature. He remembered this admirable trait in himself as he sat thinking over his future married life that night. It was one of the means by which he would be sure to win the love of his wife, and drive away her grief for the poor old captain. He took out a tiny volume from his pocket and studied it carefully by the dull light of the lamp overhead. The conductor, who knew the great Christian financier by sight, looked on reverently at a distance. It was some epitome of wisdom that he pored over: perhaps the Book of books. There was, in fact, a little mirror set in the inside of the binding. Van Ness studied the glisten on his yellow beard, the gluey softness of his blue eyes. "There never was a woman who would not yield to me," he thought, shutting the book. "But it does not matter whether she does or not," he added, his fingers searching for the marriage certificate in his pocket and closing on it with a fierce grip.

Chapter 20

Van Ness had really but slight knowledge of the places in which Jane's early life had been passed. On reaching Philadelphia he was forced to search through old directories for the houses in which the captain had lived, and go to them in turn—a tedious process enough, as the old man had migrated, as his whim or purse dictated, from Kensington to Southwark, from a close-built block in the business quarter to a tumble-down cottage on the Wissahickon. It was near night before he arrived at the old house surrounded by trees in the Neck which had been their last home in Philadelphia. Disappointment and secret rage had only made the unctuous sweetness of his manner a little coarser in flavor. The woman who came to the door adjusting a pink bow at her collar found his familiar greeting exactly suited to the level of her own breeding.

"A young lady? With blue eyes and yellow hair? Oh yes, sir. Colored pretty much like yourself. But she don't favor you, either. Come in! come in! My name's Crawford. Young lady's yer sister, likely?"

"At what time was she here?"

"Just at breakfast-time. Well, say seven. She didn't come in no fur-der than this room. Said she'd lived here with a friend, and would like to take a look ag'in at the old place. She sat there, on that settee, and looked in the fire a while, and then went out to the garden and walked up and down. I suspicioned she wa'n't right in her mind," volubly. "The idee of comin' back to look at a house and yard! I guess I was right. Somethin' wantin'—eh?" touching her forehead.

"Yes. Do you know in which direction she went, Mrs. Crawford?"

"I haven't the least notion. If I'd ha' had any intimation, now, that she had escaped from her friends, I'd ha' done all I could to help 'em. My George could hev' followed her all day, for that matter. What was the cause, now? Religious excitement? Disappintment?"

"Both, both! You did not observe her dress, I suppose?"

"Oh yes, I did. Brown waterproof and brown hat. 'Twouldn't be easy to trace her by her dress."

"Did she speak of returning here?"

"No. I wish I'd incouraged her!" her zeal reaching fever-heat in this hinted tragedy. "She come in an' thanked me very gravely, an' said she would probably never see the old house ag'in. Poor thing! She gave George some money, which wa'n't at all necessary, I'm sure."

"If she did not expect to see the house again, she meant to leave the city," said Van Ness when he was again in the street. "She will be easily traced at the railway-stations."

But in this he was disappointed. Young women dressed in the uniform travelling costume daily came and went in troops through the avenues of travel: a dozen indifferent ticket-agents had hazy recollections of this especial traveller on her way to Boston, to San Francisco, to Baltimore. Mr. Van Ness, too, found that his own social dignity and prominence sorely hindered his researches. Everybody in the city knew Pliny Van Ness by sight. It would not do for him, as for any common man, to go from office to office inquiring for the heroine of a mysterious elopement. The Christian humanitarian must keep his garments clean of suspicion as jealously as Caesar's wife.

Reporters, too, had their eyes upon him, turn which way he would, for the opinions and movements of Mr. Van Ness had long furnished welcome material for the columns of "Personals" in the morning journals. What if a hint of this episode of his marriage and his wife's disappearance should creep into the blatant newspapers? He moved, threatened, hampered, by this open-day terror, one unsuccessful day slipping into another until three weeks had gone by.

Early one chilly October morning he found himself without any definite aim knocking at Mrs. Crawford's door, and was welcomed by her with effusion, for she had supposed her chance of any share in the tragedy to be gone.

"And you hain't found her yet, eh? Dear! dear! If I'd only knowed in time! It's told on you, sir. Yes, indeed. You've aged considerable in this month."

The only real change in Van Ness was a certain new alien expression which was now and then perceptible under the blandishment of his smile, like some savage beast peeping out from behind the painted canvas of his cage. His news from the lawyer in New York was unsatisfactory; he was baffled at every turn by insignificant difficulties in his search for Jane; there was every temptation for the beast which was in him to break its bonds. But luck had turned for him.

"Dear! dear!" continued Mrs. Crawford. "Have you tried the police? Though they're of little account. She could not have come to any bodily harm. The dog would protect her."

"Dog? You said nothing about a dog. Had she that damnable brute with her?" starting up.

"A large hound, sir. Why, to be sure, I told you!—Lord! he's gone!"

Here at last was a clew! It proved effectual. The agent at the Pennsylvania Railroad office remembered distinctly the young girl who wished to take her dog with her down to some station on the coast, and the difficulty which the trainmaster meant to make about it. "But she took him," he added. "She was a very beautiful woman. Nobody cared to refuse her."

Van Ness went down to the Branch, to Beach Haven, Manasquan, all the fishing-villages along the coast, among the rest to Sutphen's Point. He talked to old Sutphen himself, his foot resting on a barnacle-eaten log where Jane herself had sat the day before. But the old man was loyal. He was stupid, stared vacantly at Van Ness, had seen no young woman and no dog: there had never been any such at the Point. Van Ness went hurriedly on to the next station, spent a couple of days in the search, and returned to Philadelphia.

"So the young lady came back before you?" said the agent, nodding familiarly as he passed the ticket-window.

"Yes. You saw her?"

"Oh, she bought her ticket of me. Yesterday, you know."

"For what point?" Van Ness's voice was so hoarse that the man heard him with difficulty.

"Richmond. Took the dog, too."

"Give me a ticket for Richmond, please. When does the next train go?"

"In half an hour. She has twenty-four hours the start of you, sir," with a significant laugh as he handed out the ticket and change.

Van Ness arrived at dawn the following morning at the little wooden shed with its garden of dahlias and lilacs which called itself a depot on the outskirts of the drowsy country town so lately the focus on which had rested the eyes of the civilized world. Two or three negroes bustled into activity as the train rolled in: an old woman dusted the rocking-chairs about the stove. They all remembered the tall, handsome young lady with the dog, who had flung about her money so freely the day before.

"I brought her breakfast, sah. I'm Dabney. Everybody knows Dabney's reliable. Mighty fine hound, sah. De young lady went on to Morganton, Nothe Callina. Oh, tank you, sah!"

Morganton is a village perched on a spur of the Blue Ridge, made dusky by shadows of overhanging hills. The garrulous landlord of the inn was ready to point out his prey to Van Ness.

"A lady? Miss Swendon, you mean? I've known her since she was a child. Captain Swendon came to the Balsam Mountings for years for the hunting. Allays brought the little girl. She's broken down terrible. Her father's death's interrupted her, powerful."

"She is here, then?" lowering his voice.

"No. She went on to the captain's camping-ground on the Old Black. Seemed as if she must go every place where he had been. He allays buried himself among the mountings. I doubt if you can find the place."

"Where Miss Swendon can go I surely can follow."

"Dunno. She's used to the mountings. P'raps you can get a guide at Asheville. It's the last place whah human beings live—high up on the Black: an old hunter, Glenn and his wife—kind, decent people, but not jest civilized. The captain was allays in cahoot with them, and they was powerful fond of Jane."

There was no regular conveyance then across the Blue Ridge to Asheville. Van Ness crossed the range on horseback with a guide: the horse broke down, and caused a delay of a day. He arrived, therefore, at the little hill-town late in the afternoon of Friday. Miss Swendon had gone up into the mountains two days before, he learned, with the old hunter Glenn, who happened to be in the village with a load of roots and peltry.

"I must go on to-night," said Van Ness urgently.

The ex-Confederate colonel who kept the inn surveyed him leisurely. "Glenn's house lies about thirty miles up in the Balsam Range," he said deliberately. "The passes are dangerous in daylight: it would be impossible to make the ascent at night. I shall not be able to find a guide for you until to-morrow."

Van Ness was exhausted in mind and body. The night's rest was tempting.

"I shall find her at this man Glenn's? She will not go farther?"

The colonel laughed: "Not unless she turns hermit or takes up her lodging with the wild beasts. Glenn's hut is the last human habitation on the mountains. You have her, sure."

"Then I will take supper and a bed."

He slept soundly that night, and sipped his coffee at breakfast comfortably, smiling now and then to himself. The silly creature was making herself happy this morning in the mountain-fastness, going over her father's old haunts, thinking that she was hidden where he would never find her. But how easily he had run her down! The horses and guide were waiting at the door. Before the sun set he would have her in his hold securely, as easily as he could grasp that bird in its cage yonder.

Glenn's house was in fact but a rambling log hut built under the shelter of one of the peaks of the Old Black. The Appalachian ranges at this point reach their highest altitude on the continent. The unbroken primeval forest came up to the very door of the hut. A few feet off a stream, the head-water of the Swannanoa, dashed over the precipice.

As the sun was setting that evening, the old hunter's wife waited in the door to meet Jane, who came slowly down the gorge, with the dog beside her. The two women stood together watching the red ball of fire go down behind Old Craggy. It threw sharp shafts of light into the heavy cloud that hung halfway up the peak, while overhead the sky was green and translucent as the sea.

The hunter's wife did not speak to Jane as she stood beside her, and did not watch her. The incurious habit of silence of these mountaineers rested the girl. They had been her friends when she was a little girl: she had come back, as sure of finding their friendship as the rock on which their house was built. She had come up with her heart and brain full of unwholesome sickness to be cured in these silent solitudes of the world. The cure was begun. Her eye was clearer, the hopeless load was lifted from her life. What did pain matter? Or death? There was about her here a great repose in which these things faded out.

She looked at the glittering stream close by, at the unending slopes of underbrush blazing scarlet with the rowan and the shonieho, and then beyond these lower hills—fold and fold of living color—to the great bare peak wrapped in clouds, a few dead trees climbing its base, which stands like a mighty warder of the Atlantic coast. The tears rose to her eyes.

"One must have a mean and selfish soul to be unhappy here," she thought. The twilight fell suddenly. The sides of the mountains went into shadow: only the sky about the peaks burned redly. Jane went in and sat down by the old hunter before the big log-fire.

"I wish you to let me stay with you," she said. "I have a little money, which will last a long time here. After it is gone I can make more, somehow."

Glenn for answer only put out his hand and touched hers gently. The hand was as bony as her father's, and his hair was as white. That comforted the girl more than any words. His wife, who was always the speaker, said, "You've always been welcome, Jane. You know that. You won't need money. We get our living out of the mountings for the taking of it. When your father was gone it was nateral for you to come straight here, an' to stay."

"Yes, I will stay," said Jane.

Presently the old man raised his hand: "Hark! There's folks coming."

"I hear nothing, father," said Mrs. Glenn.

"Yes. There's horses at the lower ford. Two of 'em. They're across now. It's more'n a year since anybody's bin up the mounting. Kin it be any one a-followin' you, Jane?"

She got up slowly: "Who could follow me?"

The next moment the hoofs of the horses rang on the shelving rocks outside. The door opened, and Van Ness stood on the threshold.

Chapter 21

The Scotia was within a few hours of Liverpool. The passengers were all gathered on deck—the women, eager and garrulous, eying each other a little curiously in their new costumes—even the most *blasé* traveller among them roused by the smell of land. Miss Fleming, however, sat quietly apart, with Mr. Neckart beside her. The other passengers were accustomed to see these two together, silent and uncommunicative even to each other. Cornelia had early understood that Neckart's ailment, whatever it was, whether mood or disease, craved quiet. She instantly suited herself to its need. Captain Swendon had always rejoiced in her as one of the most loquacious and sociable of human beings. Bruce, on the contrary, was strongly attracted by the aloofness and unconscious repose of this taciturn woman, who held herself apart from the vulgarly fashionable crowd in the cabins, not being of their kind. He fell into the habit of taking his seat near her, partly to avoid the others, partly for the comfort of being able to sleep, talk, or be silent undisturbed. After a few days he began to be conscious of a fine similarity of taste and convictions between them. Whether it was a question of political law or the color of a curling wave, Cornelia's thought about it evidently ran in the same groove as his own, though more weakly, as became the intellect of a woman. A word or a laughing glance was enough to convey this subtle sympathy between them. It had undeniably soothed and brightened the passage.

Bruce Neckart, at night, alone in his state-room, knew that he had left ambition, love, happiness, behind him—that he was cut off from all the chances of life. At night the indescribable feeling of vacancy at the base of the brain, the stricture as of an iron band about his jaws, the occasional sudden numbness of nerve and thought, as though he were stricken for the instant with extreme old age, were hints which brought his approaching fate before him as with a horror of great darkness. But on deck, in daylight, the swell lapping the vessel, his feeble appetite gratified by a well-cooked meal, there was some interest yet to be found in the Southern problem or the claims of the Pre-Raphaelites; and he was grateful to Chance for this companion who sat ready to grasp any subject which attracted him, with a woman's fine intuition, but who demanded only the personal courtesy due to an innocent, manly boy. She showed him, too, during the voyage, much womanly, personal kindness, for which, being of an honest, affectionate nature, he was grateful.

Now that they were nearing land, therefore, Mr. Neckart's thoughts as he sat beside her were wholly busied with his companion. He was heartily sorry for her. Ordinary observers, he reflected, would mistake her for one of the strong-minded Advanced Sisterhood, but he knew her to be sensitive and delicate in the extreme. He felt a certain sense of ownership in her as his discovery. How was she to find her way alone in Europe? He had meant to cut absolutely loose from every tie of his past life on landing, but this thread held him still. Could he arrange any future occasional intercourse with her? He did not mean to hamper himself at all. Still, he might be useful to her, etc., etc. In short, the pillow on which he had rested his aching head had been warm and pleasant to him, and he threw it away reluctantly. There really was no reason, he argued (according to the invariable argument of men concerning this woman), no reason whatever, why firm and fervent friendships should not exist between persons of opposite sex. He would have been insulted at a hint that this sympathy, *bonne camaraderie*, with the little woman in green beside him involved disloyalty to Jane.[1] The little woman, however, gave neither of these fine names to their traffic of sentiment. The Cornelias of their sex make no mistakes in this matter.

It was a sombre, foreboding day. The passengers were gathered on the forward deck. Neckart and Cornelia were alone, the gray fog shutting them in. She sat with her head turned from him, immovable, but he was conscious, through the strong subtle magnetism that belonged to this woman, of the powerful excitement which she controlled. He quite forgot his own trouble. This delicate, lonely creature venturing into the world! He asked her some questions as to her plans on landing, but she answered vaguely. She heard only the throb of the steamer beating out the few moments left to her. Her whole life was risked upon this voyage. Had she failed? There was but an hour left. What woman could do she had done. Good God! why must she be silent? Her whole soul had called out for this man for years: she had loved him with a man's force of passion. Why could she not speak now and tell him so? She must sit beside him dumb, lifeless, unless he put out his hand to take her!

"Half-past four," said Neckart, looking at his watch. "I am sure you are sorry the voyage is so nearly over."

She did not speak, but he caught a gleam in her eye that startled him. Under all her coldness she was a strange, vivid creature well worth study. He leaned forward eagerly.

"Your undertaking terrifies you, now that the time has come. You would rather turn back?"

She moved restlessly under his keen scrutiny, as though it hurt her. Her hands were clasped on her knees, her eyes fixed on the black line on the horizon which marked land. "No, I will go on."

"Cornelia," with warm kindness in his face and voice, "I am afraid you have overrated your devotion to your work. A woman must be possessed by her art as by a demon to enable her to endure years of solitude in a foreign country, homeless and friendless. Have you counted all the cost? When you leave me you cut yourself loose from all your old life." She turned her head away, but made no reply. "I do not believe you are strong enough, poor child!" he said presently.

Silence pleaded for her as no words of her own could have done. Neckart saw the strained eyes, the quivering chin: his interest suddenly became alive, intense—a feeling quite apart from the kindliness which his words expressed.

"I begin to think you have mistaken your vocation altogether. You are too dependent, too tender a woman, for an artist. You should have chosen a domestic life, Cornelia." And, after an embarrassed pause of a moment, "You should have married."

He saw the quick shudder: his own blood beat feverishly. He had always been curious about women. He would push the probe a little deeper: "If there had been any friend who was more to you than your art?—"

She turned her head slowly. The bleached face and burning eyes fastened on his own told her story before she spoke: "I have had no friend but you, Bruce."

Neckart started to his feet, hot from head to foot like a blushing girl. He paced the deck dumb with shame and confusion. It was long before he found courage to look at her. Her hands were clasped over her face: she was sobbing in a helpless, strengthless way that seemed to put her on the ground at his feet. He looked toward the land. Would it never come nearer? Finally, feeling himself wholly a scoundrel, and moved by a great compassion and as great annoyance, he pushed the green cloak aside and sat down hastily on the bench beside her, beginning to talk rapidly. If the limb must come off, the quicker the better.

"I understand just what you mean, Miss Fleming. You need a friend, an adviser, being here in Europe alone. Of course you turn to me, remembering old times in Delaware, and—and—" She had stopped sobbing now, and was watching him breathlessly, her eyes following his lips as he spoke. Neckart, looking at her, broke down.

"How can I do it?" he thought. "This woman's whole life has been given to me, and I did not know it!—It's natural," he began again aloud, "that you should turn to me. You know how gladly I would be your friend—"

She shook her head, her straining eyes on his. "Yes, gladly— thankfully!" (Surely, it was only right to soften the blow.) "You cannot know how—how dear you have always been to me, Cornelia. But I can have nothing to do with friendship or any other relation which makes a man's life worth endurance. I am barred out from so much of my birthright by my blood."

"What do you mean, Bruce?"

"You know the fate of the Davidges: I need not go over the story. God knows it is not a pleasant subject for me to dwell upon. But for the last year I have had unmistakable proof that I have the hereditary disease. That is the reason why I have given up my business and every tie in life, and expatriated myself."

As he spoke she rose, shaken with excitement; her face took on a new meaning; for the moment she was a young and beautiful woman: "Oh,

Bruce! Bruce! you are all wrong! Is it possible that you have never been undeceived? There is not a drop of the Davidge blood in your veins!"

"What do you mean?"

"I have heard the story from my mother a hundred times. Your father was married twice—the first time in Maryland, where you were born. Your mother died at your birth. He came to Kent county and married Miss Davidge, who never had any children. It was the first symptom of her insanity that she conceived the idea that you were her own son, and your father willingly humored her in the belief. You were deceived too as a child, lest you might betray the real facts to her. But I thought when you were a man you would be told the truth."

"How could I?" said Neckart, bewildered. "My father died when I was a boy of ten, and my mother—But she was not my mother!" His eyes filled: he turned hastily away. It seemed to him as if the dear old mother had just then died to him.

Cornelia timidly touched his arm: "But you do not understand. You are not a Davidge. You are free from the Davidge disease."

"Free?" It was not easy to turn back the convictions and terrors of a lifetime in a moment. He stared at her stunned: "Then these symptoms have been only caused by overwork, as the doctors said? I—I am like other men?"

"Yes."

"Merciful God!"

Cornelia leaned over the taffrail. Would he come to her? The blood ebbed weakly in her veins; the rush of the water below roared like thunder; as the minutes passed a deadly sickness came into her breast. She looked to find him. He was at the other end of the deck, talking with the captain, his swarthy face glowing, his eyes like coals of fire.

"The Russia is the first steamer to New York," she heard the captain say. "You can board her to-night. This is a very sudden resolution, Mr. Neckart?"

"Yes. But I must return to my business at once. There are other matters too which—matters which I have neglected."

"But your health? You mentioned a cerebral disorder which required rest?"

"Oh, I am much better! The sea-voyage—I am another man, sir!"

He walked down the deck, his back toward her. It was the heavy figure, the swinging awkward gait, which she remembered twenty years ago on the old farm-road. The world was born anew to him: health, work, chances—he had but to stretch out his hands and clutch them all again, and under all was the sweet triumphant passion.

"Jane! Jane!"

His eyes strained back over the long waste of water. But as for Cornelia, he had forgotten that she was in the world.

When the people were leaving the steamer to go on the tug, she came up to him. It was easier to bear another turn of the rack than be utterly dropped out of remembrance.

"We part here, Mr. Neckart," with an admirably cordial little smile, holding out her gloved hand.

Neckart stammered with sudden remorse and pity: "'Pon my soul, Miss Fleming, I forgot that you were going ashore! Forgive me. But a man reprieved with the axe at his neck can't be expected to have his senses at call."

"You go back, then?"

"Oh, immediately! I must regain my—my work. What can I do for you?" zealously. "Your baggage, now? There will be nothing dutiable, of course. Will you have it sent to London or direct to the Continent? You told me your plans, but—"

"You have forgotten them," smiling. "The baggage is already on its way. You forget I am one of the capable, self-reliant sisterhood. No. You can do nothing for me but to say good-bye."

Neckart caught her hand and wrung it vehemently, but it lay with its smooth kid covering passive in his palm. He began to say something to her about her art and success, but the words seemed a ghastly mockery and died in his throat.

"Oh, I shall succeed, undoubtedly, but in a low grade. My ability is of inferior quality. I know all my limitations," with a sudden metallic laugh.

"You will return in a year or two, and—"

"No, I shall not return. I shall never see you again," looking for the first time in his face.

Neckart glanced beyond her to the strange city, vast and dreary in the twilight and drizzle and falling soot. The docks were swarming with life. Some of their fellow-passengers had already landed and been met by eager friends, and were driven away to their homes. This woman was going friendless into the night and crowd. She was so little and lonely and hardly used! But what could he do? He had not a minute to lose if he would board the Russia.

"Miss Fleming, I owe a fresh lease of life to you. I shall always think of you with gratitude."

"What I gave you was a free gift," she said in a very quiet voice. "I want no gratitude in return for it. Good-bye."

"Good-bye."

She suddenly raised his hand and kissed it.

"Cornelia!"

But she was gone, and in a moment was lost in the hurrying crowds, on which a sullen rain was beginning to fall.

Before midnight Neckart was ploughing his way back. His brain was quite clear—no threats of paralysis or sudden age. He lay awake building honest air-castles—new plans for the paper, dreams of happiness for Jane as fresh and sweet as a boy's of his first love. But through them all the kiss on his hand burned like fire. He rubbed it again and again angrily.

He wanted no guilty damned spot about him when he came to Jane.

Chapter 22

When the door of the hut opened Bruno growled furiously. Mr. Van Ness appeared on the threshold, smiling, benign, a goodly sight, from his blond head and the yellow topaz on his snowy shirtfront to the polished boots.

"Down, Bruno, down!" said Jane.

The old hunter observed that though she stood erect she could not bring her voice above a whisper. She looked at Van Ness like a kid that the dogs were going to tear to death. Glenn came up hastily between her and the stranger. He had the dog's sudden antipathy to him and to his smile.

"What is your business?"

Van Ness advanced and held out his hand cordially. The mountains had had their effect upon him: his irritated nerves lay now quieted out of sight in the thick cool flesh. As he ascended the heights he had laid his plans. Gentleness first, force if need be: gentle measures would no doubt suffice. The law would ensure to him immediate possession of his wife. She had the devilish obstinacy of a mule, but she was his wife. He would bring her to love him at last, and their future life would be eminently respectable and comfortable. Laidley's estate must yield now, on an average—? The remainder of the ride had passed in pleasant calculation. Never had his temper been more serene or firm than when he presented himself before his wife.

"What's your business?" said the old man.

"My business," gently, "is with that lady. I have followed her here from New York, and I thank you heartily, sir, for taking care of her."

"Of course I'll take care of Jane. I'll not allow her to be follered or disturbed, neyther.—Do you want to see this man, child?"

Jane did not hear him. Her eyes were fastened on the handsome figure, all light and benignity. She had thought she was done with it for ever. It seemed to her now as if it never would leave her sight again.

"You kin see clearly that you're unwelcome to her," said Glenn. "Wife, take Jane into her own room until this gentleman is gone."

"When I go," said Van Ness with a pleasant, airy wave of the hand, "she goes with me. You are kind, my dear sir, but unreasonable. I have a claim upon this lady which even you will allow is sufficient."

"What claim has he on you, Jane?" turning his back abruptly on Van Ness. "Has he any right to talk in this way?"

"Yes. I am his wife."

"Wife! Married! Not accordin' to law?"

"There is the certificate."

At the sight of this slip of paper, and with the rustle of it in Glenn's hand, her strength ebbed away from Jane. It was the Law. Her prejudices and dislikes seemed suddenly insignificant, helpless, in this mighty force. It had the same effect on the ignorant, law-abiding mountaineer.

"I don't see but as it's correct," turning it over, perplexed. "She's yer legal wife."

"No matter ef she were his wife a hundred times," cried his wife: "she shall not go back ef she chooses to stay. P'raps he's abused her. He shall not force her away."

"I have no wish to force her to leave you," in the same gentle, cheerful tone. "Be rational, dear friends. I leave Jane to answer whether I have ever used toward her a word or action that was not loving and tender."

"No," said Jane, dully.

"Do you know anything of me which would justify your flight? Answer me candidly. Is there a single reason why you should not honor and respect me as your husband?"

Jane was silent. The law within her gave a savage answer. But what was that but blind prejudice? She must answer according to the judgment of the outside world.

"Is there any reason?"

"No—none."

Van Ness nodded cheerfully, and motioned the hunter and his wife confidentially to his side: "I will explain the matter to you precisely as it stands," his light eyes looking over their heads to Jane.

She stood irresolutely a moment, and then went into the little room which had been set apart for her. She could not draw her breath so near to him.

Van Ness, peering through the open door, saw that there was but one narrow window inside, opening over a sheer descent of rocks. "It is quite natural that you should love Jane and wish to defend her, as you knew her when she was a child," he said, raising his voice that she might hear. "But you do not understand. She married me of her own free will by the bedside of her dying father. His last act was to give her to me with his blessing. You can judge whether he would have chosen an unworthy husband for her."

"'Tain't likely," said Glenn. But his wife shook her head.

"An hour after his death Jane escaped: left her dead father—left me whom she loved. The only rational way of accounting for her course is that the nervous strain had proved too much for her, and that she was temporarily insane. You can question her whether I have stated the facts correctly."

The old people glanced doubtfully in at the tall figure standing motionless at the open window.

"She don't contradict you in nothin', sir. I'm sorry ef I was onjust to you," said the old man slowly.

"I honor you for it! You could have no claim to my friendship as strong as your affection for my wife."

"Yes," with deliberation, "we've allays been powerful fond of Jane. But marriage is marriage. We won't interfere. Them as God hes jined together—"

Van Ness rose: "I shall take her with me to Asheville. Her mental trouble may make her seem disinclined to go. But firmness and affectionate care will soon restore her." He walked to the door: "Come, my dear wife."

Jane turned and faced him. Her very lips seemed withered: "I have given you the money."

"I want *you*."

Van Ness waited smiling, without a word after that, his white hands held out.

"Come, my pretty!" whispered the old woman, stroking her arm soothingly. "Suppose you don't like him so much at first? You'll grow into it. Hundreds of women marry without love. You must give up to the law."

The law, the whole world, were against her.

Van Ness came closer, step by step, with the inexorable steadiness of Fate in his eye. Mrs. Glenn drew back and left them alone.

"You married me."

"I wanted to give you the money. There was my mistake."

"You cannot repair it. There is no one to help you."

She looked out at the bare peaks and the sky near at hand, and raised her arms, clasping her hands back of her head. Her lips moved. "God will help me," Van Ness thought he heard her say.

He put his hand on her shoulder: "Come. We must return to-night, at least part of the way," with quiet authority.

He drew her toward him, stooped to kiss her lips.

At that moment there was a loud knocking at the outer door, and a man and woman entered. Van Ness saw them. His hand fell from Jane's arm, his countenance relaxed: for a moment he stood unnerved: then with quick decision he stepped boldly forward to meet them, drawing to the door of the chamber behind him.

"Charlotte?"

"Yes," with a shrug, "or Princess Trebizoff, Madame Varens, what you choose. By any other name I am as dear to you. Heavens! what a chase!" perching herself airily on the settle in front of the fire. "I am one living ache.—I can't congratulate you on your roads, madam. But your scenery! Ah, that goes to the heart!"

Mr. Neckart stood beside her, calmly waiting until Van Ness should turn to him. The great reformer was brought to bay: he was alert, prompt, ready.

"You followed me here, Mr. Neckart?" turning sharply.

"Yes."

"For what purpose?"

"To bring your wife to you," glancing at Charlotte.

"I inferred that was the story which this poor creature had imposed upon you. Surely, you know her character, Neckart? Why, she has levied blackmail for years by just such ingenious devices. I did not suppose any statement of hers would bear a minute's investigation from a shrewd, practical man like yourself. So she really deceived you, eh?" with a discordant laugh.

Charlotte, drying her dainty feet at the fire, looked contemptuously over her shoulder at him.

"There is no need of any discussion in the matter," said Neckart dryly. "We are not here to play melodrama. The matter is easily understood. I returned from Europe last week, and went direct to the Hemlock Farm. From the servants I heard the details of the forced marriage and of Jane's flight. I followed her."

"How did you find her here?"

"Betty Nichols knew that she was coming."

"Damn her! She hid it from me, her husband!"

Neckart stepped hastily forward, then controlled himself and drew back: "She had given the route to Charlotte also. I overtook her at Baltimore. She had stopped to obtain legal proof of your marriage to her in 1847. We followed an hour behind you from Richmond."

Even in this imminent moment Van Ness secretly wondered how this passionate brute of a Neckart held himself in check and talked coolly to the man who had stolen from him the woman that he loved. It would have been in character for him to tear his life out, like Bruno. But this was admirable self-command! It really gratified Van Ness's taste, tottering on the verge of ruin as he was. The truth was, that Neckart was conscious of little else than that Jane was in the hut. The rage against this scoundrel which had maddened him through the long journey had strangely died out. He had not harmed her. He was like a fangless snake, to be trampled under foot at any moment.

But she was there! He had caught a glimpse of the proud, delicate head and its crown of yellow hair behind the door as Van Ness closed it.

The door moved. It opened, and she came out among them. Neckart rose, his head bent upon his breast. He was deaf and blind for the time—could not tell whether she spoke to him or not.

She went directly up to Van Ness: "I am not your wife?"

He cowered for a moment. Then, rapidly shifting his defence, he stood up, benevolent, impregnable: "I do not deny that I was once married to this woman. It was a mad error of my youth, long since repented of. I was divorced from her last June."

"Ta, ta, Pliny, take care!" interrupted Charlotte. "The application for divorce was not made until after your marriage to Miss Swendon. I told you you would not risk a criminal trial for her sake. But I underrated your affection. You did it."

"Then I am free?" said Jane.

"You are free," said Charlotte.

Jane turned to the door and went into the open air without a word.

"I took a good deal of trouble to come here," resumed Charlotte, brushing some dust from her flounces, "to tell her that. I shouldn't have done it for other woman. But you remember that day when I was shamming death, how she kissed me, Pliny? I didn't forget that kiss."

Van Ness stood silent, hesitating. The firelight shone upon his tall figure, the dainty gray clothes, the shining stone, like a watchful evil eye, upon his breast. He was a perfect presentation of prosperity and peace. He looked at Neckart, but he was looking through the open door at a slight figure moving among the rocks.

Van Ness rubbed his hands softly. "I do not see," he said with unctuous precision, "that further discussion will be of any use in this matter. I was evidently mistaken as to point of time in the divorce. No one who knows me will suspect me of any worse error than a mistake. I will accompany you to Asheville, Charlotte, with pleasure. I owe you no grudge for the bitter wrong you have done me."

Charlotte rose and laughed good-naturedly: "You have your virtues, no doubt, Pliny. So have I. I always thought we were well mated. Shall we continue one? You may have to fall back upon my blackmailing devices, after all. I forgot to tell you that there was an inquiry last week into the disposition of the funds entrusted to you for the Home for Friendless Children, and that they were reported *nil.*"

For the first time in his life Van Ness blenched. The story of the marriage could be smothered. But this was total ruin.

"The sooner you go the better," said the hunter, tapping him on the shoulder. "Ef I understand right, you're not the kind of man as ought to pizen these mountings long."

Van Ness moved heavily to the door. But he turned on the threshold with a sickly smile: "I forgive you your rudeness, my friend. It is not my nature to bear malice.—Farewell, Mr. Neckart. You have mistaken my motives in this matter. But I shall think of you kindly.—I shall bear you all to the throne of grace in my prayers." He shook his hand as if scattering blessings, and went out with a lofty step and head erect.

Charlotte lingered and went up to Neckart.

"You are going to cling to that poor wretch?" he said.

"Well, he's down now, you see. There's nobody but me to stay by him. And I can always draw on him when I'm out of funds."

"You will remember what I told you of the school in Indiana? You could live in respectability and comfort; bring your boy home too."

"My boy? Home?" Her eyes filled with tears. "These are very tempting words, Mr. Neckart. But oh-h! Respectability is such a bore! I must go my own gait to the end;" and with a merry laugh and shrug she followed Van Ness.

When they were out of sight down the gorge, Neckart rose and went slowly out to the cleft in the rock where the girl sat alone.

"Jane," he said, "the way is open between us at last. Will you come to me?"

I cannot write Finis to the story of any of these people. They are all alive today, and the current of each life goes on with very little change.

You may still see Van Ness on the platform at all large religious or benevolent meetings in the great cities. There was much talk of the missing funds, but he quieted it satisfactorily. Cynical reporters throw out hints of ugly shadows in his life, but his disciples gather more solidly about him, trust their souls to his direction and their money to his pockets. Simple followers of Jesus fear to condemn a light which shines so splendidly in the market-place, and men who are not His followers accept it as Christianity, and damn the religion as spurious and a fraud.

Charlotte is just now the successful leader of an English opera-bouffe company which is travelling in the West. She gave the proceeds of her benefit in every town to the poor last winter, which was supposed by all respectable people to be an advertising trick. But it was not. The little woman would do more than that to buy herself an entrance into the heaven where her boy is going. She would do anything, in fact, but lead a decent life.

Miss Fleming is still in Rome. She belongs to the modern school which regards the nice reproduction of drapery and dry goods as the highest art. She sends home pictures, which sometimes gain a place by sufferance in a dark corner at the spring exhibition.

Mr. Neckart once bought one, a *Lady's Toilette*.

"A fair specimen of the millinery cult," he said, showing it to Judge Rhodes. "Poor Cornelia! Why is it that she never, even by chance, paints a clean-minded woman?" He sent a cheque for double the price asked for it. But he threw the picture on the market again, not wishing to take it home. He had married a singularly clean-minded woman.

Cornelia's first impulse was to send the cheque back. But, instead, she bought a ring with a single costly ruby in it, and has worn it ever since, though she has been hungry for bread many a time. Hungry or not, she makes her studio one of the pleasantest resorts for the young artists in Rome. She has cut her hair short, wears a jaunty velvet coat and man's collar: her arms are bony, but she bares them, and still shoots languishing glances from out of the crowsfeet. The young men laugh to each other. "A good fellow, Corny," they say, "but what a pity that she is not a man!"

The Home for Friendless Children is at last a reality in New York, though Van Ness is not a director. It was established by the editor Neckart, whose wife, it is said, endowed it with her own fortune. This charitable deed left them with but a very moderate competency. Neckart managed to buy in the Hemlock Farm, out of his income, for her and the boy.

He drives them over once a week to see the children in the Home, each of whom Jane knows and tries to spoil.

"You are glad that we made this act of reparation, Jane?" he said to her one day.

"Reparation?" She hesitated, and then said, "I know that I made many mistakes when I was a law to myself. You are my law now, Bruce."

"But you are satisfied that it was right to give back the money?" he insisted.

"Oh, of course! The money was unlucky! It made you uncomfortable too. And I look on it as a free gift from Swendon here to the poor little babies," taking her boy on her knee and stroking his curls. "But," she added in a low voice, "the money was mine. I was quite right when I burned the will."

Neckart laughed good-humoredly, and touched the horses with his whip. There is no man living who loves his wife more tenderly; and Jane is the most simple and prosaic of women. Yet there are times when she seems, even to him, a woman whose acquaintance he has scarcely made, and whom he can never hope to know better.

Notes

Chapter 1

1. Davis experimented with dialect, usually to designate African American or regional speech patterns.
2. Winfield Scott was a general in the U.S. Army. He commanded the southern forces in the Mexican-American War (1846–1848).
3. Atropos is one of the three fates of Greek mythology.
4. Probably a reference to Byron's *Childe Harold's Pilgrimage*, Canto III, which reads:

> But ever and anon of griefs subdued
> There comes a token like a scorpion's sting,
> Scarce seen, but with fresh bitterness imbued;
> And slight withal may be the things which bring
> Back on the heart the weight which it would fling
> Aside for ever: it may be a sound—
> A tone of music—summer's eve—or spring—
> A flower—the wind—the ocean—which shall wound,
> Striking the electric chain wherewith we are darkly bound.

In his reference to a wind harp, the judge may be conflating, and misunderstanding, the ideas of several romantic poets. Coleridge's "Eolian Harp" uses the harp as a metaphor for art, and in "Ode to the West Wind," Shelley uses wind to signify revolutionary force.

5. Homeopathy refers generally to alternative approaches to medicine. See James C. Whorton's *Nature's Cures: The History of Alternative Medicine in America* (Oxford: Oxford University Press, 2002). Influenced by the ideas of Franz Mesmer and Emanuel Swedenborg, spiritualism was a popular nineteenth-century belief in the ability to communicate with the dead through séances; the practice was popular among many early women's rights advocates. For more information about spiritualism in Davis's cultural moment, see Bret E. Carroll, *Spiritualism in Antebellum America* (Bloomington: Indiana University Press, 1997); Ann Braude, *Radi-*

cal Spirits: Spiritualism and Women's Rights in Nineteenth-Century America
(Bloomington: Indiana University Press, 2001).

Chapter 2

1. Combe may be a reference to George Combe, author of *A System of Phrenology* (1853). Combe popularized phrenology, the pseudoscience that attempted to interpret personality characteristics from the shape of the skull.
2. At the request of King Saul, the Witch of Endor summoned Samuel's ghost. See I Samuel 28.3–25.
3. The language in this passage suggests the qualities of mesmerism. Energy (often described as electricity or a magnetic force) links animate and inanimate objects. See Whorton, *Nature's Cures*.
4. Here, Davis reverses the familiar trope of a male mesmerist who controls a female subject. See Hawthorne's *The Blithedale Romance* for one such example; the "Veiled Lady" was "a phenomenon in the mesmeric line" unlike "nowadays" when "in the management of his 'subject,' 'clairvoyant,' or 'medium,' the exhibitor affects the simplicity and openness of scientific experiment" (40). Davis revisits the mesmerist in "Mesmerism vs. Common Sense" (1881); here, the practical Ellen Wynn discovers that a male mesmerist is "an ungodly fraud" (54). Like in *A Law Unto Herself,* marriage and property play an important role in the deception; the mesmerist attempts to "cheat poor, credulous Lee [Page] out of her jewels . . . and force her nearly into marriage" (57).
5. Night refers to the Greek goddess of night, Nyx. Her many offspring include Thanatos (death) and Hypnos (sleep).
6. Alexander Cabanel (1823–1889) was a French painter whose works include *The Birth of Venus* (1863).
7. The "evil eye" refers to a malevolent look as well as the powerful gaze associated with mesmerism.

Chapter 3

1. The divine cow Audhumbla is a Norse mythological figure associated with creation.
2. Epictetus (AD 55–AD 135) was a Stoic philosopher in ancient Greece.

Chapter 4

1. The Captain borrows the phrase "the dangerous classes" from the title of Charles Loring Brace's *The Dangerous Classes of New York* (1872).
2. An anchorite withdraws from society to lead a religious life as a monk or a hermit; like the Catholic priest, the anchorite refuses sexual relation-

ships. Both references suggest that Neckart plans to lead a celibate life to avoid passing insanity to another generation, a decision consistent with late nineteenth-century eugenic ideas.

3. Old Chrysostom refers to St. John Chrysostom, an anchorite who became a priest noted for his eloquence in the early Church. He was eventually exiled after a legal dispute with his enemies. According to legend, while he was a hermit, he met a princess who convinced him to let her into his cave. Unable to withstand the temptation, they conceived a child.

4. The *Argyle* sank off the coast of New Jersey on January 28, 1855.

5. La Pérouse refers to Jean-François de Galaup, comte de La Pérouse (1741–c.1788), a French navigator who explored the Pacific and wrote *A Voyage Round the World* (published posthumously in 1801).

Chapter 5

1. See Matthew 19:21; Mark 10:21; Luke 18:22. In this passage, a wealthy young man asks Jesus what he should do to achieve eternal life. Since the young man already honors the Ten Commandments, Jesus tells him to sell his possessions and give to the poor.

Chapter 6

1. Latin for at the moment of death.

2. This line is from Shakespeare's *The Merchant of Venice*: "As who should say, 'I am Sir Oracle, / And when I ope my lips let no dog bark!'" (Act 1.1. 99–100).

3. The physical description of Neckart and the reference to Jane as his "little friend" echo Charlotte Brontë's *Jane Eyre* (1847).

4. Aslauga and Ingeborg are Scandinavian names. Aslauga may be a reference to the title character of "Aslagua's Knight" by Friedrich Heinrich Karl la Motte-Fouqué, a German romantic writer. "Aslagua's Knight" is also a chapter title in Louisa May Alcott's *Jo's Boys* (1886).

5. This line is from Ben Jonson's lyric poem, "A Celebration of Charis: Part IV. Triumph."

6. Admirable Crichton refers to the talented Scotsman, James Crichton, who was the subject of the historical novel *Crichton* (1836) by William Harrison Ainsworth. The phrase "the Admirable Crichton" also appears in William Makepeace Thackeray's *Vanity Fair* (1847).

7. See Lamentations 4:2. Davis also uses *Earthen Pitchers* for the title of a novella serialized in *Scribner's Monthly* from November 1873 to April 1874. Two female characters prefigure Jane Swendon and Cornelia Fleming in interesting ways.

Chapter 8

1. Aristides (530 BC–468 BC) was an Athenian statesman known for his sense of justice.
2. A Brahmin is a scholar in traditional Hindu society. In nineteenth-century America, the term may also refer to an upper-class, well-educated Bostonian.
3. Rabies.
4. The phrase "dangerous classes" likely refers to Charles Loring Brace's *The Dangerous Classes of New York* (1872).
5. Wilhelm Richard Wagner (1813–1883) is a German composer known for his powerful operas. *Cloisonné* refers to a type of decorative enamel used on vases and other items. *En rapport* means to be in agreement with.
6. *Flux de bouche* refers to the quality of good speech or writing; powerful and effective use of language.
7. Congress passed a Naval Appropriations Bill in 1867 in an attempt to regulate campaign finance.

Chapter 10

1. Etruscans art dates from the ninth to the second century BC and includes a variety of forms. *Capo di Monte* is a type of Italian porcelain first produced in 1743. *Henri Deux* may refer to an antique in the Renaissance (or Henri II) style.
2. The Captain echoes Charles Loring Brace's descriptions of friendless children and orphans in *The Dangerous Classes of New York* (1872). Brace urges his readers to "think of these bitter and friendless children of the poor, in the great city" (122).
3. In *Bits of Gossip* (1904), Davis uses a similar metaphor to describe the Transcendentalists, especially Ralph Waldo Emerson and Bronson Alcott, after she met them during a visit to Concord in 1863. In a chapter titled "Boston in the Sixties," she explains, "Their theories were like beautiful bubbles blown from a child's pipe, floating overhead, with queer reflections on them of sky and earth and human beings, all in a glow of fairy color and all a little distorted" (39–40).

Chapter 11

1. A beautiful, idyllic setting, Happy Valley is the starting point for Rasselas's journey in Samuel Johnson's *Rasselas* (1759).
2. The reference to Arcadia suggests an idyllic, rural retreat or a Utopian community.
3. See Luke 10:25–37.

Chapter 12

1. Christina (1626–1689) was the queen of Sweden from 1633 to 1654 when she abdicated the throne to convert to Roman Catholicism.
2. *The Facts on File Dictionary of Allusions* defines "a law unto oneself" as "disregarding the wishes and conventions of others in favor of what one wants or believes" (289). The entry notes the biblical origins of the phrase in Romans 2:14: "For when the Gentiles, which have not the law, do by nature the things contained in the law, these, having not the law, are a law unto themselves." According to the entry, the Gentiles "moral nature" can stand in for the "law of Moses."

Chapter 13

1. See *Hamlet* 2.2.280.
2. The phrase "To the laborers belong the spoils" may be an ironic misquote and misattribution of the expression "To the victors belong the spoils." New York senator William L. Marcy apparently said, "To the victors belong the spoils" when Jackson Democrats won the 1828 presidential election.
3. See the story of Hagar and Sarah in Genesis 16. The power dynamics, especially the legal implications, parallel that of Charlotte and Jane. I am indebted to Jessica Hanson for this observation.

Chapter 14

1. Signor Blitz (1810–1877) was a well-known magician and ventriloquist.

Chapter 16

1. Una is a character in Edmund Spenser's *The Faerie Queen* (1590). According to the *Spenser Encyclopedia*, her "main function is to be Redcrosse's companion and to encourage him at moments of extreme moral and spiritual anger" (704). She is also noted for her fearlessness because she survives an encounter with a lion who becomes her protector.
2. French for extra attention or extravagant attention.
3. Reynard refers to Reynard the Fox, a sly, trickster figure who appears in numerous folktales.

Chapter 17

1. For the Sermon on the Mount, See Matthew chapters 5–7.
2. As a *femme sole* (an unmarried woman of legal age), Jane can legally make a gift of her property.
3. Jane describes a variation of the "The Frog Prince," often published as the first story in the Grimm brothers' collection of fairy tales. In the origi-

nal tale, the princess throws the frog against the wall, the frog turns into a handsome prince, and the two marry at her father's request. Davis's version emphasizes the legal implications of marriage as a property relationship. See *The Annotated Brothers Grimm* for the history of the tale and its variations.

Chapter 21

1. *Bonne camaraderie* refers to friendship.

In the Legacies of Nineteenth-Century American Women Writers series

To order or obtain more information
on these or other University
of Nebraska Press titles, visit
nebraskapress.unl.edu.